ARCHIE COMIC PUBLICATIONS, INC.

MICHAEL I. SILBERKLEIT
Chairman and Co-Publisher

RICHARD H. GOLDWATER
President and Co-Publisher

VICTOR GORELICK
Vice President /
Managing Editor

FRED MAUSSER
Vice President /
Director of Circulation

Americana Series Editor: **PAUL CASTIGLIA**

Americana Series Art Director: **JOSEPH PEPITONE**

Front Cover Illustration: **REX W. LINDSEY**

Cover colored by: **HEROIC AGE**

Production Manager: **CARYN WIMBERT**

Archie characters created by **JOHN L. GOLDWATER**

The likenesses of the original Archie characters
created by **BOB MONTANA**

Archie Americana Series, BEST OF THE SEVENTIES, Volume 4, 1998. Printed in Canada. Published by Archie Comic Publications, Inc., 325 Fayette Avenue, Mamaroneck, New York 10543. The individual characters names and likenesses are the exclusive trademarks of Archie Comic Publications, Inc. All stories previously published and copyrighted by Archie Comic Publications, Inc. (or its predecessors) in magazine form in 1970-1979. This compilation copyright © 1998 Archie Comic Publications, Inc. All rights reserved. Nothing may be reprinted in whole or part without written permission from Archie Comic Publications, Inc.

ISBN 1-879794-05-5

TABLE OF CONTENTS

INTRODUCTION BY SHIRLEY JONES

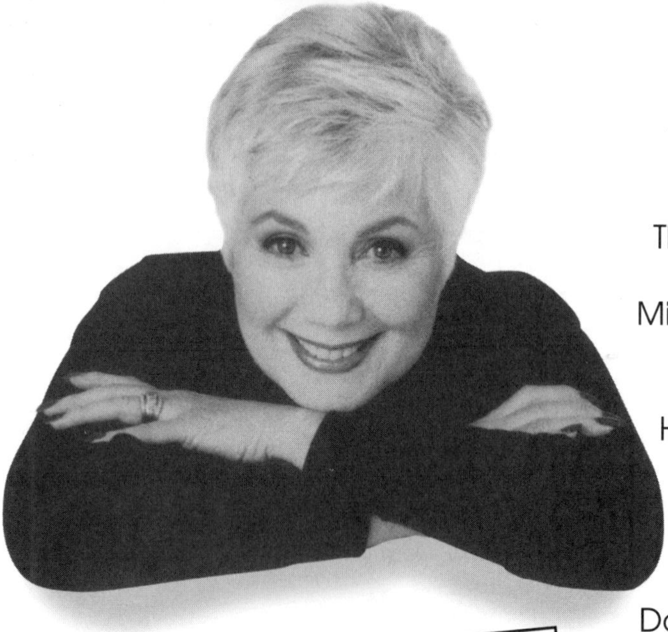

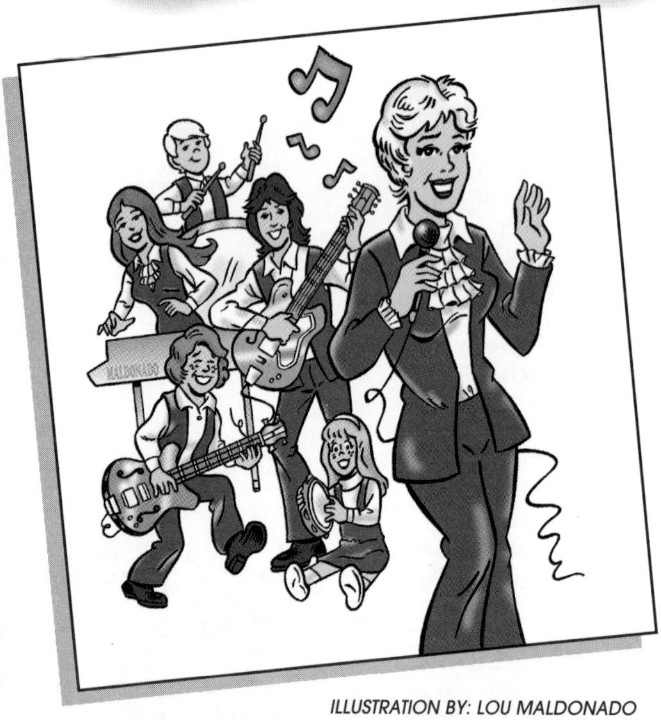
MALDONADO

ILLUSTRATION BY: LOU MALDONADO

*Multi-talented performer Shirley Jones is star of both stage and screen, having appeared in such musical classics as **South Pacific, Oklahoma, Carousel** and **The Music Man**. She won an Oscar for her role in **Elmer Gantry**, and is perhaps best known for her portrayal of pop singer Shirley Partridge, the "hippest" TV mom of the seventies, on the hit series, **The Partridge Family**.*

The slick and saucy `70s –
contentious, fierce, and free,
Apollo, Cher, Cambodia, Mel Brooks,
and Wounded Knee;
Bobby Fisher, Annie Hall,
Iran, and Son of Sam,
Jim Jones, My Lai, and Attica,
Mark Spitz, and Viet Nam.

The Beatles split, Stallone's a hit,
And Roots, the very first;
Miss Thatcher's in and Nixon's out,
And where is Patty Hearst?

Hank Aaron's hits, Sinatra quits,
Picasso paints in heaven;
Old Ali wins, and Agnew sins,
Bye-Bye, Chicago Seven.

Dallas, Network, Wonder Woman,
Cheech and Hutch, and Seaver;
Those Cuckoo's hoots,
and Leisure suits,
And big Travolta fever.
Communism, Exorcism,
So long, J. Paul Getty;
CB noise and Mood Ring toys,
Jaws and Helen Reddy.
The 3-mile stir, The Way We Were,
A hundred hostage barters;
Crazy Glue, and Scooby Doo,
The White House sheds the Carters.
The legends fade like Gatorade,
We never thought we'd lose;
Hendrix, Chaplin, Crosby, Presley,
Groucho, Truman, Hughes.
Krupa, Coward, Janis, Benny,
Hoover even goes,
Peron, De Gaulle, Ben Gurion,
And ageless Gypsy Rose.
And so we view the `70s
With Archie and his friends;
I have to say they made my day,
And so my story ends.

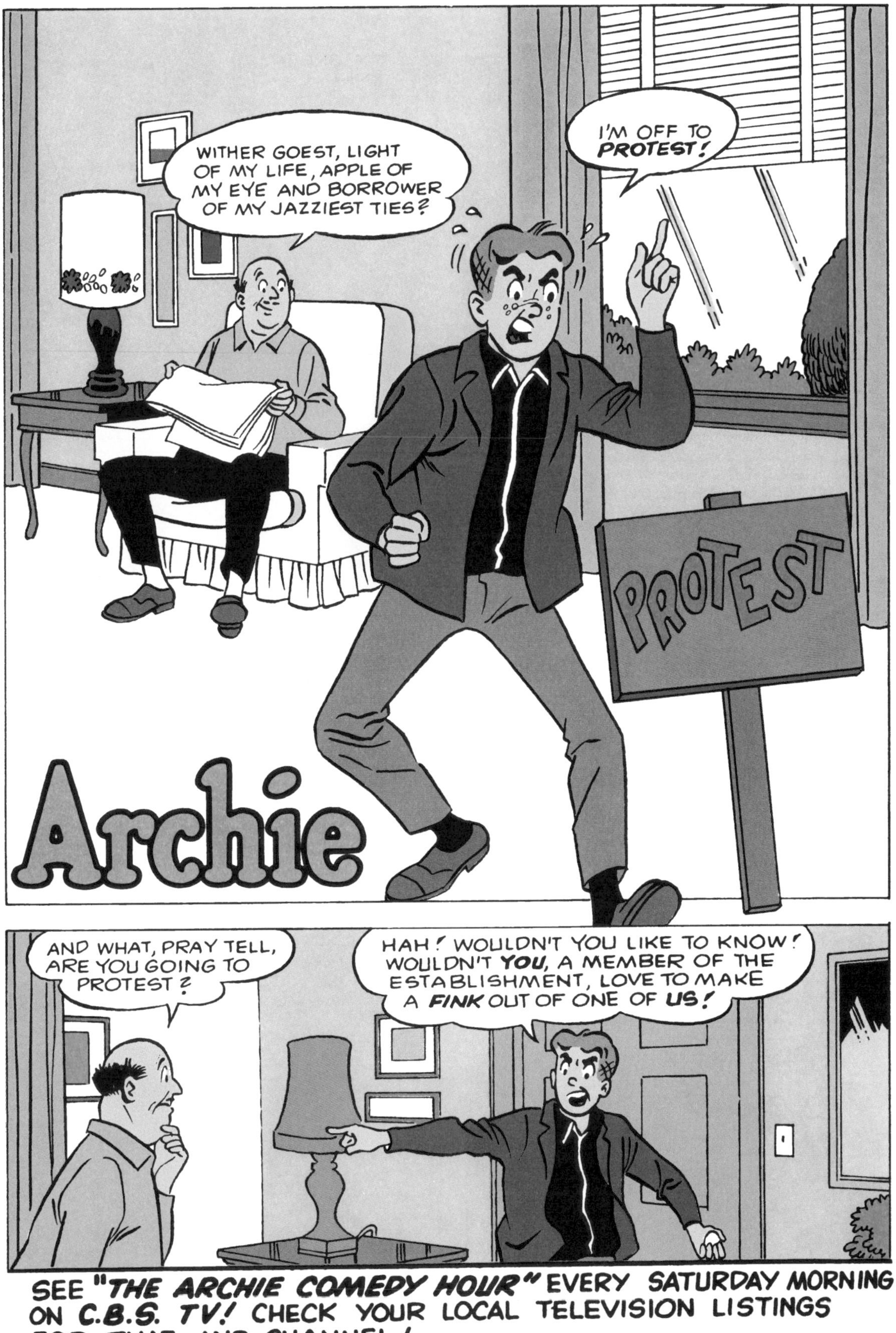
WITHER GOEST, LIGHT OF MY LIFE, APPLE OF MY EYE AND BORROWER OF MY JAZZIEST TIES?
I'M OFF TO PROTEST!
PROTEST
Archie
AND WHAT, PRAY TELL, ARE YOU GOING TO PROTEST?
HAH! WOULDN'T YOU LIKE TO KNOW! WOULDN'T YOU, A MEMBER OF THE ESTABLISHMENT, LOVE TO MAKE A FINK OUT OF ONE OF US!

SEE "*THE ARCHIE COMEDY HOUR*" EVERY SATURDAY MORNING ON *C.B.S. TV!* CHECK YOUR LOCAL TELEVISION LISTINGS FOR TIME AND CHANNEL!

Originally presented in LIFE WITH ARCHIE #93, January, 1970

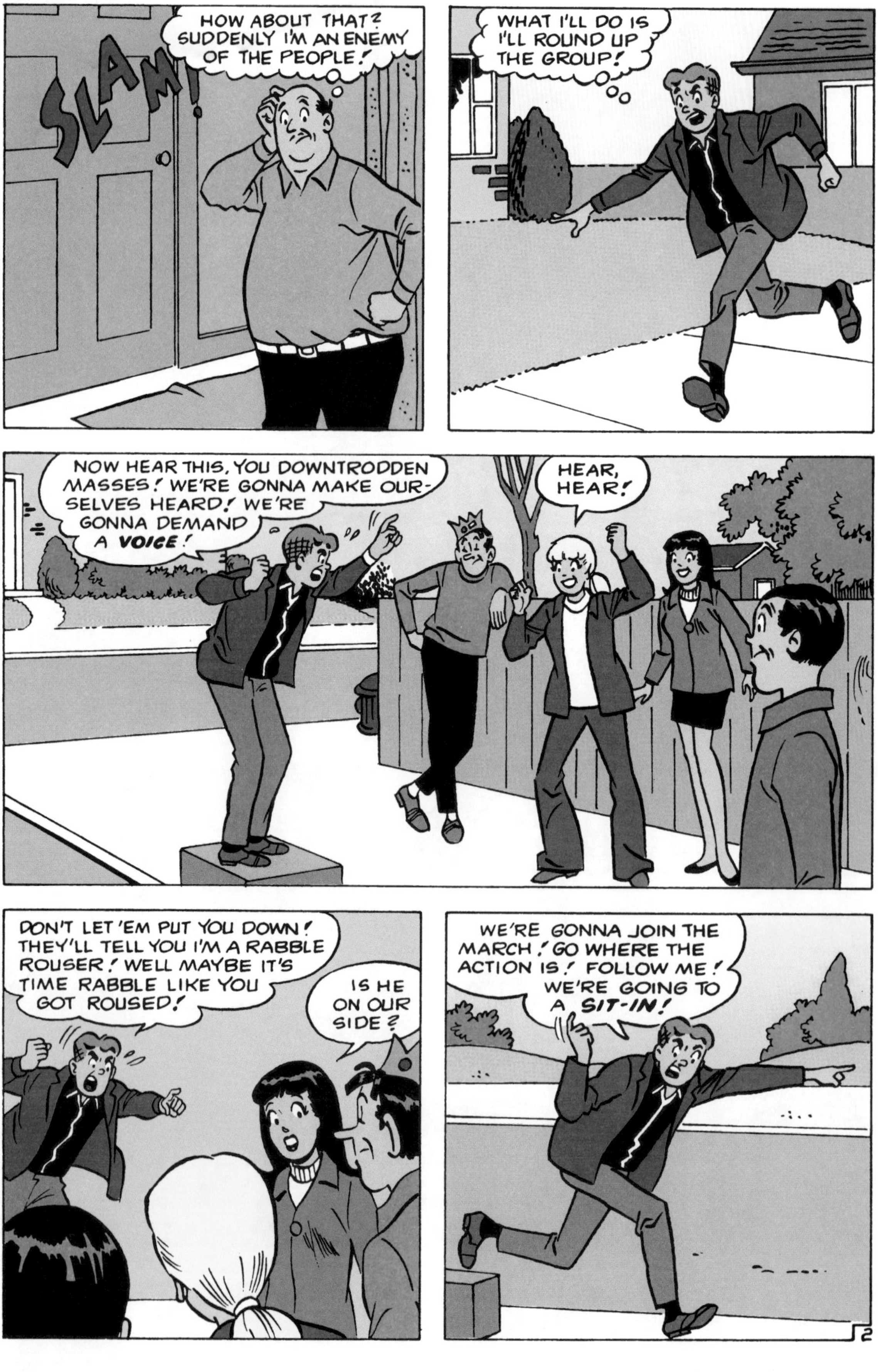
SLAM!
HOW ABOUT THAT? SUDDENLY I'M AN ENEMY OF THE PEOPLE!
WHAT I'LL DO IS I'LL ROUND UP THE GROUP!
NOW HEAR THIS, YOU DOWNTRODDEN MASSES! WE'RE GONNA MAKE OURSELVES HEARD! WE'RE GONNA DEMAND A VOICE!
HEAR, HEAR!
DON'T LET 'EM PUT YOU DOWN! THEY'LL TELL YOU I'M A RABBLE ROUSER! WELL MAYBE IT'S TIME RABBLE LIKE YOU GOT ROUSED!
IS HE ON OUR SIDE?
WE'RE GONNA JOIN THE MARCH! GO WHERE THE ACTION IS! FOLLOW ME! WE'RE GOING TO A SIT-IN!
2

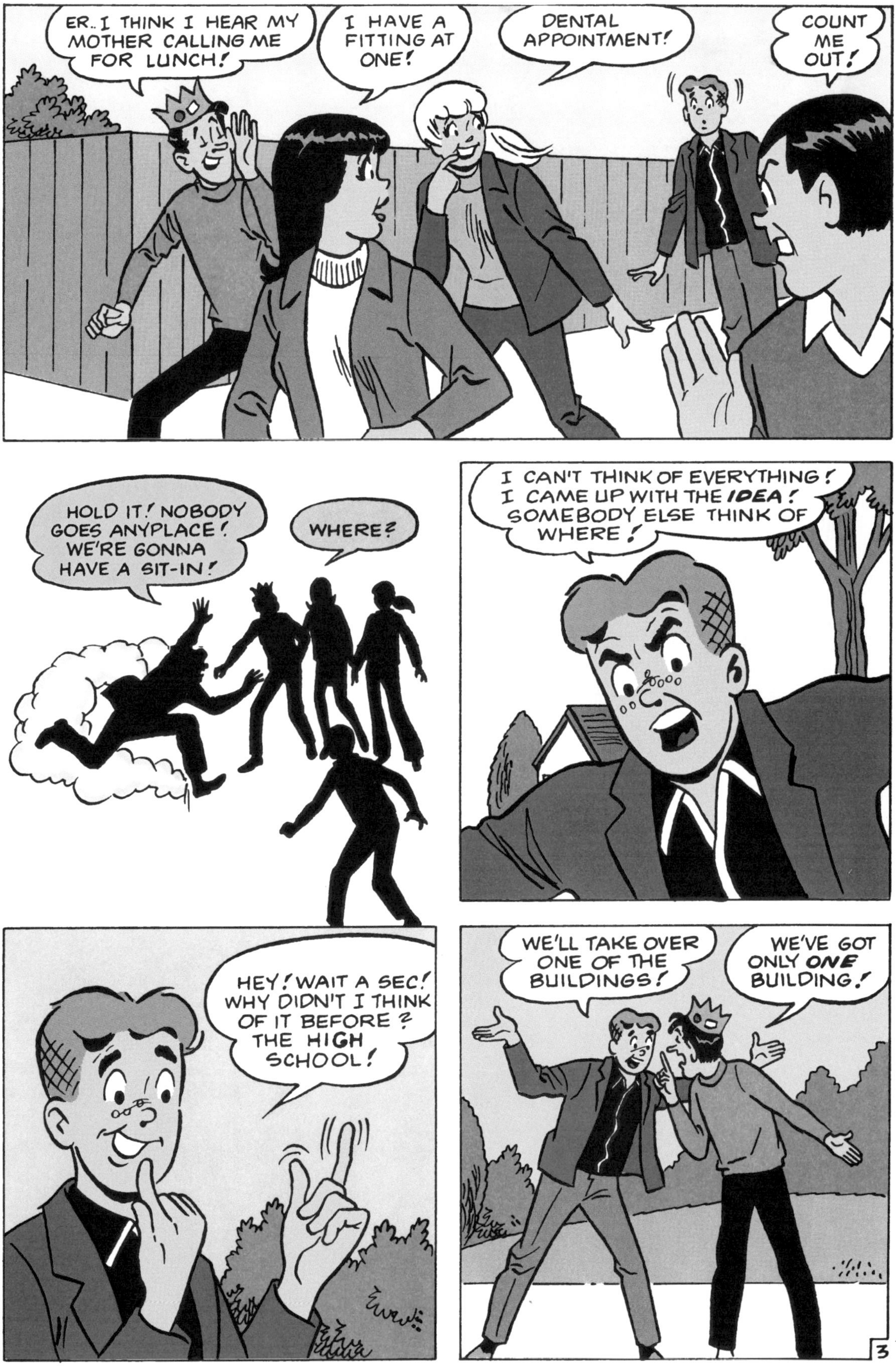
ER.. I THINK I HEAR MY MOTHER CALLING ME FOR LUNCH!
I HAVE A FITTING AT ONE!
DENTAL APPOINTMENT!
COUNT ME OUT!
HOLD IT! NOBODY GOES ANYPLACE! WE'RE GONNA HAVE A SIT-IN!
WHERE?
I CAN'T THINK OF EVERYTHING! I CAME UP WITH THE IDEA! SOMEBODY ELSE THINK OF WHERE!
HEY! WAIT A SEC! WHY DIDN'T I THINK OF IT BEFORE? THE HIGH SCHOOL!
WE'LL TAKE OVER ONE OF THE BUILDINGS!
WE'VE GOT ONLY ONE BUILDING!
3

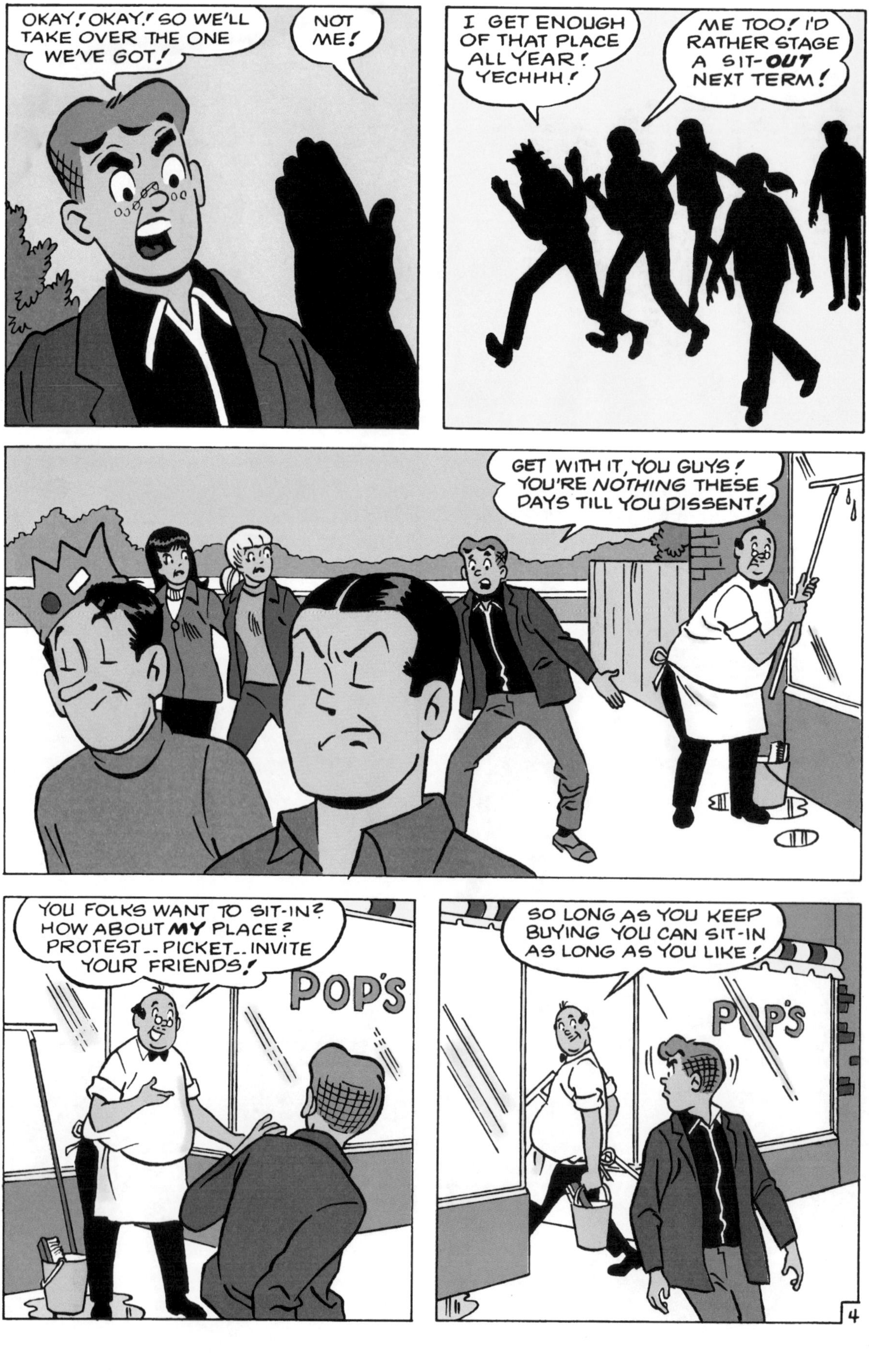

OKAY! OKAY! SO WE'LL TAKE OVER THE ONE WE'VE GOT!
NOT ME!
I GET ENOUGH OF THAT PLACE ALL YEAR! YECHHH!
ME TOO! I'D RATHER STAGE A SIT-**OUT** NEXT TERM!
GET WITH IT, YOU GUYS! YOU'RE *NOTHING* THESE DAYS TILL YOU DISSENT!
YOU FOLKS WANT TO SIT-IN? HOW ABOUT **MY** PLACE? PROTEST.. PICKET.. INVITE YOUR FRIENDS!
POP'S
SO LONG AS YOU KEEP BUYING YOU CAN SIT-IN AS LONG AS YOU LIKE!
POP'S
4

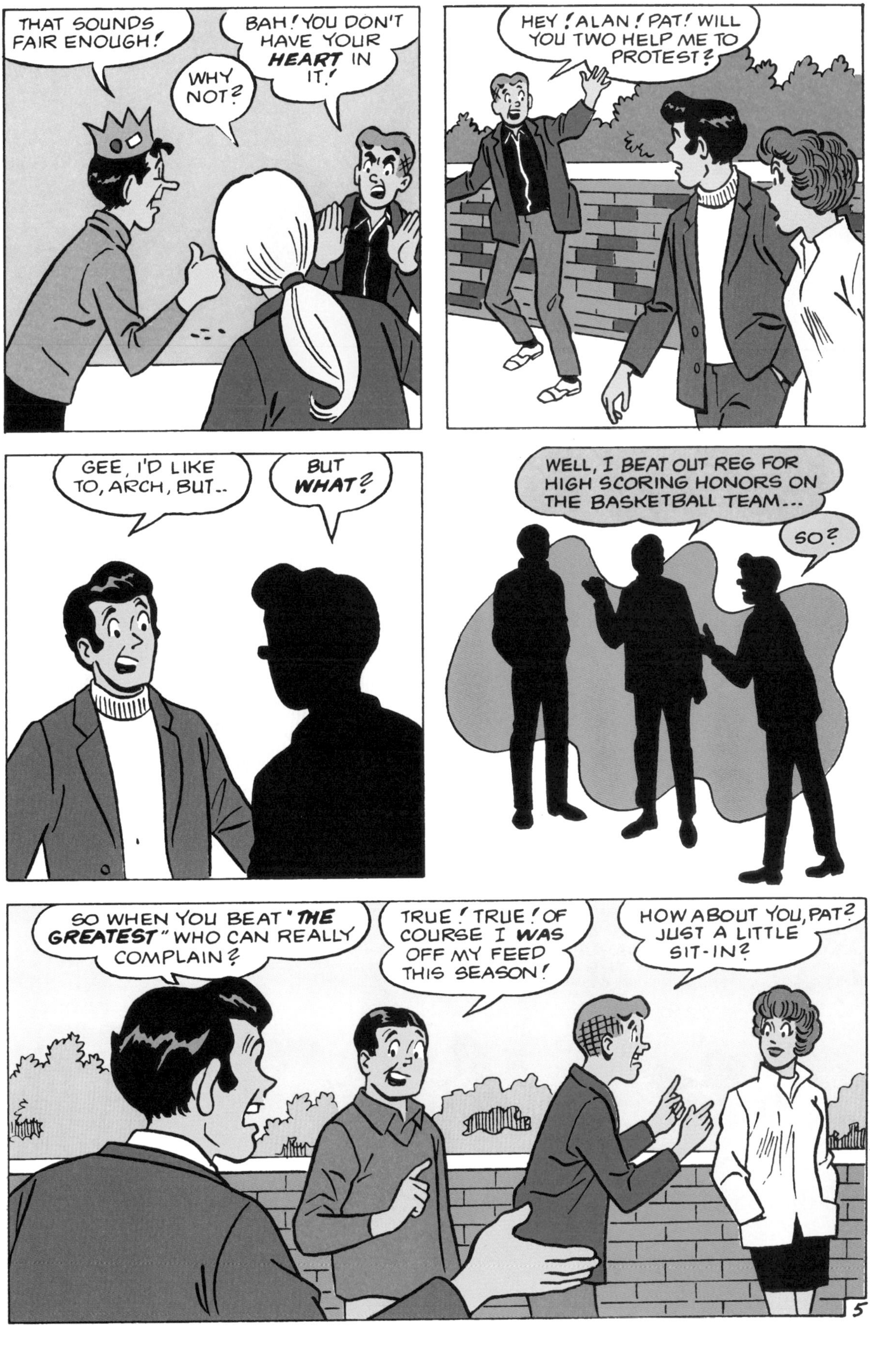
THAT SOUNDS FAIR ENOUGH!
WHY NOT?
BAH! YOU DON'T HAVE YOUR HEART IN IT!
HEY! ALAN! PAT! WILL YOU TWO HELP ME TO PROTEST?
GEE, I'D LIKE TO, ARCH, BUT..
BUT WHAT?
WELL, I BEAT OUT REG FOR HIGH SCORING HONORS ON THE BASKETBALL TEAM...
SO?
SO WHEN YOU BEAT "THE GREATEST" WHO CAN REALLY COMPLAIN?
TRUE! TRUE! OF COURSE I WAS OFF MY FEED THIS SEASON!
HOW ABOUT YOU, PAT? JUST A LITTLE SIT-IN?
5

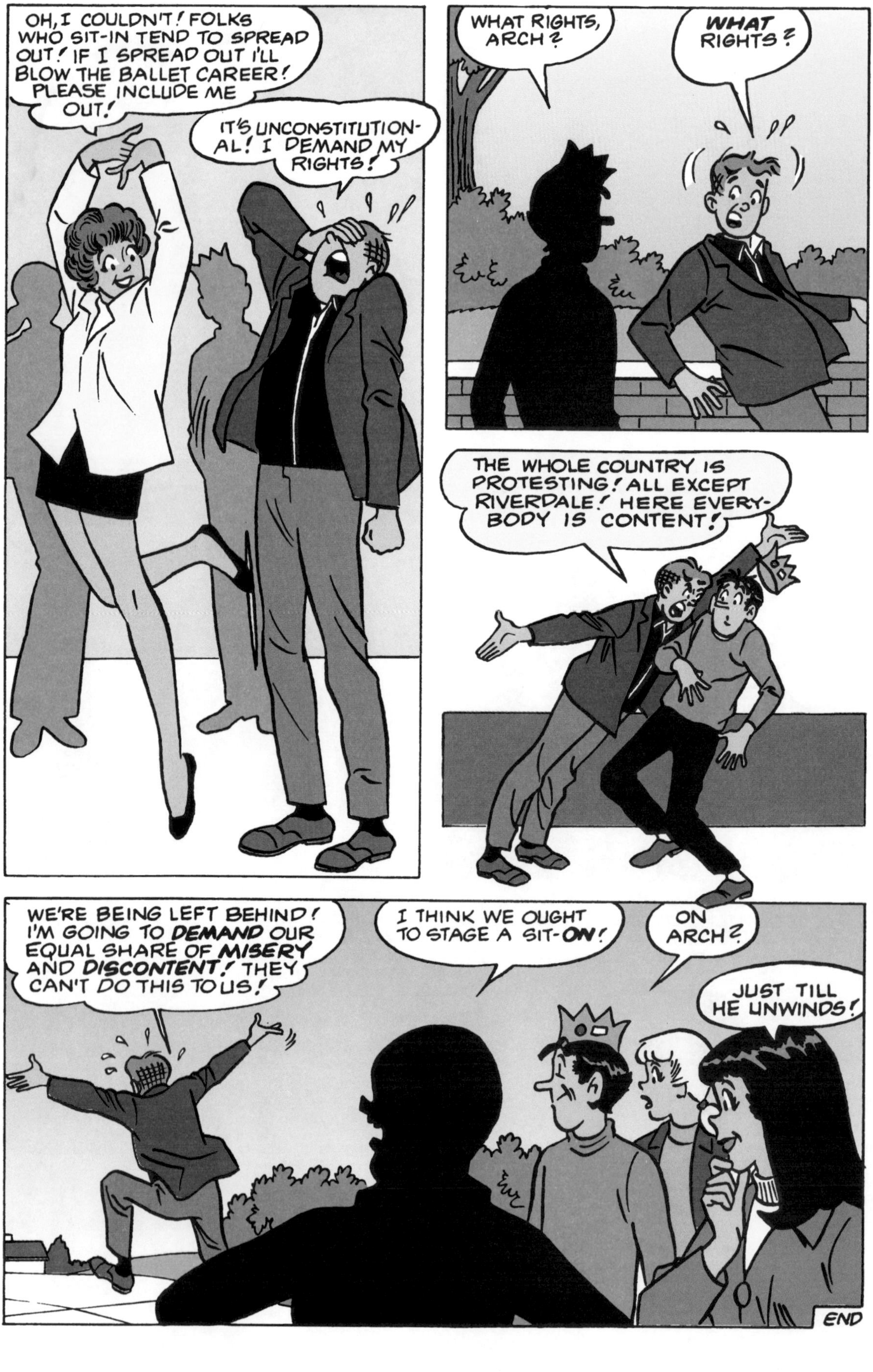
OH, I COULDN'T! FOLKS WHO SIT-IN TEND TO SPREAD OUT! IF I SPREAD OUT I'LL BLOW THE BALLET CAREER! PLEASE INCLUDE ME OUT!
IT'S UNCONSTITUTION-AL! I DEMAND MY RIGHTS!
WHAT RIGHTS, ARCH?
WHAT RIGHTS?
THE WHOLE COUNTRY IS PROTESTING! ALL EXCEPT RIVERDALE! HERE EVERY-BODY IS CONTENT!
WE'RE BEING LEFT BEHIND! I'M GOING TO DEMAND OUR EQUAL SHARE OF MISERY AND DISCONTENT! THEY CAN'T DO THIS TO US!
I THINK WE OUGHT TO STAGE A SIT-ON!
ON ARCH?
JUST TILL HE UNWINDS!
END

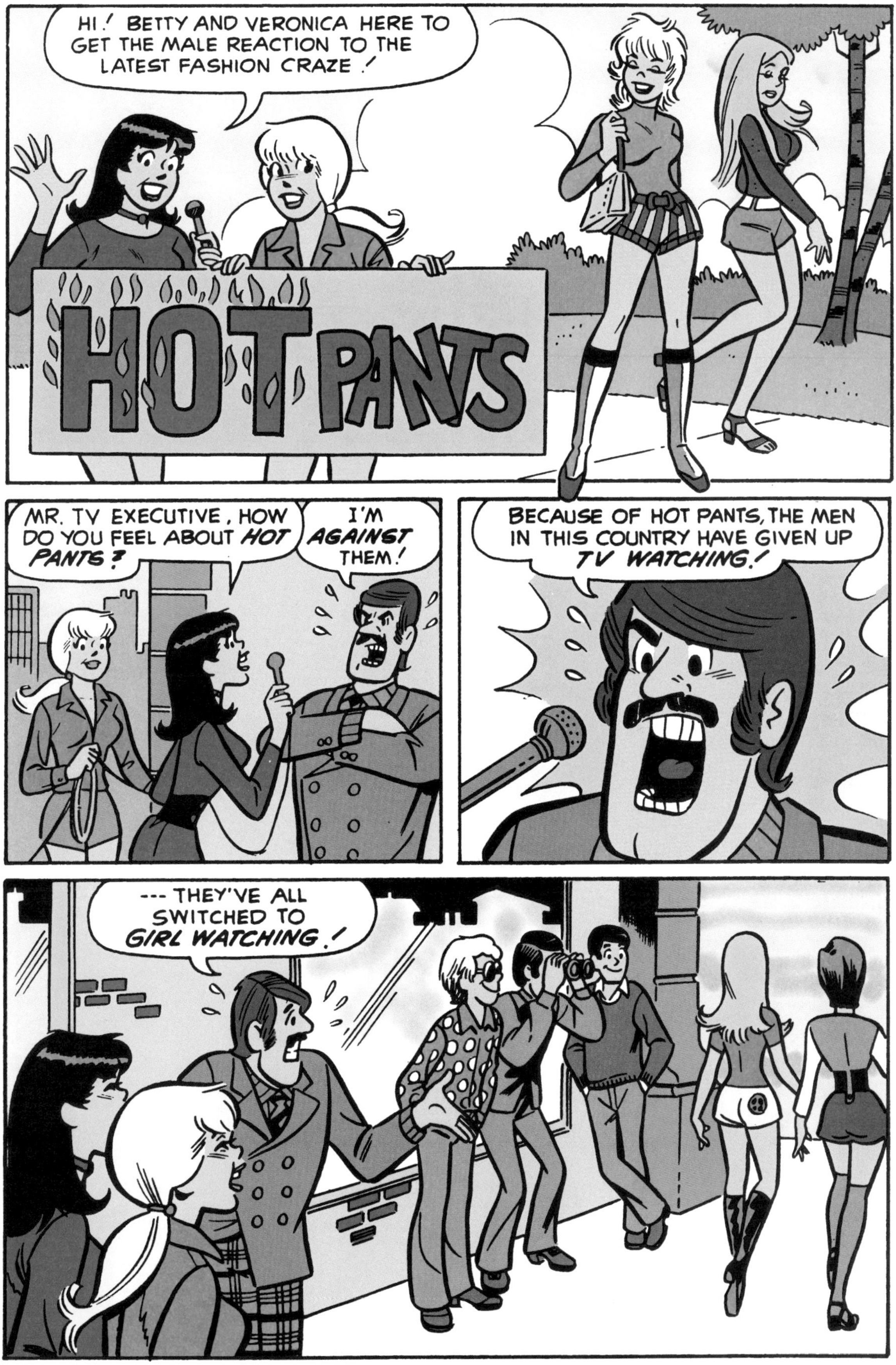
HI! BETTY AND VERONICA HERE TO GET THE MALE REACTION TO THE LATEST FASHION CRAZE!
HOT PANTS
MR. TV EXECUTIVE, HOW DO YOU FEEL ABOUT *HOT PANTS?*
I'M *AGAINST* THEM!
BECAUSE OF HOT PANTS, THE MEN IN THIS COUNTRY HAVE GIVEN UP *TV WATCHING!*
--- THEY'VE ALL SWITCHED TO *GIRL WATCHING!*

Originally presented in LAUGH #248, November, 1971

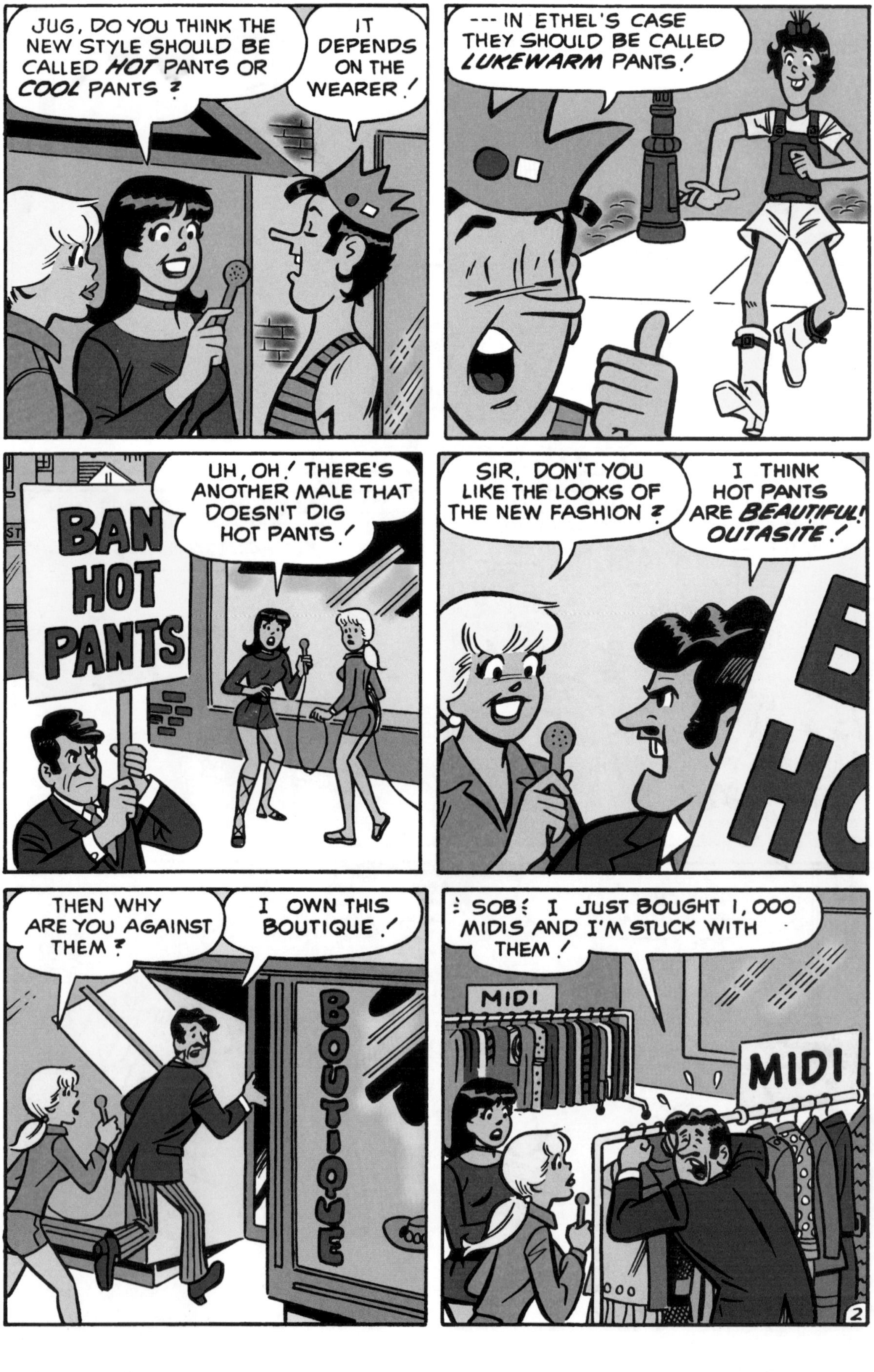

JUG, DO YOU THINK THE NEW STYLE SHOULD BE CALLED HOT PANTS OR COOL PANTS ?
IT DEPENDS ON THE WEARER !
--- IN ETHEL'S CASE THEY SHOULD BE CALLED LUKEWARM PANTS !
BAN HOT PANTS
UH, OH ! THERE'S ANOTHER MALE THAT DOESN'T DIG HOT PANTS !
SIR, DON'T YOU LIKE THE LOOKS OF THE NEW FASHION ?
I THINK HOT PANTS ARE BEAUTIFUL! OUTASITE !
THEN WHY ARE YOU AGAINST THEM ?
I OWN THIS BOUTIQUE !
BOUTIQUE
: SOB : I JUST BOUGHT 1,000 MIDIS AND I'M STUCK WITH THEM !
MIDI
MIDI
2

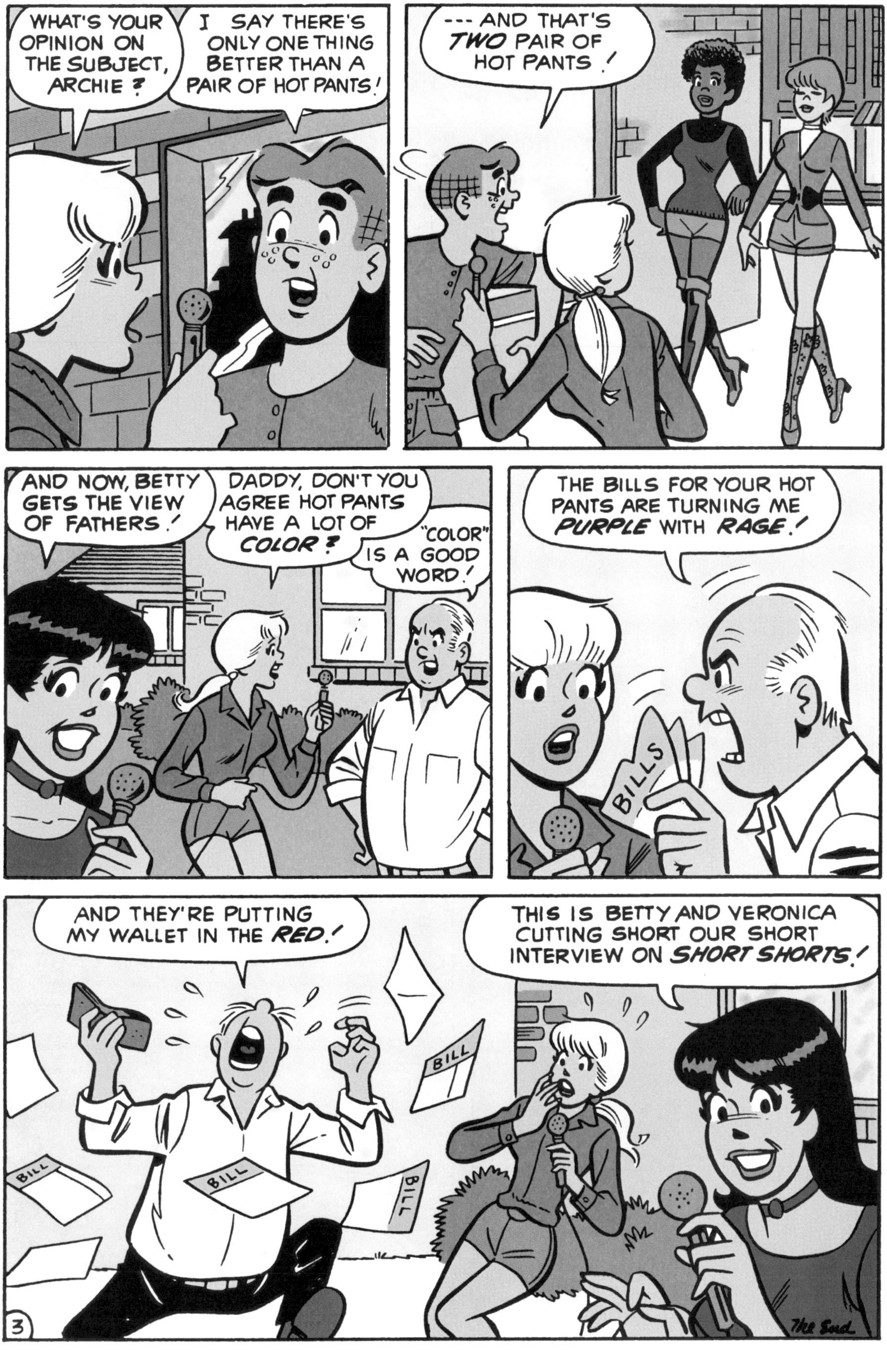
WHAT'S YOUR OPINION ON THE SUBJECT, ARCHIE ?
I SAY THERE'S ONLY ONE THING BETTER THAN A PAIR OF HOT PANTS!
--- AND THAT'S TWO PAIR OF HOT PANTS!
AND NOW, BETTY GETS THE VIEW OF FATHERS!
DADDY, DON'T YOU AGREE HOT PANTS HAVE A LOT OF COLOR ?
"COLOR" IS A GOOD WORD!
THE BILLS FOR YOUR HOT PANTS ARE TURNING ME PURPLE WITH RAGE!
BILLS
AND THEY'RE PUTTING MY WALLET IN THE RED!
THIS IS BETTY AND VERONICA CUTTING SHORT OUR SHORT INTERVIEW ON SHORT SHORTS!
BILL
BILL
BILL
BILL
3
The End

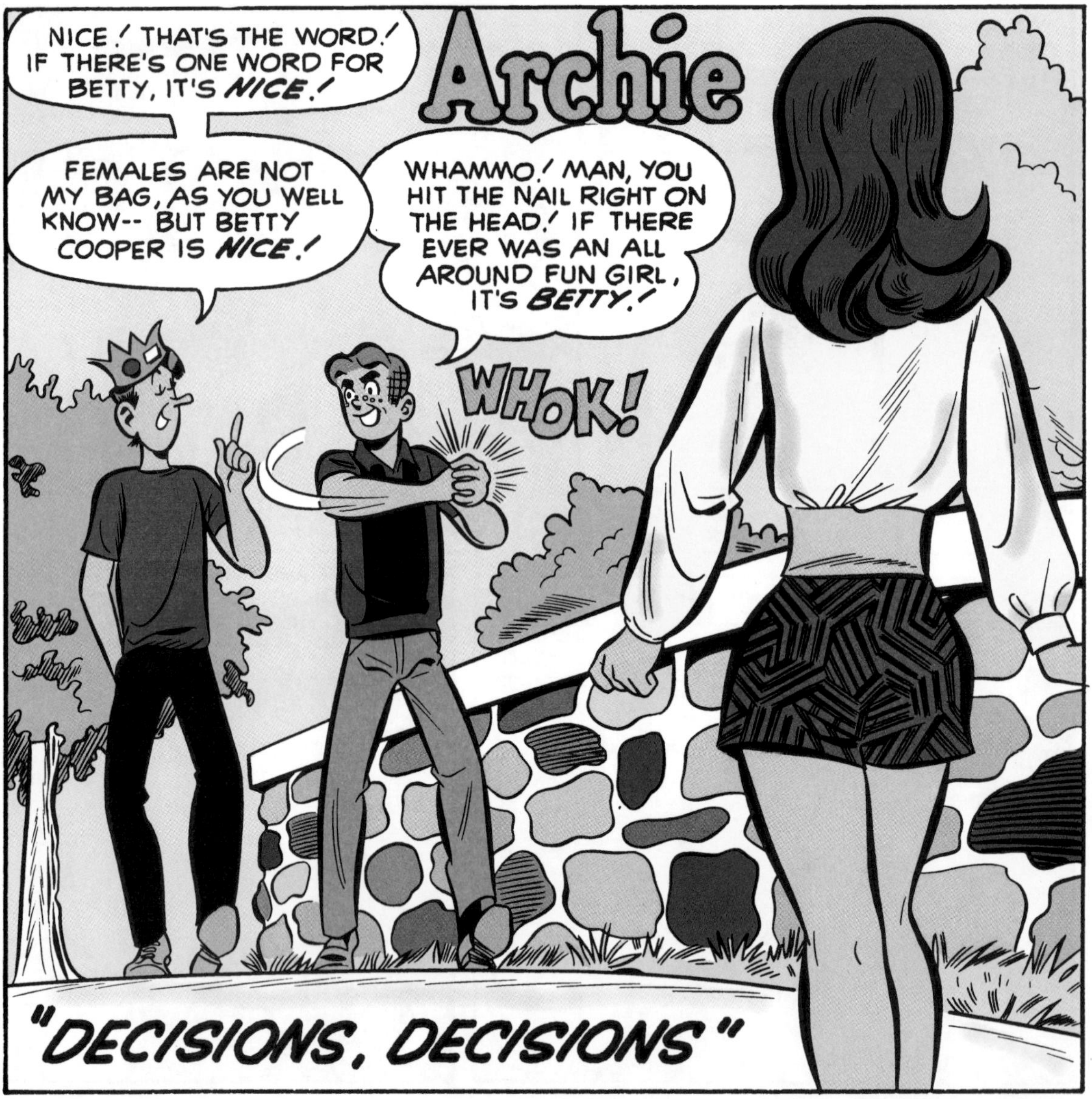
Archie
NICE! THAT'S THE WORD! IF THERE'S ONE WORD FOR BETTY, IT'S NICE!
FEMALES ARE NOT MY BAG, AS YOU WELL KNOW-- BUT BETTY COOPER IS NICE!
WHAMMO! MAN, YOU HIT THE NAIL RIGHT ON THE HEAD! IF THERE EVER WAS AN ALL AROUND FUN GIRL, IT'S BETTY!
WHOK!
"DECISIONS, DECISIONS"

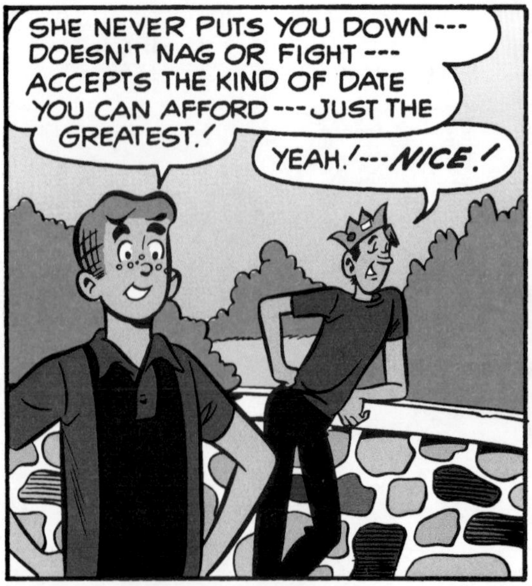
SHE NEVER PUTS YOU DOWN--- DOESN'T NAG OR FIGHT--- ACCEPTS THE KIND OF DATE YOU CAN AFFORD---JUST THE GREATEST!
YEAH!---NICE!

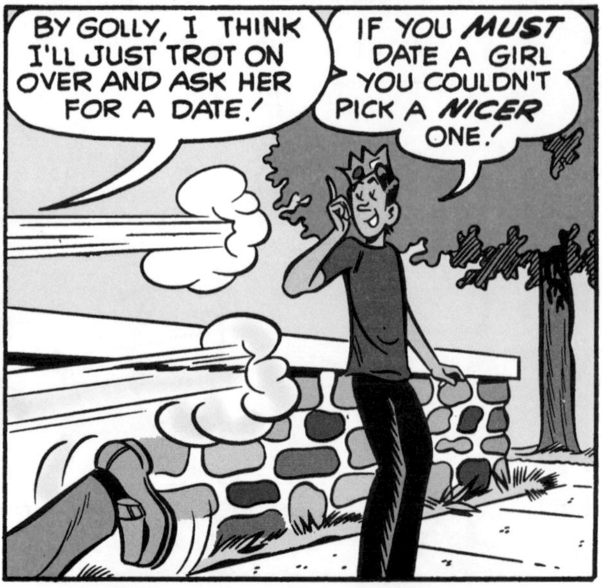
BY GOLLY, I THINK I'LL JUST TROT ON OVER AND ASK HER FOR A DATE!
IF YOU MUST DATE A GIRL YOU COULDN'T PICK A NICER ONE!

Originally presented in ARCHIE #214, December, 1971

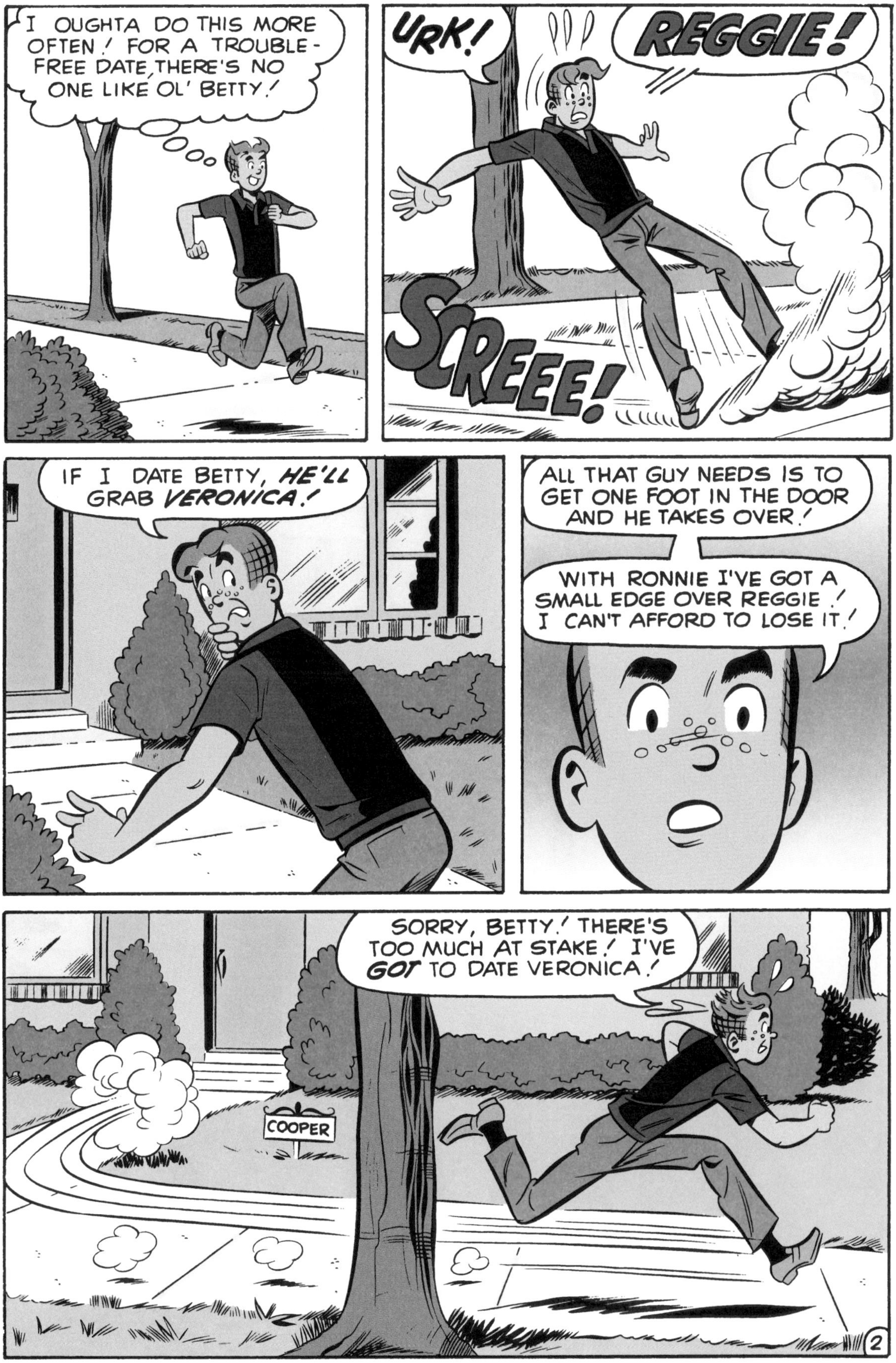
I OUGHTA DO THIS MORE OFTEN! FOR A TROUBLE-FREE DATE, THERE'S NO ONE LIKE OL' BETTY!
URK!
REGGIE!
SCREEEE!
IF I DATE BETTY, HE'LL GRAB VERONICA!
ALL THAT GUY NEEDS IS TO GET ONE FOOT IN THE DOOR AND HE TAKES OVER!
WITH RONNIE I'VE GOT A SMALL EDGE OVER REGGIE! I CAN'T AFFORD TO LOSE IT!
SORRY, BETTY! THERE'S TOO MUCH AT STAKE! I'VE GOT TO DATE VERONICA!
COOPER
2

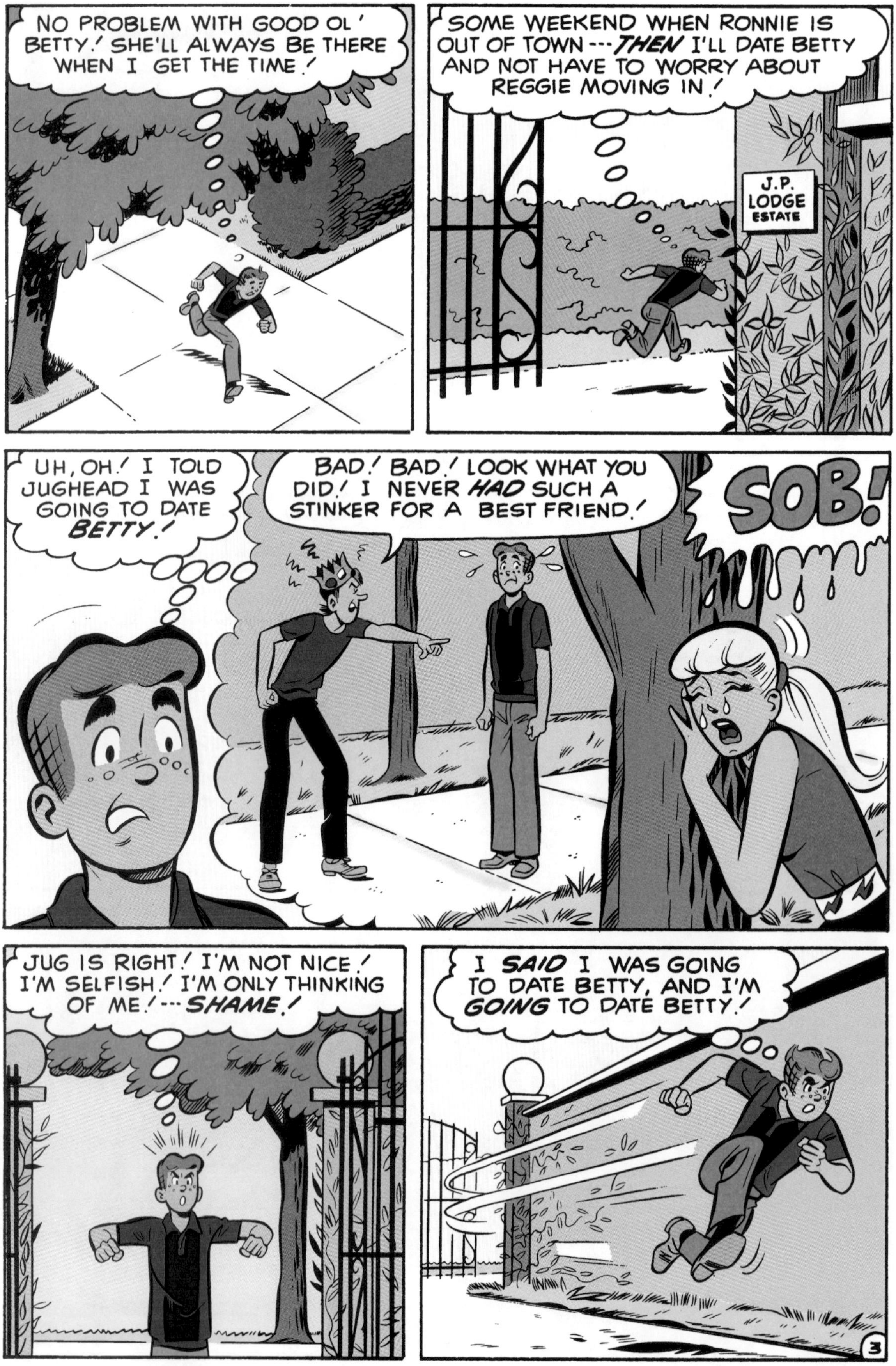
NO PROBLEM WITH GOOD OL' BETTY! SHE'LL ALWAYS BE THERE WHEN I GET THE TIME!
SOME WEEKEND WHEN RONNIE IS OUT OF TOWN --- THEN I'LL DATE BETTY AND NOT HAVE TO WORRY ABOUT REGGIE MOVING IN!
J.P. LODGE ESTATE
UH, OH! I TOLD JUGHEAD I WAS GOING TO DATE BETTY!
BAD! BAD! LOOK WHAT YOU DID! I NEVER HAD SUCH A STINKER FOR A BEST FRIEND!
SOB!
JUG IS RIGHT! I'M NOT NICE! I'M SELFISH! I'M ONLY THINKING OF ME! --- SHAME!
I SAID I WAS GOING TO DATE BETTY, AND I'M GOING TO DATE BETTY!
3

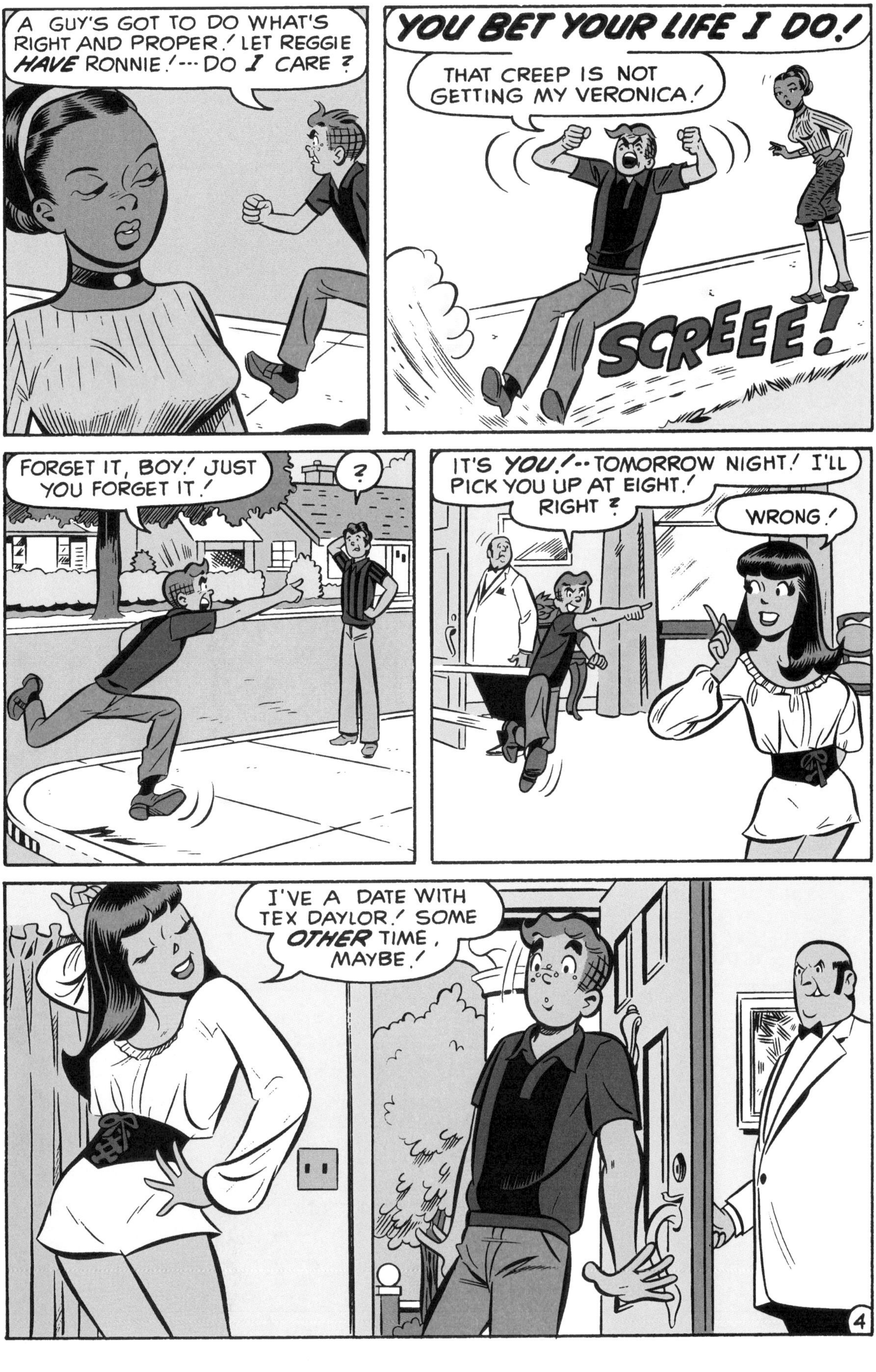
A GUY'S GOT TO DO WHAT'S RIGHT AND PROPER! LET REGGIE HAVE RONNIE! --- DO I CARE?
YOU BET YOUR LIFE I DO!
THAT CREEP IS NOT GETTING MY VERONICA!
SCREEEE!
FORGET IT, BOY! JUST YOU FORGET IT!
?
IT'S YOU! -- TOMORROW NIGHT! I'LL PICK YOU UP AT EIGHT! RIGHT?
WRONG!
I'VE A DATE WITH TEX DAYLOR! SOME OTHER TIME, MAYBE!
4

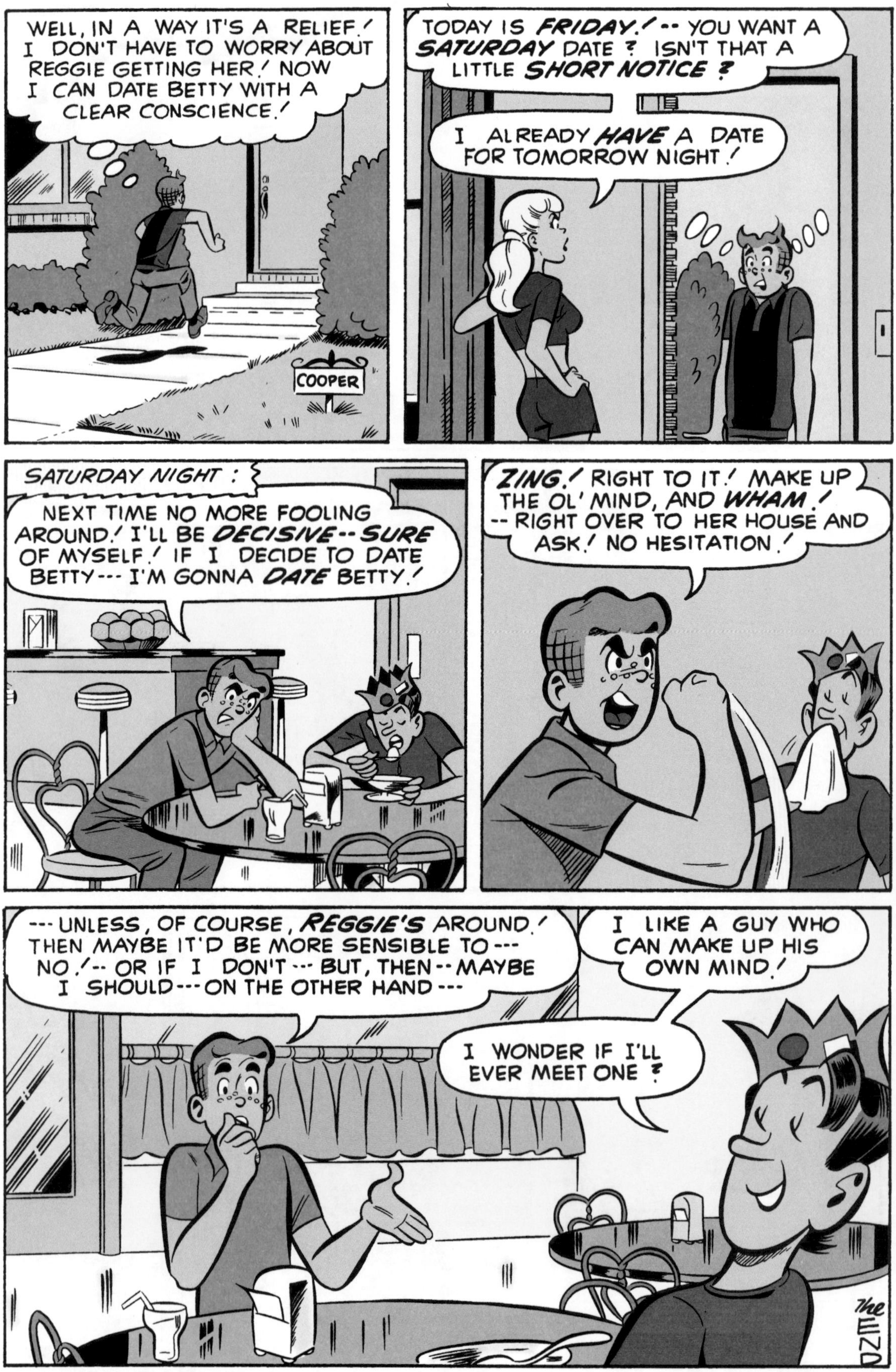
WELL, IN A WAY IT'S A RELIEF! I DON'T HAVE TO WORRY ABOUT REGGIE GETTING HER! NOW I CAN DATE BETTY WITH A CLEAR CONSCIENCE!
COOPER
TODAY IS FRIDAY! -- YOU WANT A SATURDAY DATE ? ISN'T THAT A LITTLE SHORT NOTICE ?
I ALREADY HAVE A DATE FOR TOMORROW NIGHT!
SATURDAY NIGHT :
NEXT TIME NO MORE FOOLING AROUND! I'LL BE DECISIVE -- SURE OF MYSELF! IF I DECIDE TO DATE BETTY --- I'M GONNA DATE BETTY!
ZING! RIGHT TO IT! MAKE UP THE OL' MIND, AND WHAM! -- RIGHT OVER TO HER HOUSE AND ASK! NO HESITATION!
--- UNLESS, OF COURSE, REGGIE'S AROUND! THEN MAYBE IT'D BE MORE SENSIBLE TO --- NO! -- OR IF I DON'T --- BUT, THEN -- MAYBE I SHOULD --- ON THE OTHER HAND ---
I LIKE A GUY WHO CAN MAKE UP HIS OWN MIND!
I WONDER IF I'LL EVER MEET ONE ?
THE END

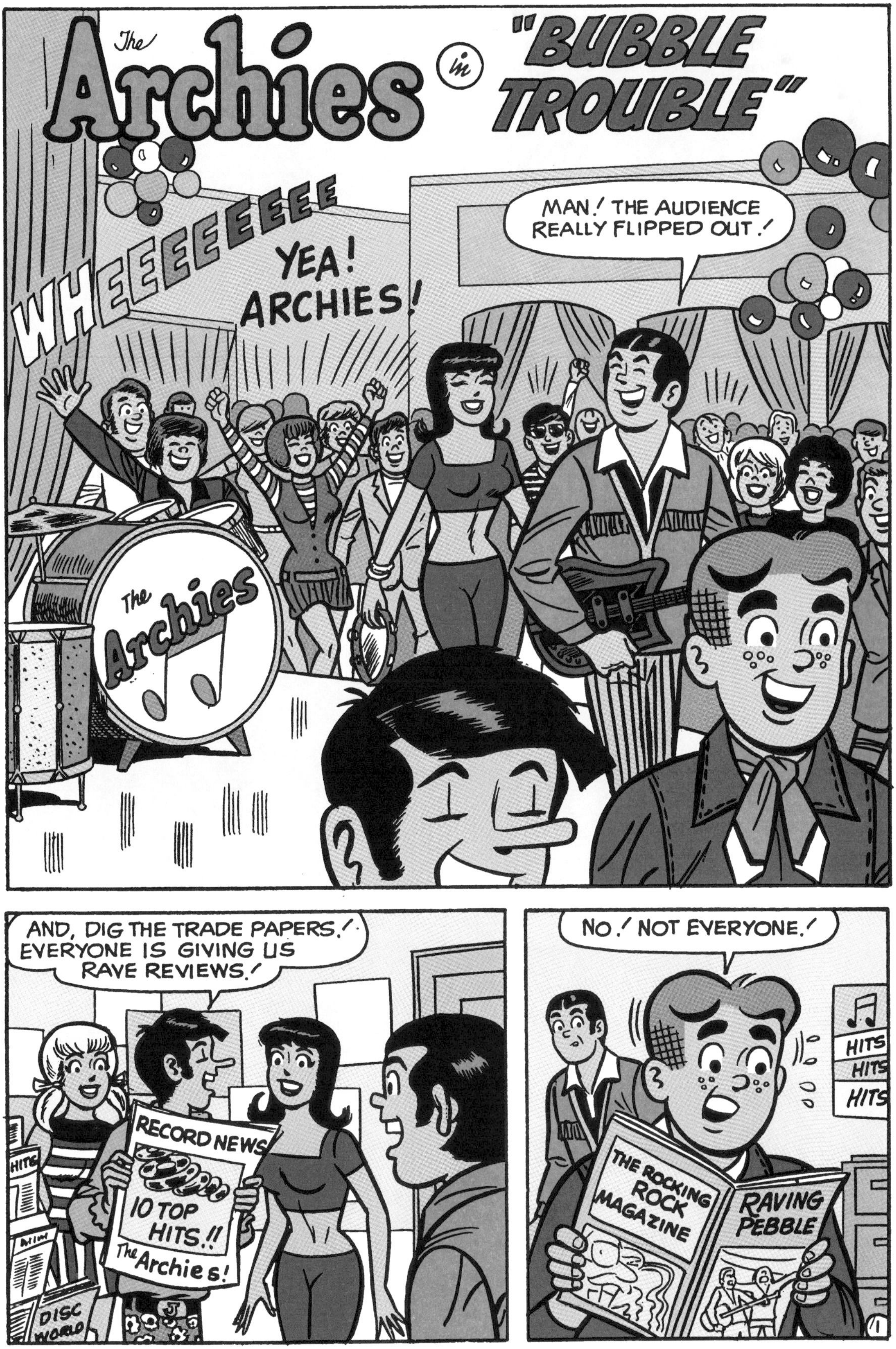
The Archies in "BUBBLE TROUBLE"
WHEEEEEEEEE
YEA! ARCHIES!
MAN! THE AUDIENCE REALLY FLIPPED OUT!
The Archies
AND, DIG THE TRADE PAPERS! EVERYONE IS GIVING US RAVE REVIEWS!
RECORD NEWS
10 TOP HITS!!
The Archies!
DISC WORLD
NO! NOT EVERYONE!
HITS
HITS
HITS
THE ROCKING ROCK MAGAZINE
RAVING PEBBLE

Originally presented in EVERYTHING'S ARCHIE #21, April, 1972

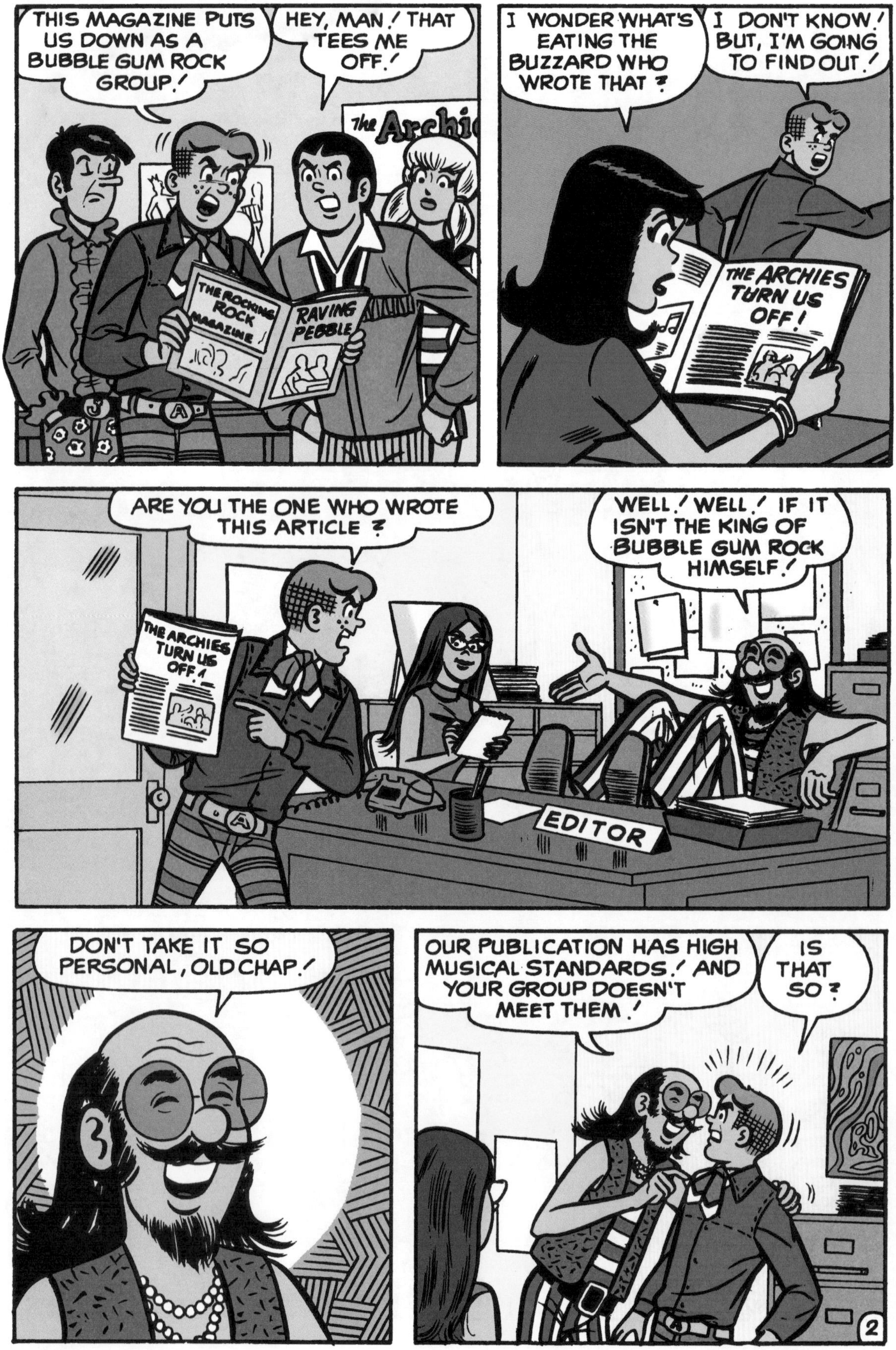
THIS MAGAZINE PUTS US DOWN AS A BUBBLE GUM ROCK GROUP!
HEY, MAN! THAT TEES ME OFF!
THE ROCKING ROCK MAGAZINE
RAVING PEBBLE
I WONDER WHAT'S EATING THE BUZZARD WHO WROTE THAT?
I DON'T KNOW! BUT, I'M GOING TO FIND OUT!
THE ARCHIES TURN US OFF!
ARE YOU THE ONE WHO WROTE THIS ARTICLE?
WELL! WELL! IF IT ISN'T THE KING OF BUBBLE GUM ROCK HIMSELF!
THE ARCHIES TURN US OFF!
EDITOR
DON'T TAKE IT SO PERSONAL, OLD CHAP!
OUR PUBLICATION HAS HIGH MUSICAL STANDARDS! AND YOUR GROUP DOESN'T MEET THEM!
IS THAT SO?
2

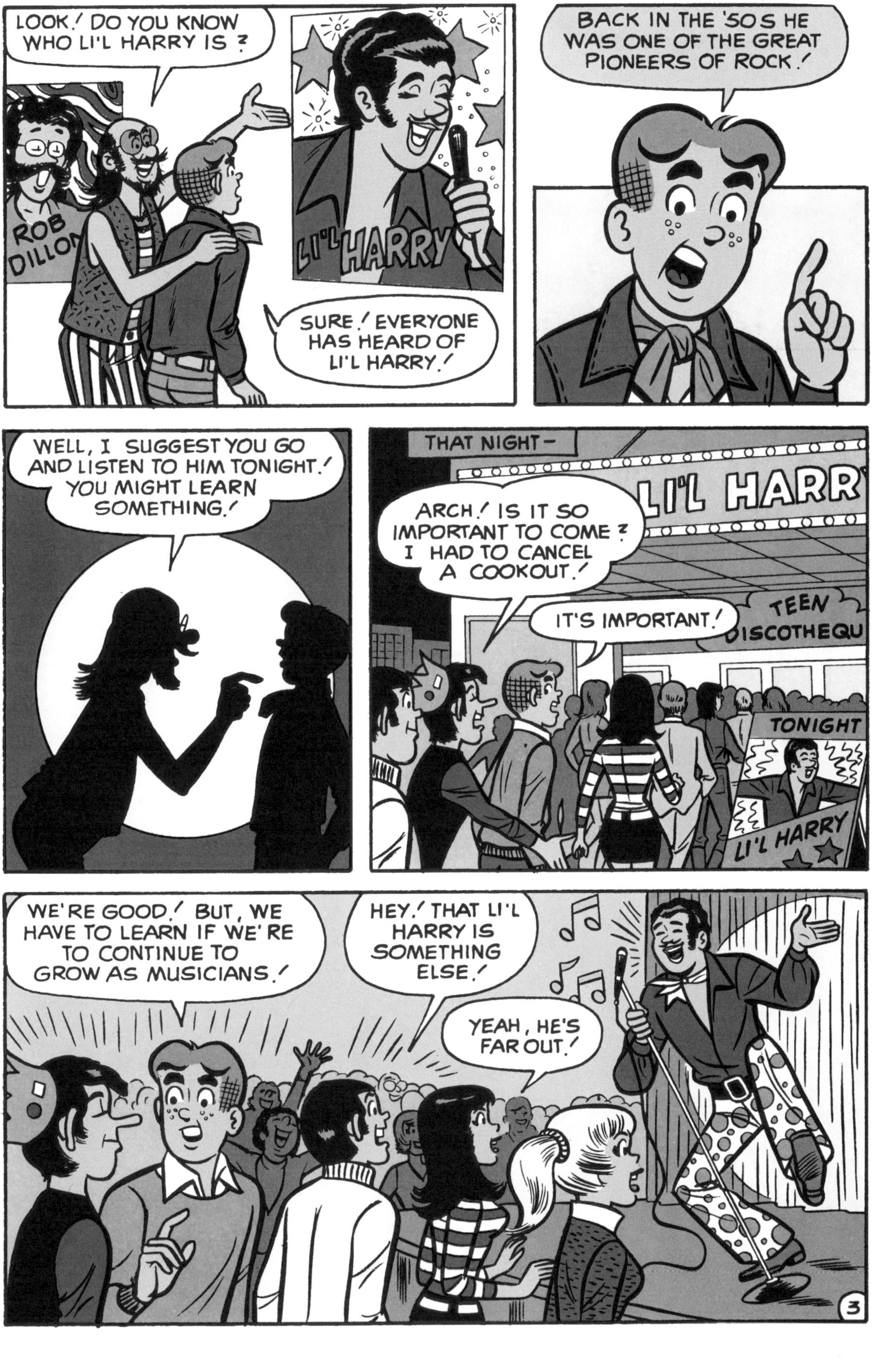
LOOK! DO YOU KNOW WHO LI'L HARRY IS ?
ROB DILLON
LI'L HARRY
SURE! EVERYONE HAS HEARD OF LI'L HARRY!
BACK IN THE '50S HE WAS ONE OF THE GREAT PIONEERS OF ROCK!
WELL, I SUGGEST YOU GO AND LISTEN TO HIM TONIGHT! YOU MIGHT LEARN SOMETHING!
THAT NIGHT—
LI'L HARR
ARCH! IS IT SO IMPORTANT TO COME ? I HAD TO CANCEL A COOKOUT!
IT'S IMPORTANT!
TEEN DISCOTHEQU
TONIGHT
LI'L HARRY
WE'RE GOOD! BUT, WE HAVE TO LEARN IF WE'RE TO CONTINUE TO GROW AS MUSICIANS!
HEY! THAT LI'L HARRY IS SOMETHING ELSE!
YEAH, HE'S FAR OUT!
3

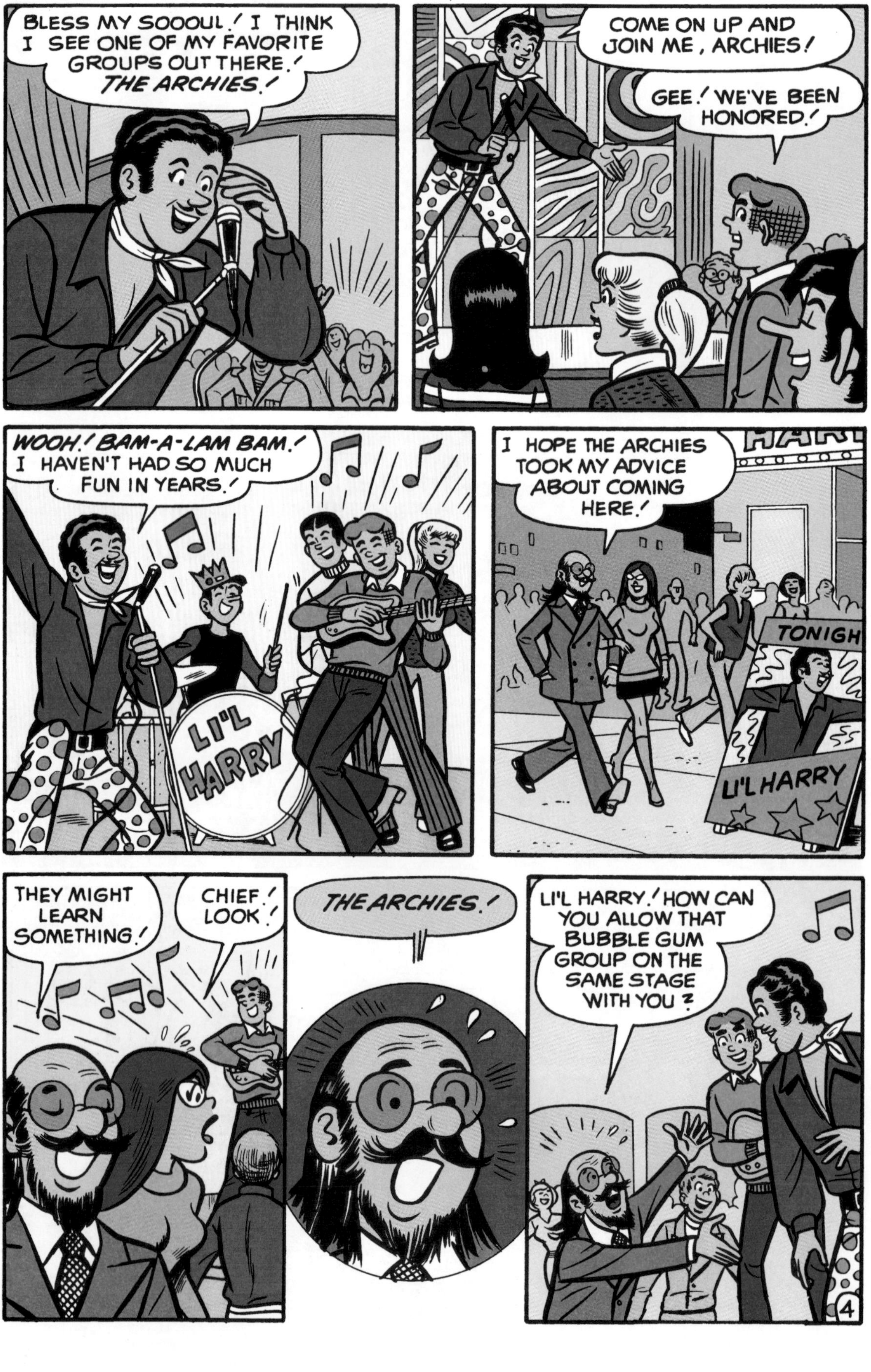
BLESS MY SOOOUL! I THINK I SEE ONE OF MY FAVORITE GROUPS OUT THERE! THE ARCHIES!
COME ON UP AND JOIN ME, ARCHIES!
GEE! WE'VE BEEN HONORED!
WOOH! BAM-A-LAM BAM! I HAVEN'T HAD SO MUCH FUN IN YEARS!
LI'L HARRY
I HOPE THE ARCHIES TOOK MY ADVICE ABOUT COMING HERE!
TONIGH
LI'L HARRY
THEY MIGHT LEARN SOMETHING!
CHIEF! LOOK!
THE ARCHIES!
LI'L HARRY! HOW CAN YOU ALLOW THAT BUBBLE GUM GROUP ON THE SAME STAGE WITH YOU?
4

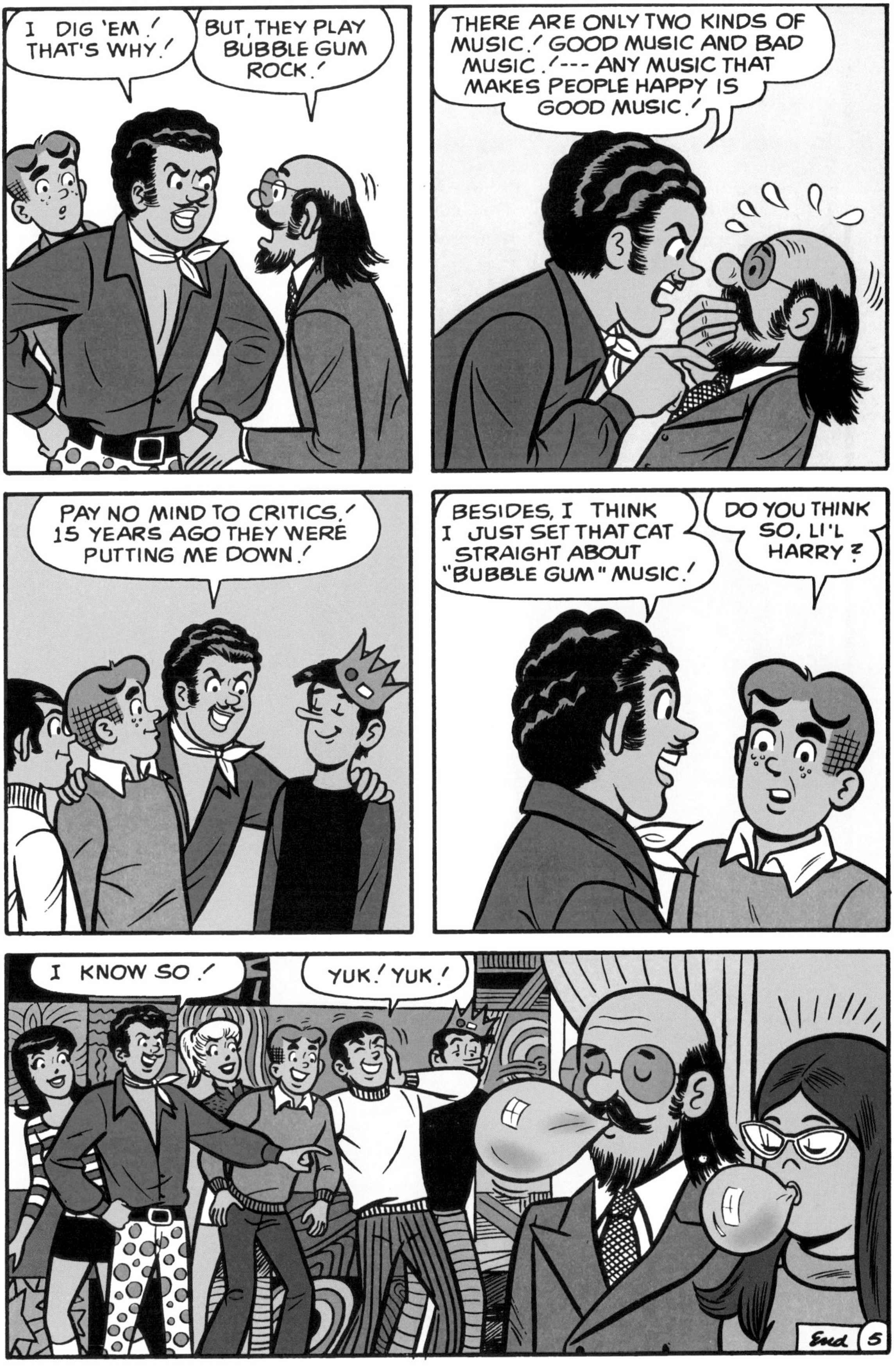
I DIG 'EM! THAT'S WHY!
BUT, THEY PLAY BUBBLE GUM ROCK!
THERE ARE ONLY TWO KINDS OF MUSIC! GOOD MUSIC AND BAD MUSIC!--- ANY MUSIC THAT MAKES PEOPLE HAPPY IS GOOD MUSIC!
PAY NO MIND TO CRITICS! 15 YEARS AGO THEY WERE PUTTING ME DOWN!
BESIDES, I THINK I JUST SET THAT CAT STRAIGHT ABOUT "BUBBLE GUM" MUSIC!
DO YOU THINK SO, LI'L HARRY?
I KNOW SO!
YUK! YUK!
End
5

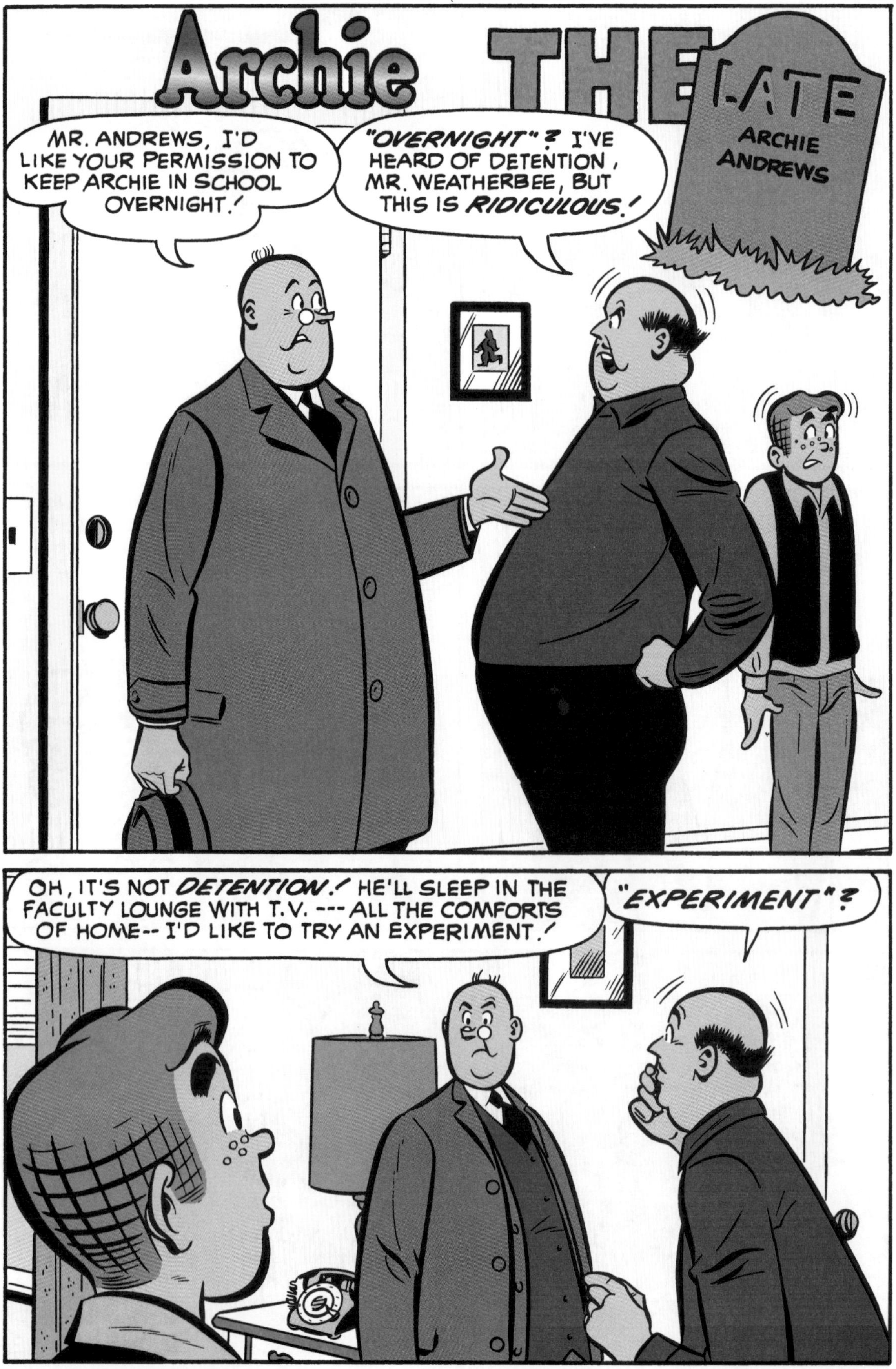
Archie
THE LATE
ARCHIE ANDREWS
MR. ANDREWS, I'D LIKE YOUR PERMISSION TO KEEP ARCHIE IN SCHOOL OVERNIGHT!
"OVERNIGHT"? I'VE HEARD OF DETENTION, MR. WEATHERBEE, BUT THIS IS RIDICULOUS!
OH, IT'S NOT DETENTION! HE'LL SLEEP IN THE FACULTY LOUNGE WITH T.V. --- ALL THE COMFORTS OF HOME-- I'D LIKE TO TRY AN EXPERIMENT!
"EXPERIMENT"?

Originally presented in ARCHIE #217, April, 1972

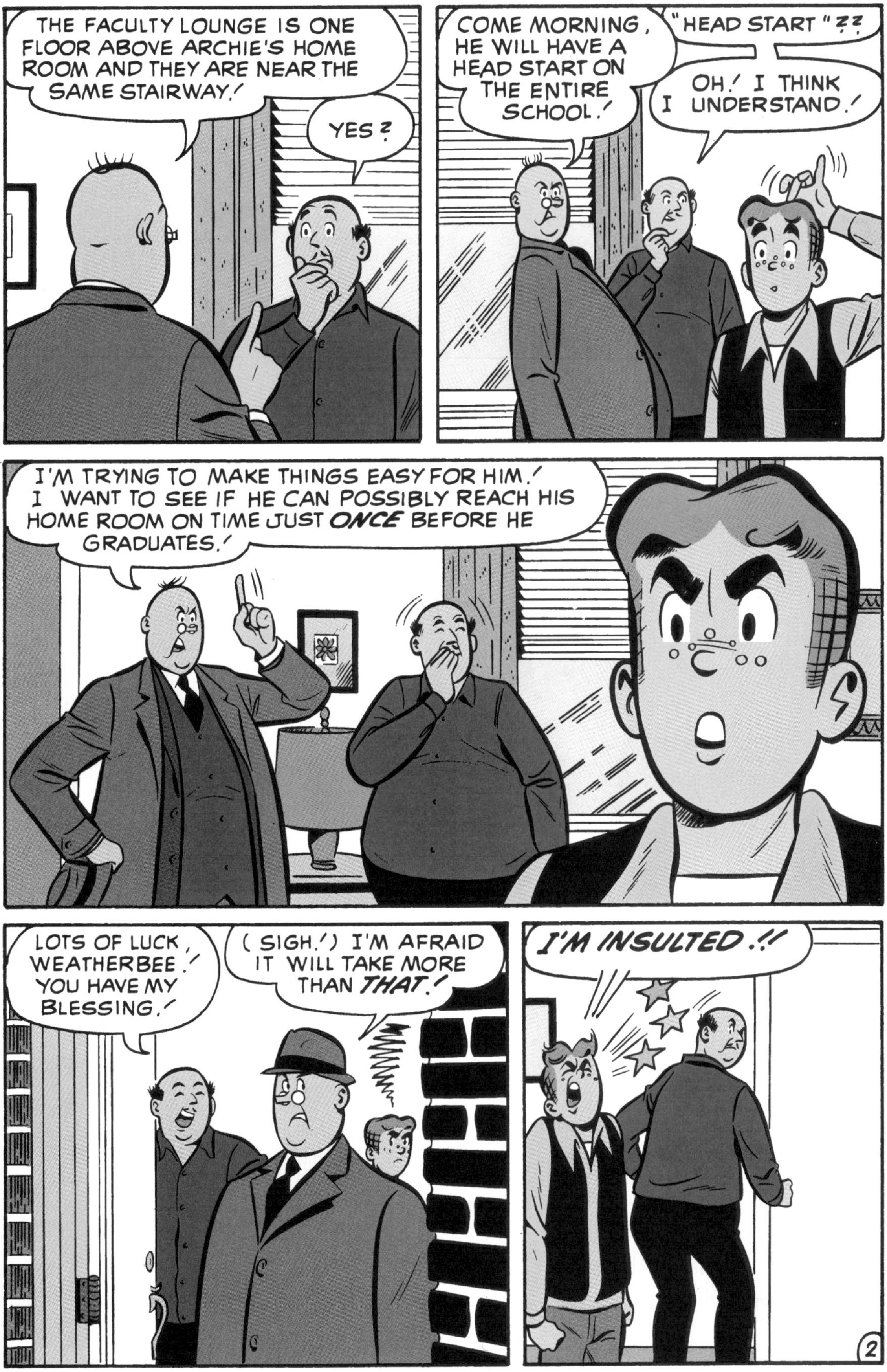
THE FACULTY LOUNGE IS ONE FLOOR ABOVE ARCHIE'S HOME ROOM AND THEY ARE NEAR THE SAME STAIRWAY!
YES?
COME MORNING, HE WILL HAVE A HEAD START ON THE ENTIRE SCHOOL!
"HEAD START"??
OH! I THINK I UNDERSTAND!
I'M TRYING TO MAKE THINGS EASY FOR HIM! I WANT TO SEE IF HE CAN POSSIBLY REACH HIS HOME ROOM ON TIME JUST ONCE BEFORE HE GRADUATES!
LOTS OF LUCK, WEATHERBEE! YOU HAVE MY BLESSING!
(SIGH!) I'M AFRAID IT WILL TAKE MORE THAN THAT!
I'M INSULTED!!
2

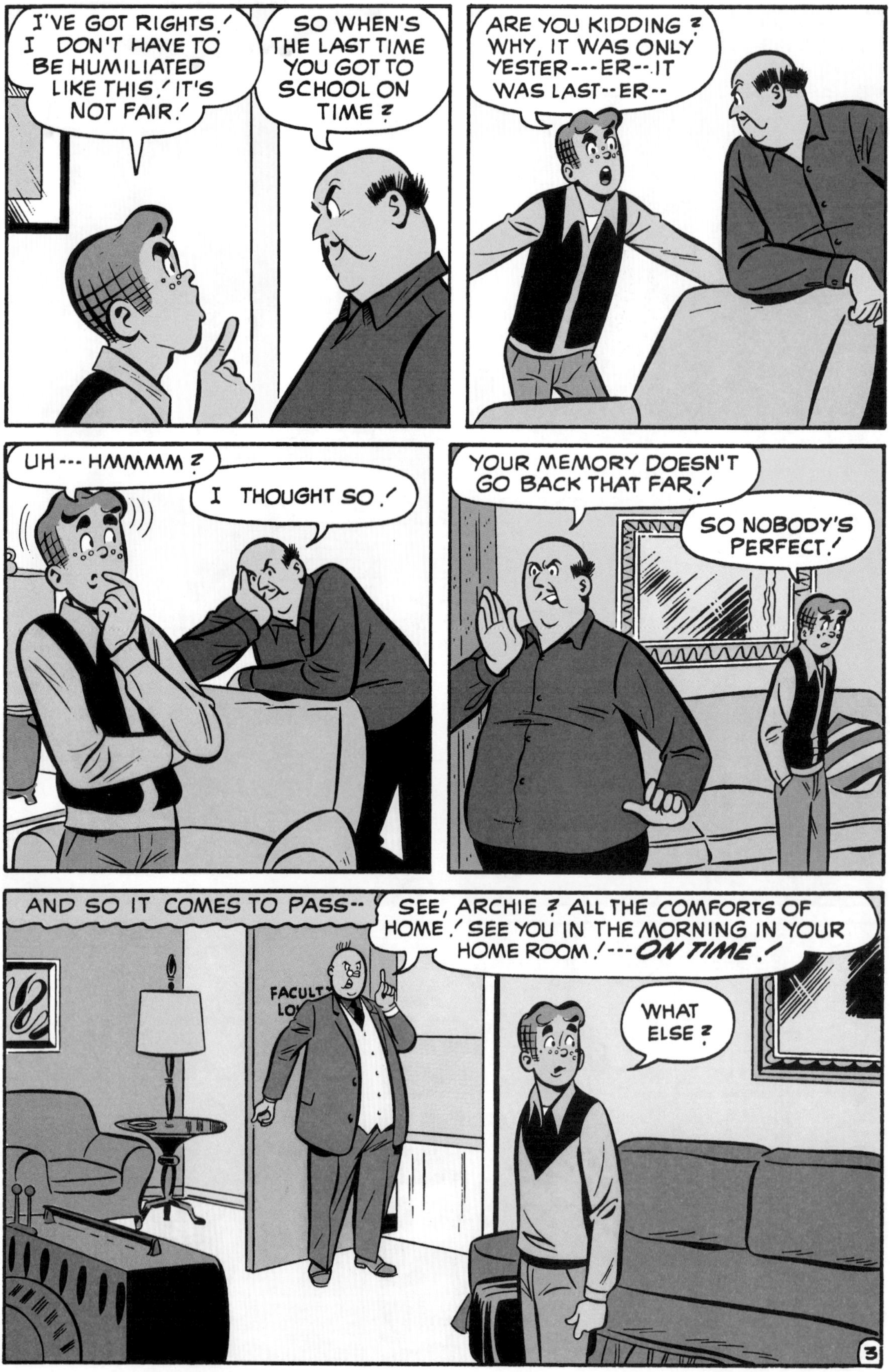
I'VE GOT RIGHTS! I DON'T HAVE TO BE HUMILIATED LIKE THIS! IT'S NOT FAIR!
SO WHEN'S THE LAST TIME YOU GOT TO SCHOOL ON TIME?
ARE YOU KIDDING? WHY, IT WAS ONLY YESTER---ER--IT WAS LAST--ER--
UH--- HMMMM?
I THOUGHT SO!
YOUR MEMORY DOESN'T GO BACK THAT FAR!
SO NOBODY'S PERFECT!
AND SO IT COMES TO PASS--
SEE, ARCHIE? ALL THE COMFORTS OF HOME! SEE YOU IN THE MORNING IN YOUR HOME ROOM!---ON TIME!
WHAT ELSE?
3

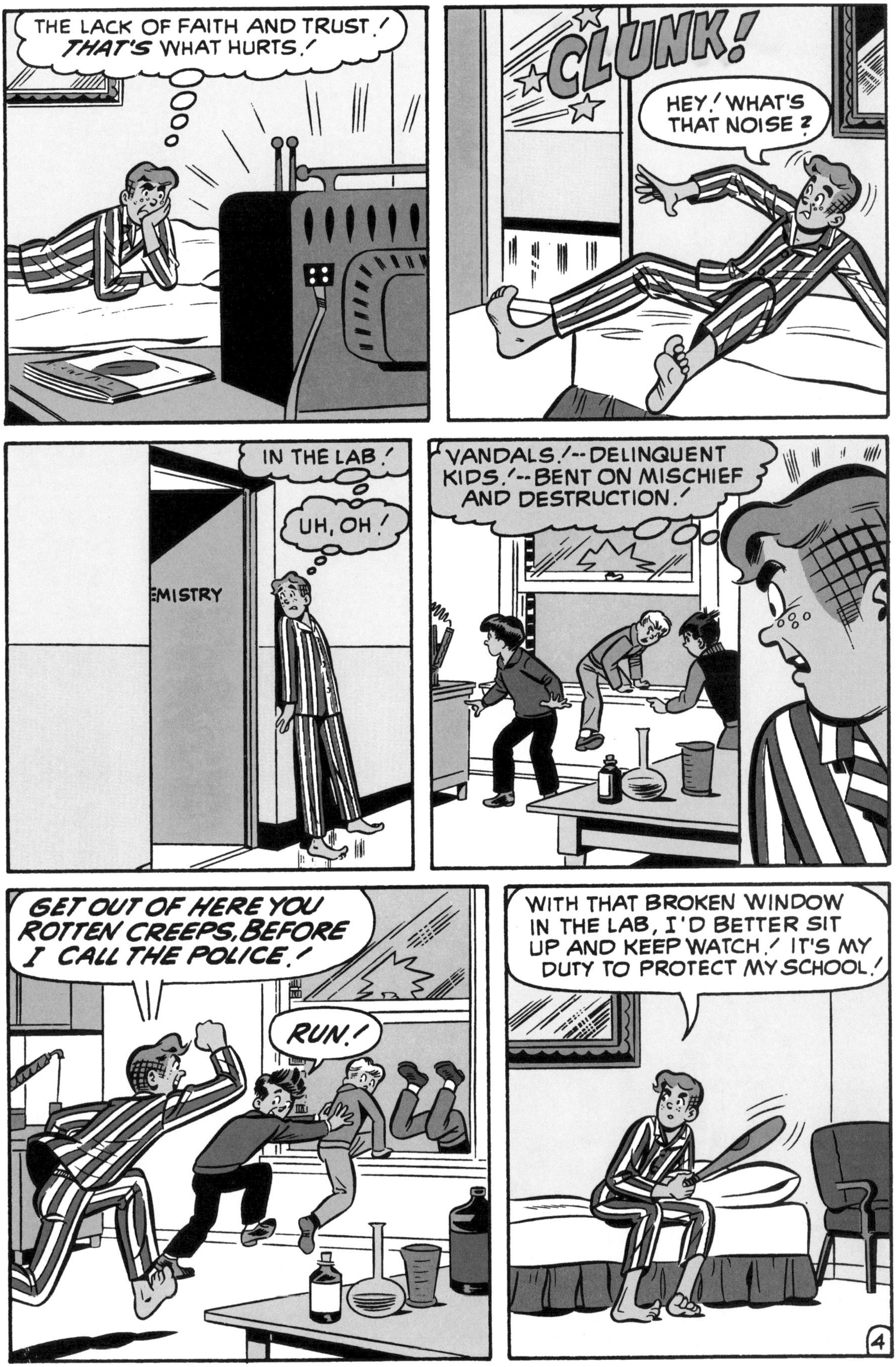
THE LACK OF FAITH AND TRUST! THAT'S WHAT HURTS!
CLUNK!
HEY! WHAT'S THAT NOISE?
IN THE LAB!
UH, OH!
EMISTRY
VANDALS!--DELINQUENT KIDS!--BENT ON MISCHIEF AND DESTRUCTION!
GET OUT OF HERE YOU ROTTEN CREEPS, BEFORE I CALL THE POLICE!
RUN!
WITH THAT BROKEN WINDOW IN THE LAB, I'D BETTER SIT UP AND KEEP WATCH! IT'S MY DUTY TO PROTECT MY SCHOOL!
4

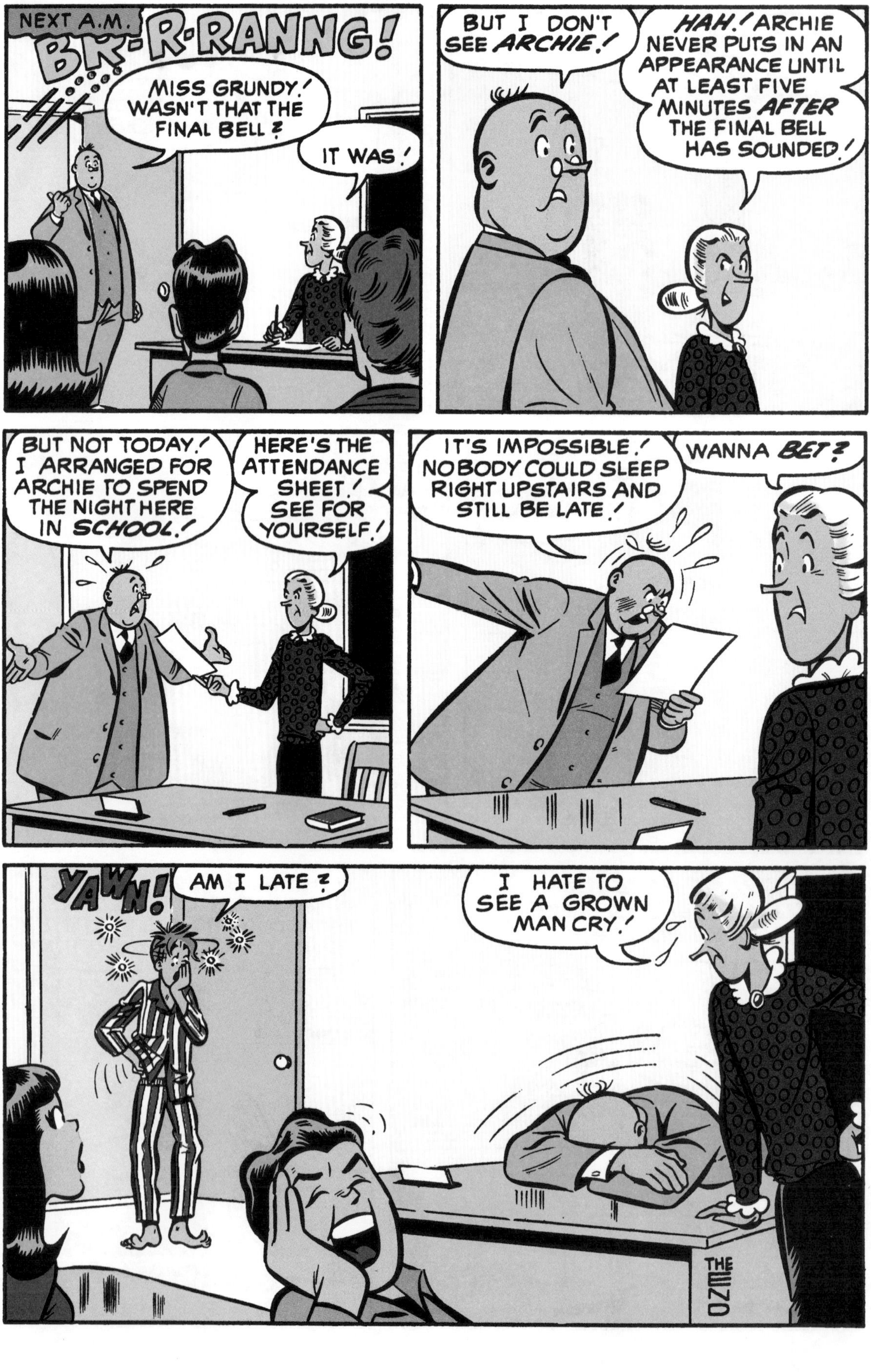
NEXT A.M.
BR-R-RANNG!
MISS GRUNDY! WASN'T THAT THE FINAL BELL?
IT WAS!
BUT I DON'T SEE ARCHIE!
HAH! ARCHIE NEVER PUTS IN AN APPEARANCE UNTIL AT LEAST FIVE MINUTES AFTER THE FINAL BELL HAS SOUNDED!
BUT NOT TODAY! I ARRANGED FOR ARCHIE TO SPEND THE NIGHT HERE IN SCHOOL!
HERE'S THE ATTENDANCE SHEET! SEE FOR YOURSELF!
IT'S IMPOSSIBLE! NOBODY COULD SLEEP RIGHT UPSTAIRS AND STILL BE LATE!
WANNA BET?
YAWN!
AM I LATE?
I HATE TO SEE A GROWN MAN CRY!
THE END

A GALLERY OF CLASSIC 1970s COVERS

ARCHIE SERIES
Archie's Girls
Betty and Veronica
15¢
NOV.
MOTHER, WE WANT TO HELP CLEAN UP OUR ENVIRONMENT!
HOW ABOUT STARTING WITH YOUR ROOM?
FIGHT
OLLUTION
DOWN WITH POLLUTION

BETTY & VERONICA #179
(November, 1970)

ARCHIE SERIES
Archie's Girls
Betty and Veronica
15¢
DEC.
NO 180
RONNIE, ISN'T THIS THE GROOVIEST BOUTIQUE?
YES! WE'LL HAVE TO COME BACK SOMETIME AND LOOK AT THE CLOTHES!
MINI SALE

BETTY & VERONICA #180
(December, 1970)

ARCHIE GIANT SERIES MAGAZINE Presents
The World of Jughead
25¢
GIANT
SERIES
POP ART EXHIBIT
JUGHEAD, THIS BURGER IS A WORK OF ART!
ARCHIE, EVERY BURGER IS A WORK OF ART!
"BURGER" by DANDY WARHOG

ARCHIE GIANT SERIES #183
(February, 1971)

FEB.
1976
ARCHIE
SERIES
25¢
Archie
ISN'T ARCHIE A DEAD-RINGER FOR JOE NAMATH?
THAT'S HIS TROUBLE! I WISH HE WAS A LIVE-RINGER!
COACH

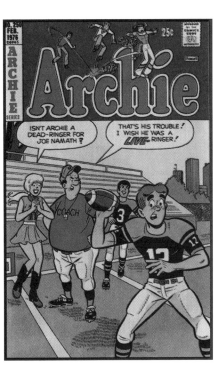

ARCHIE #250
(February, 1976)

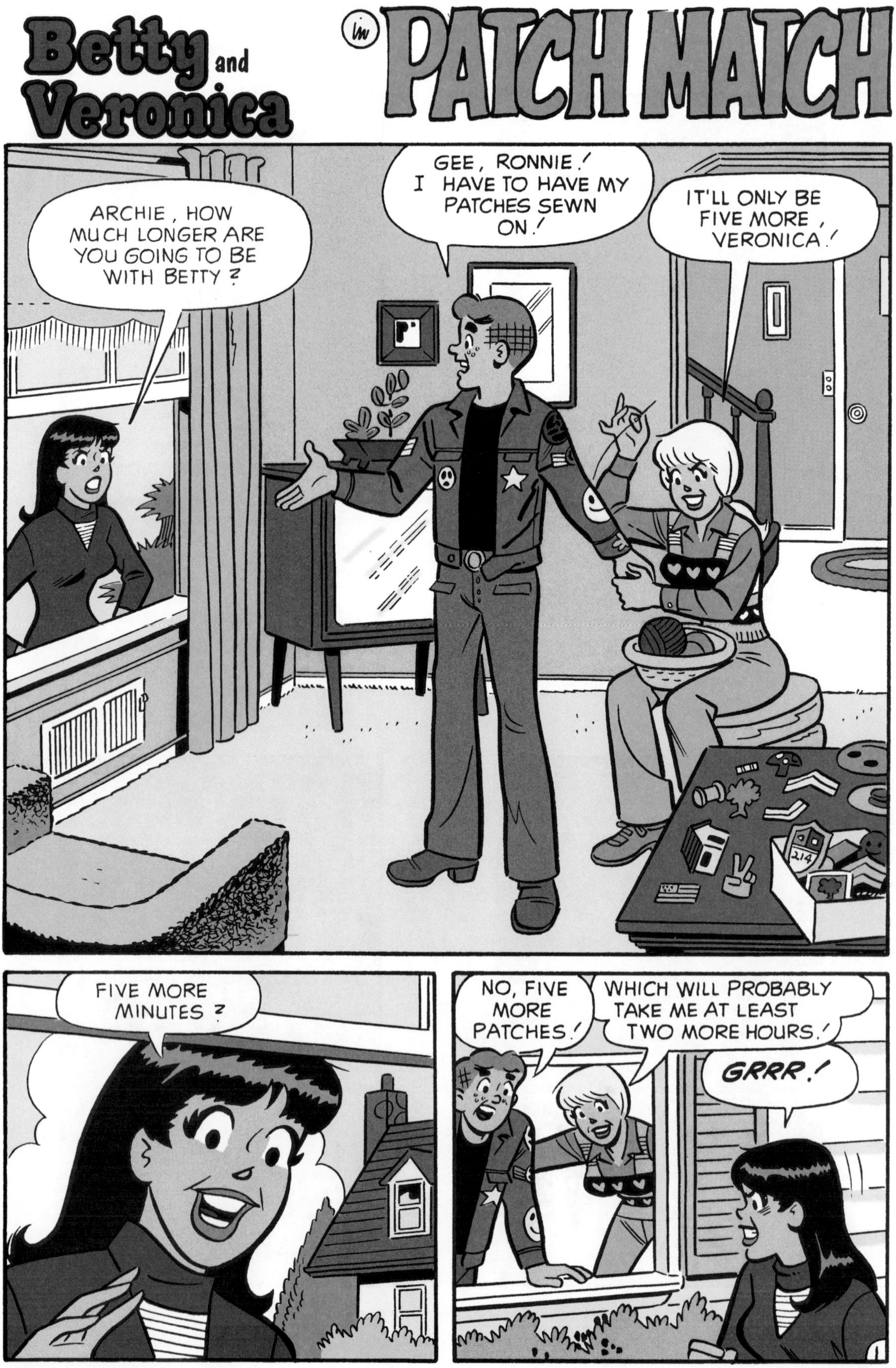
Betty and Veronica
in PATCH MATCH
ARCHIE, HOW MUCH LONGER ARE YOU GOING TO BE WITH BETTY?
GEE, RONNIE! I HAVE TO HAVE MY PATCHES SEWN ON!
IT'LL ONLY BE FIVE MORE, VERONICA!
FIVE MORE MINUTES?
NO, FIVE MORE PATCHES!
WHICH WILL PROBABLY TAKE ME AT LEAST TWO MORE HOURS!
GRRR!

Originally presented in BETTY & VERONICA #198, June, 1972

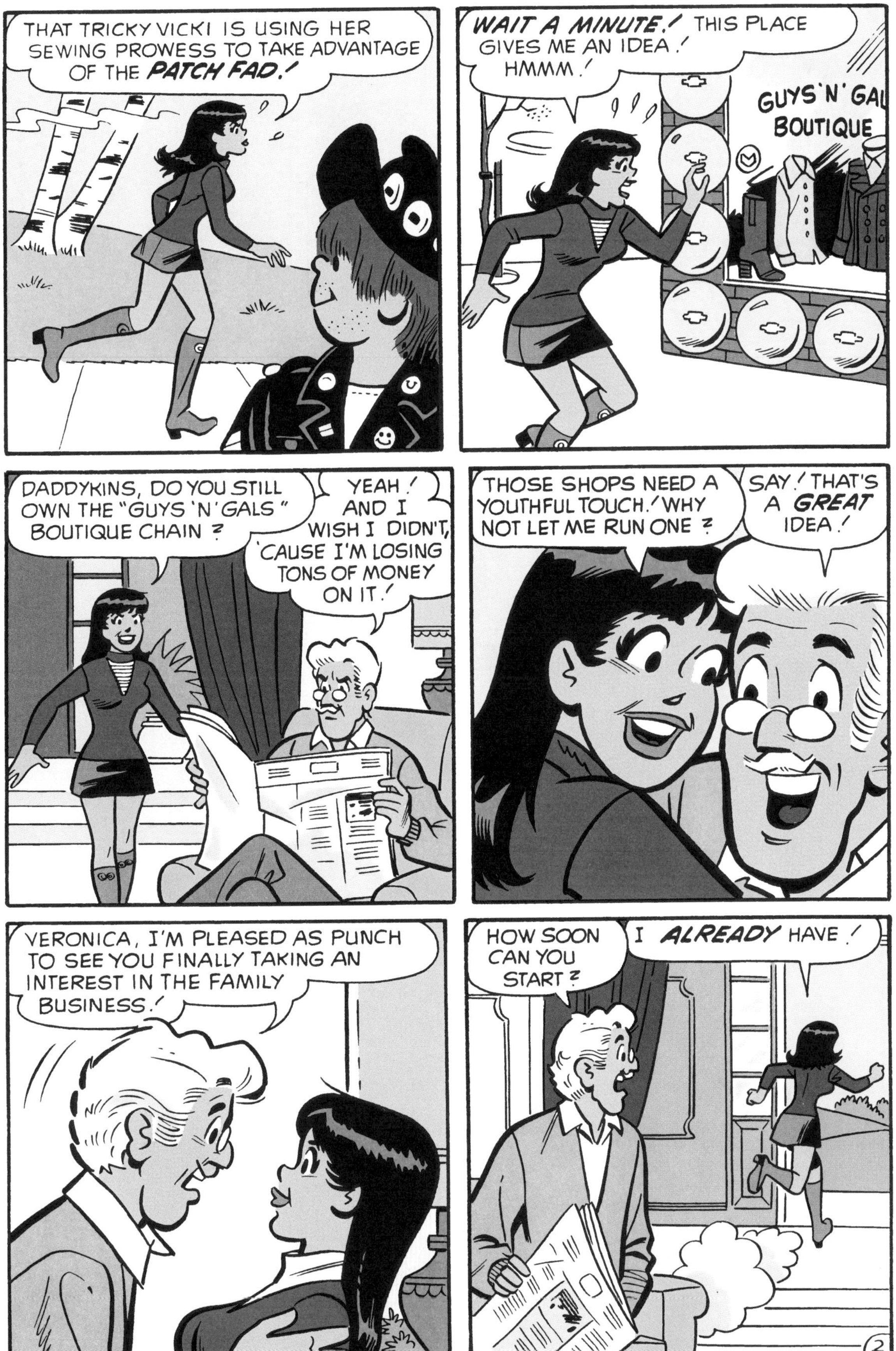
THAT TRICKY VICKI IS USING HER SEWING PROWESS TO TAKE ADVANTAGE OF THE PATCH FAD!
WAIT A MINUTE! THIS PLACE GIVES ME AN IDEA! HMMM!
GUYS 'N' GAL
BOUTIQUE
DADDYKINS, DO YOU STILL OWN THE "GUYS 'N' GALS" BOUTIQUE CHAIN?
YEAH! AND I WISH I DIDN'T, 'CAUSE I'M LOSING TONS OF MONEY ON IT!
THOSE SHOPS NEED A YOUTHFUL TOUCH! WHY NOT LET ME RUN ONE?
SAY! THAT'S A GREAT IDEA!
VERONICA, I'M PLEASED AS PUNCH TO SEE YOU FINALLY TAKING AN INTEREST IN THE FAMILY BUSINESS!
HOW SOON CAN YOU START?
I ALREADY HAVE!
2

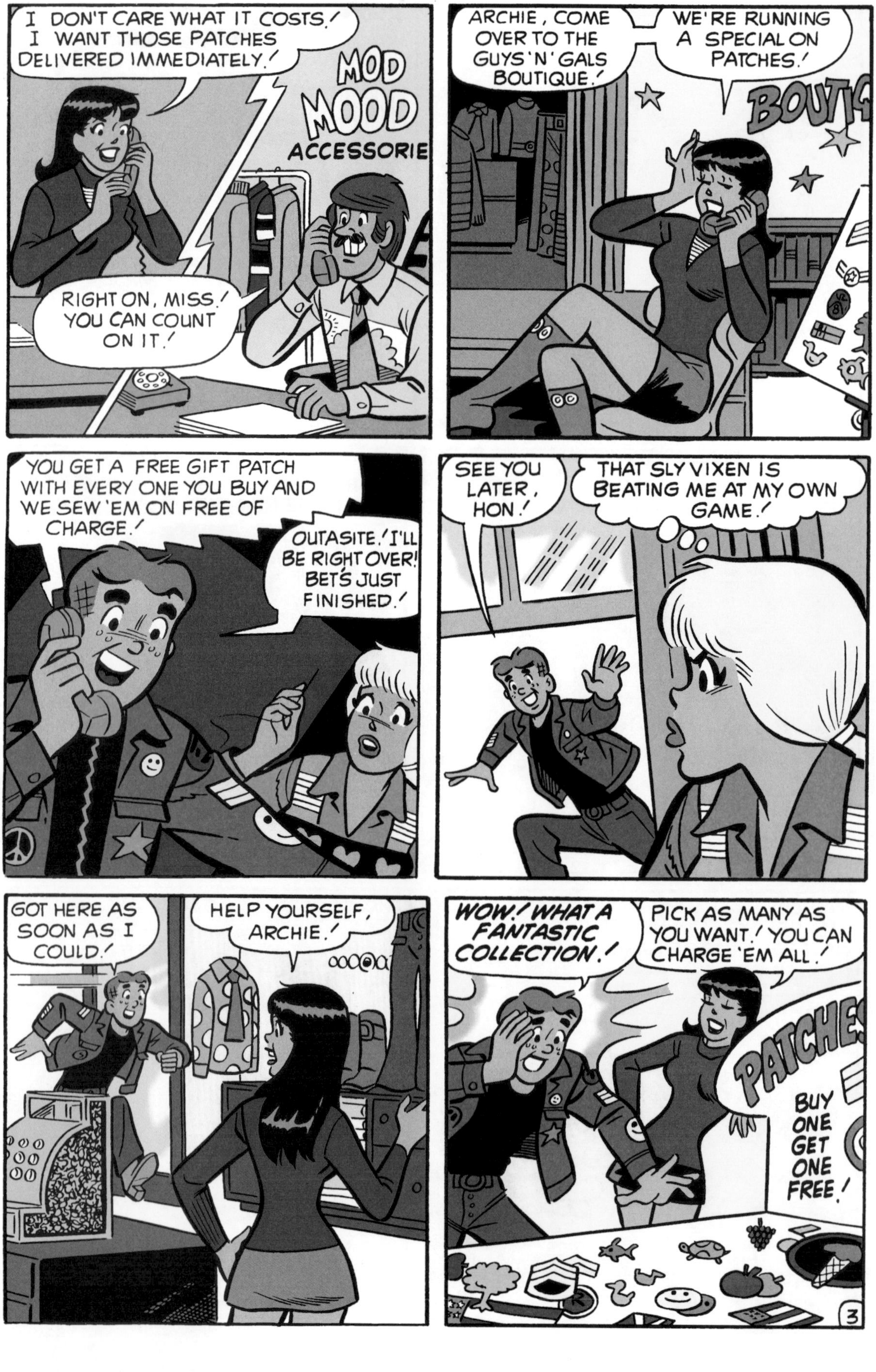
I DON'T CARE WHAT IT COSTS! I WANT THOSE PATCHES DELIVERED IMMEDIATELY!
MOD MOOD ACCESSORIE
RIGHT ON, MISS! YOU CAN COUNT ON IT!
ARCHIE, COME OVER TO THE GUYS 'N' GALS BOUTIQUE!
WE'RE RUNNING A SPECIAL ON PATCHES!
BOUTIQ
YOU GET A FREE GIFT PATCH WITH EVERY ONE YOU BUY AND WE SEW 'EM ON FREE OF CHARGE!
OUTASITE! I'LL BE RIGHT OVER! BET'S JUST FINISHED!
SEE YOU LATER, HON!
THAT SLY VIXEN IS BEATING ME AT MY OWN GAME!
GOT HERE AS SOON AS I COULD!
HELP YOURSELF, ARCHIE!
WOW! WHAT A FANTASTIC COLLECTION!
PICK AS MANY AS YOU WANT! YOU CAN CHARGE 'EM ALL!
PATCHES
BUY ONE GET ONE FREE!
3

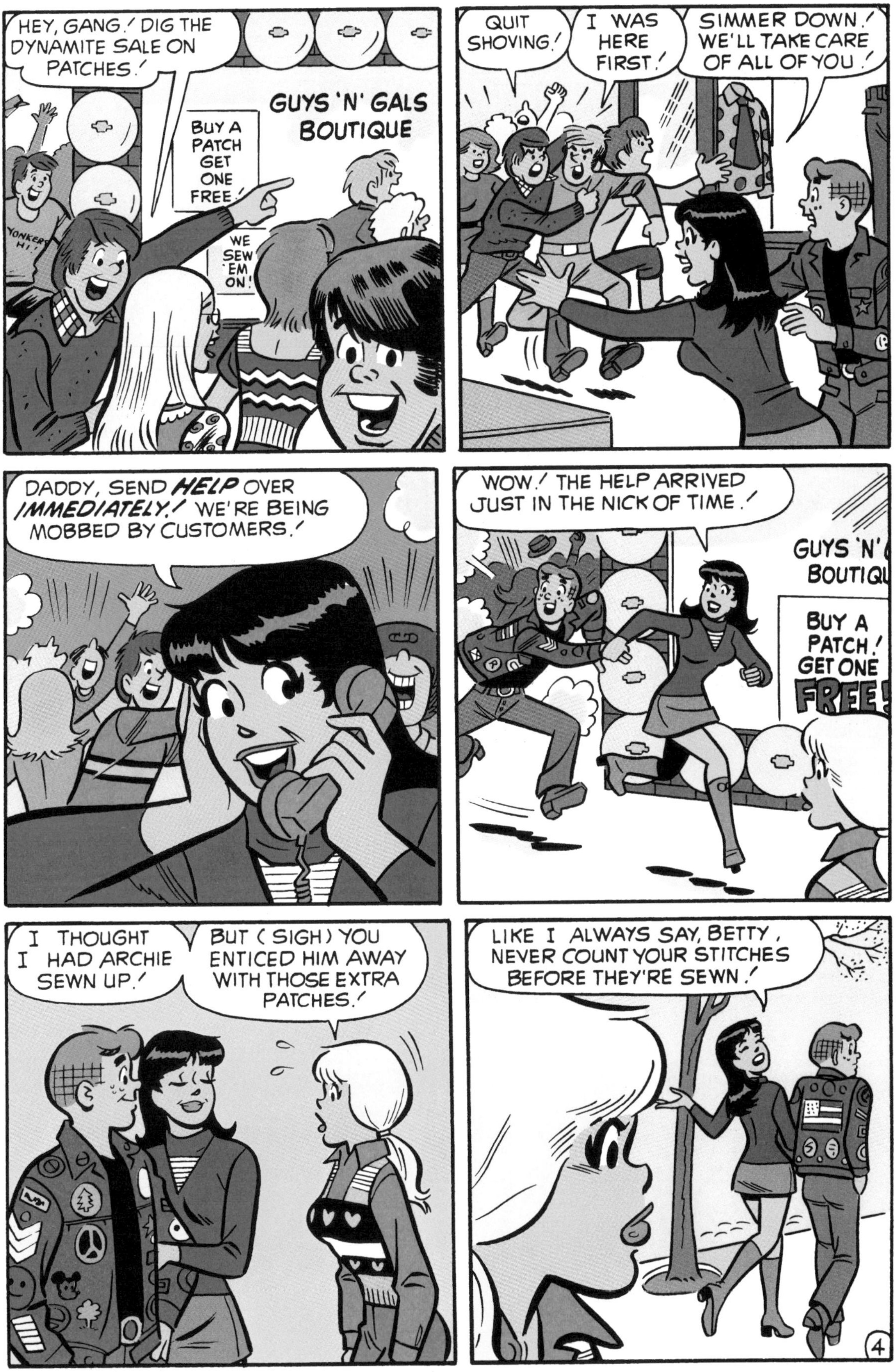
HEY, GANG! DIG THE DYNAMITE SALE ON PATCHES!
GUYS 'N' GALS BOUTIQUE
BUY A PATCH GET ONE FREE!
WE SEW 'EM ON!
YONKERS HI!
QUIT SHOVING!
I WAS HERE FIRST!
SIMMER DOWN! WE'LL TAKE CARE OF ALL OF YOU!
DADDY, SEND HELP OVER IMMEDIATELY! WE'RE BEING MOBBED BY CUSTOMERS!
WOW! THE HELP ARRIVED JUST IN THE NICK OF TIME!
GUYS 'N'
BOUTIQU
BUY A PATCH! GET ONE FREE!
I THOUGHT I HAD ARCHIE SEWN UP!
BUT (SIGH) YOU ENTICED HIM AWAY WITH THOSE EXTRA PATCHES!
LIKE I ALWAYS SAY, BETTY, NEVER COUNT YOUR STITCHES BEFORE THEY'RE SEWN!
4

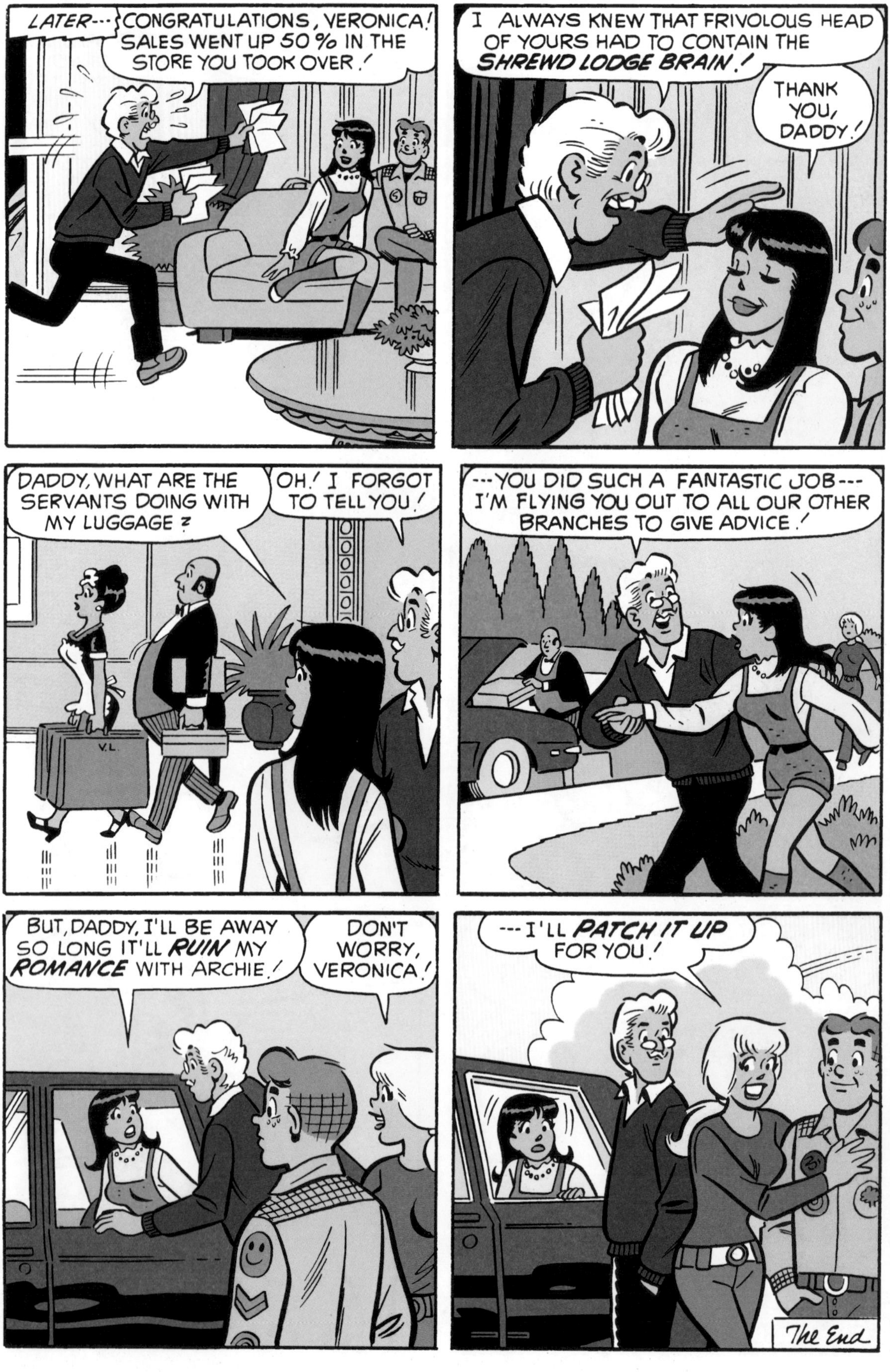
LATER---
CONGRATULATIONS, VERONICA! SALES WENT UP 50% IN THE STORE YOU TOOK OVER!
I ALWAYS KNEW THAT FRIVOLOUS HEAD OF YOURS HAD TO CONTAIN THE SHREWD LODGE BRAIN!
THANK YOU, DADDY!
DADDY, WHAT ARE THE SERVANTS DOING WITH MY LUGGAGE?
OH! I FORGOT TO TELL YOU!
V.L.
---YOU DID SUCH A FANTASTIC JOB--- I'M FLYING YOU OUT TO ALL OUR OTHER BRANCHES TO GIVE ADVICE!
BUT, DADDY, I'LL BE AWAY SO LONG IT'LL RUIN MY ROMANCE WITH ARCHIE!
DON'T WORRY, VERONICA!
---I'LL PATCH IT UP FOR YOU!
The End

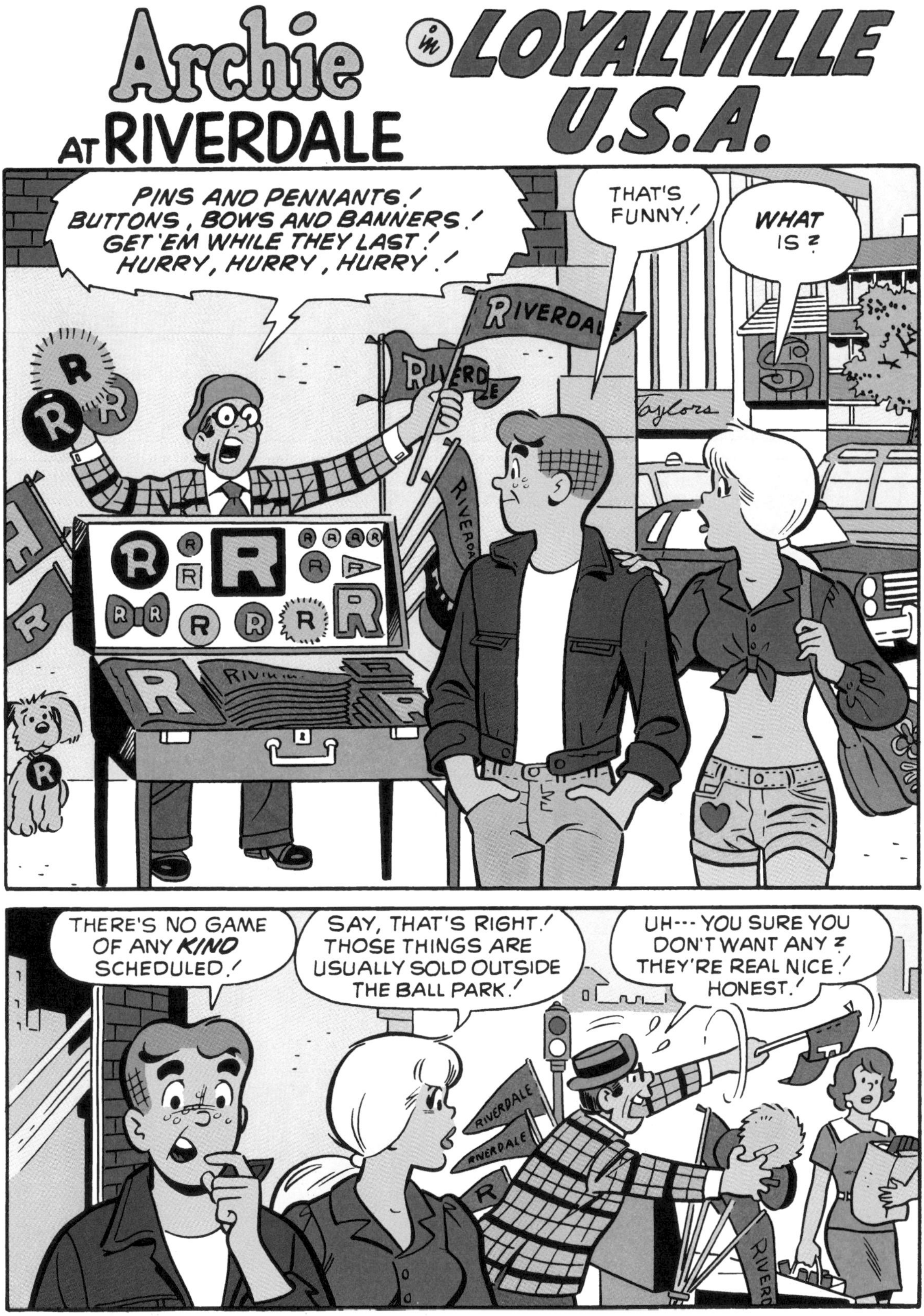
Archie AT RIVERDALE
in LOYALVILLE U.S.A.
PINS AND PENNANTS! BUTTONS, BOWS AND BANNERS! GET 'EM WHILE THEY LAST! HURRY, HURRY, HURRY!
THAT'S FUNNY!
WHAT IS?
RIVERDALE
Taylors
THERE'S NO GAME OF ANY KIND SCHEDULED!
SAY, THAT'S RIGHT! THOSE THINGS ARE USUALLY SOLD OUTSIDE THE BALL PARK!
UH--- YOU SURE YOU DON'T WANT ANY? THEY'RE REAL NICE! HONEST!
RIVERDALE
RIVERDALE

Originally presented in EVERYTHING'S ARCHIE #26, June, 1973

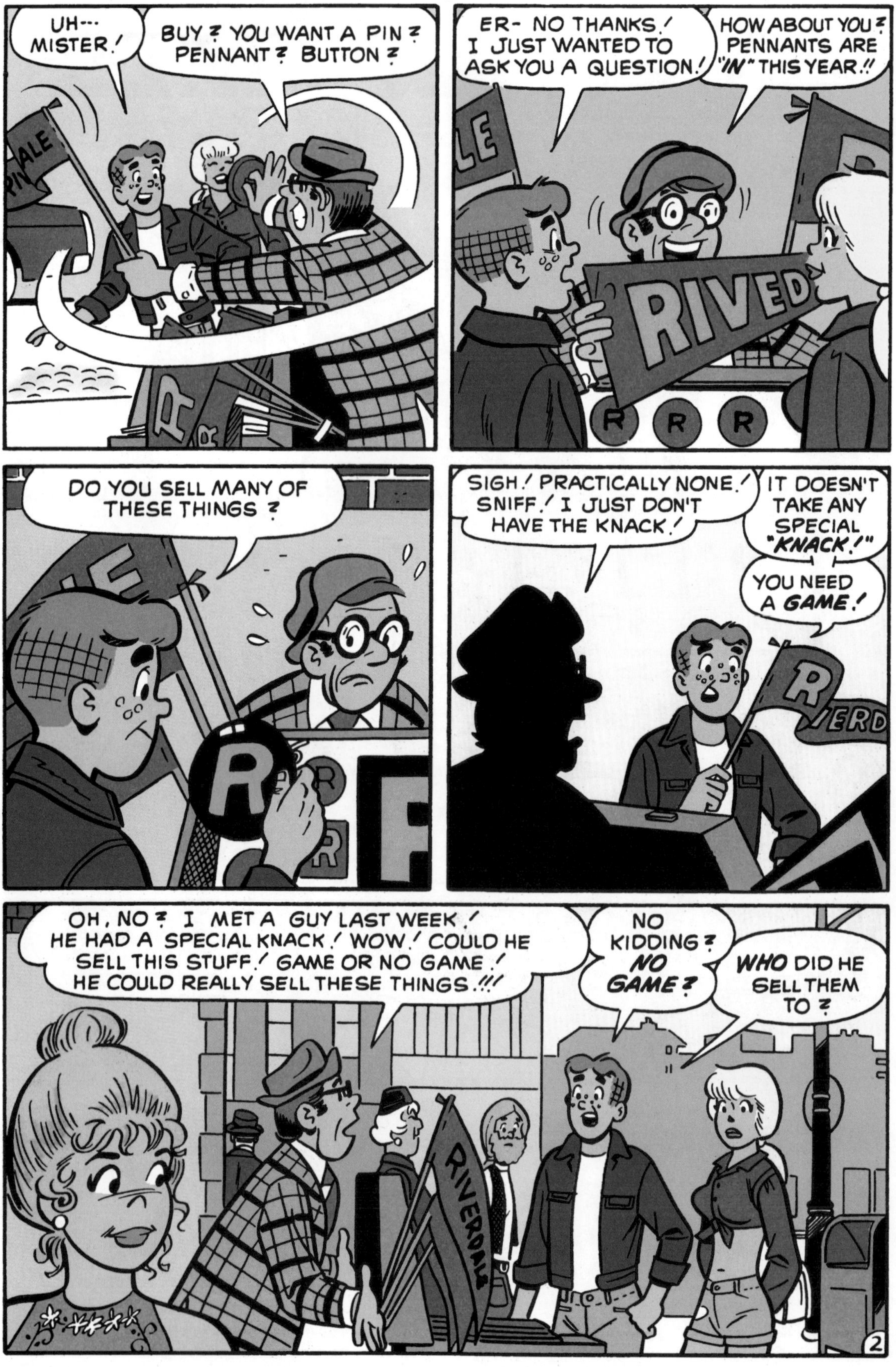
UH--- MISTER!
BUY? YOU WANT A PIN? PENNANT? BUTTON?
ER- NO THANKS! I JUST WANTED TO ASK YOU A QUESTION!
HOW ABOUT YOU? PENNANTS ARE "IN" THIS YEAR!!
RIVED
R
DO YOU SELL MANY OF THESE THINGS?
R
SIGH! PRACTICALLY NONE! SNIFF! I JUST DON'T HAVE THE KNACK!
IT DOESN'T TAKE ANY SPECIAL "KNACK!"
YOU NEED A GAME!
R
ERD
OH, NO? I MET A GUY LAST WEEK! HE HAD A SPECIAL KNACK! WOW! COULD HE SELL THIS STUFF! GAME OR NO GAME! HE COULD REALLY SELL THESE THINGS!!!
NO KIDDING? NO GAME?
WHO DID HE SELL THEM TO?
RIVERDALE
2

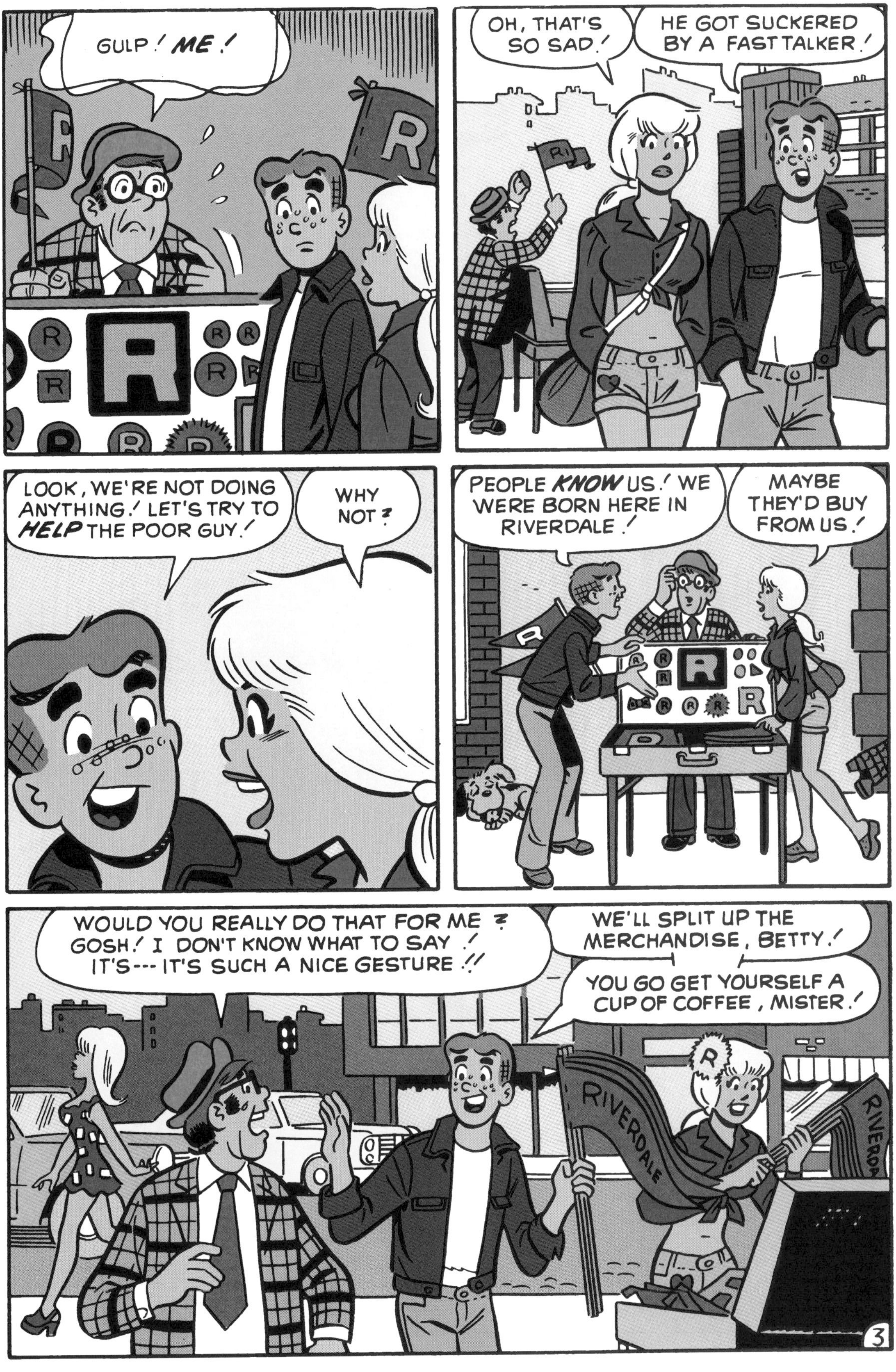
GULP! ME!
OH, THAT'S SO SAD!
HE GOT SUCKERED BY A FAST TALKER!
LOOK, WE'RE NOT DOING ANYTHING! LET'S TRY TO HELP THE POOR GUY!
WHY NOT?
PEOPLE KNOW US! WE WERE BORN HERE IN RIVERDALE!
MAYBE THEY'D BUY FROM US!
WOULD YOU REALLY DO THAT FOR ME? GOSH! I DON'T KNOW WHAT TO SAY! IT'S--- IT'S SUCH A NICE GESTURE!!
WE'LL SPLIT UP THE MERCHANDISE, BETTY!
YOU GO GET YOURSELF A CUP OF COFFEE, MISTER!
RIVERDALE
RIVERDALE
RIVERDA
3

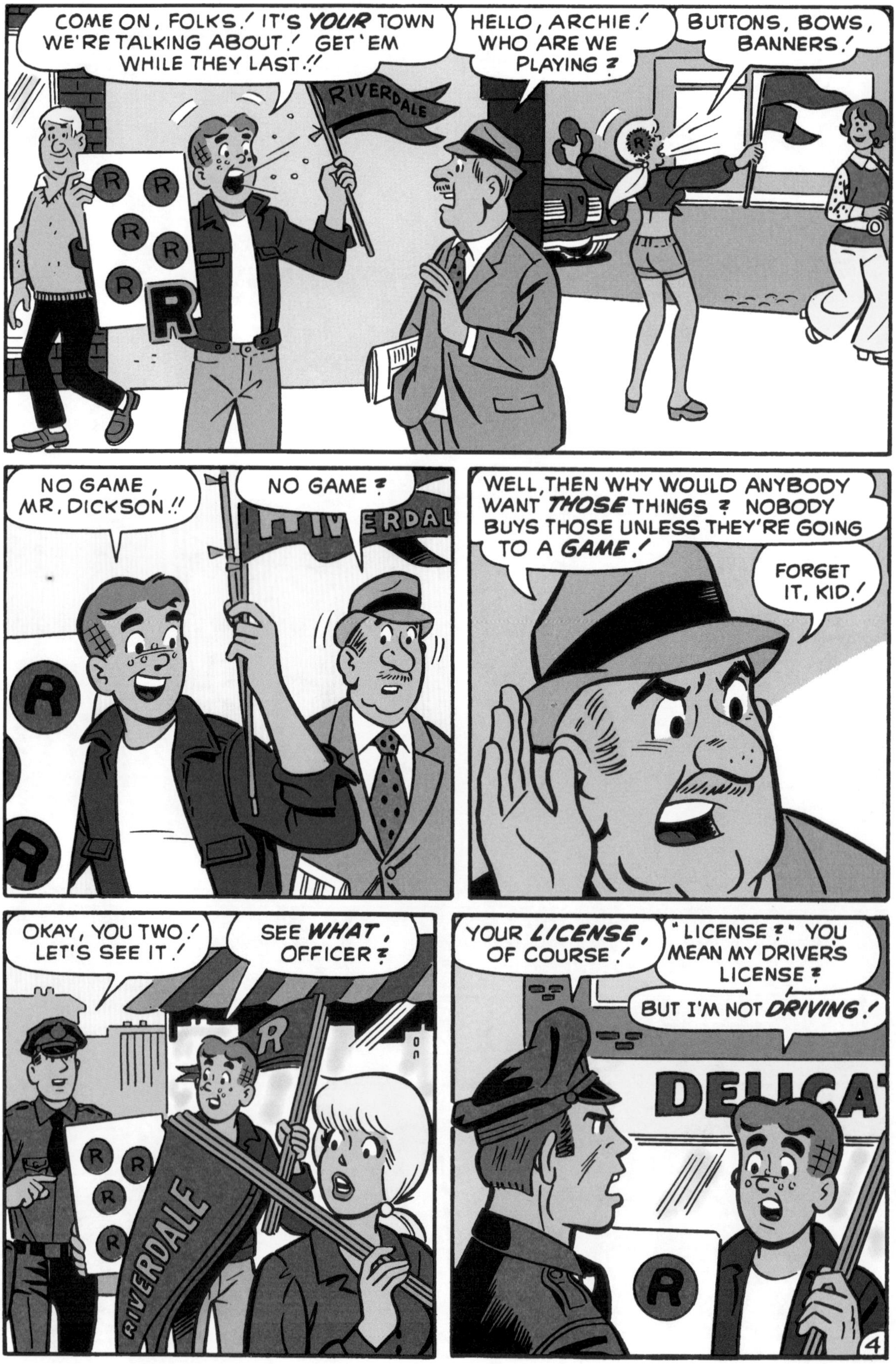
COME ON, FOLKS.! IT'S YOUR TOWN WE'RE TALKING ABOUT.! GET 'EM WHILE THEY LAST.!!
RIVERDALE
HELLO, ARCHIE.! WHO ARE WE PLAYING ?
BUTTONS, BOWS, BANNERS.!
NO GAME, MR. DICKSON.!!
NO GAME ?
WELL, THEN WHY WOULD ANYBODY WANT THOSE THINGS ? NOBODY BUYS THOSE UNLESS THEY'RE GOING TO A GAME.!
FORGET IT, KID.!
OKAY, YOU TWO.! LET'S SEE IT.!
SEE WHAT, OFFICER ?
RIVERDALE
YOUR LICENSE, OF COURSE.!
"LICENSE ?" YOU MEAN MY DRIVER'S LICENSE ?
BUT I'M NOT DRIVING.!
DELICA
4

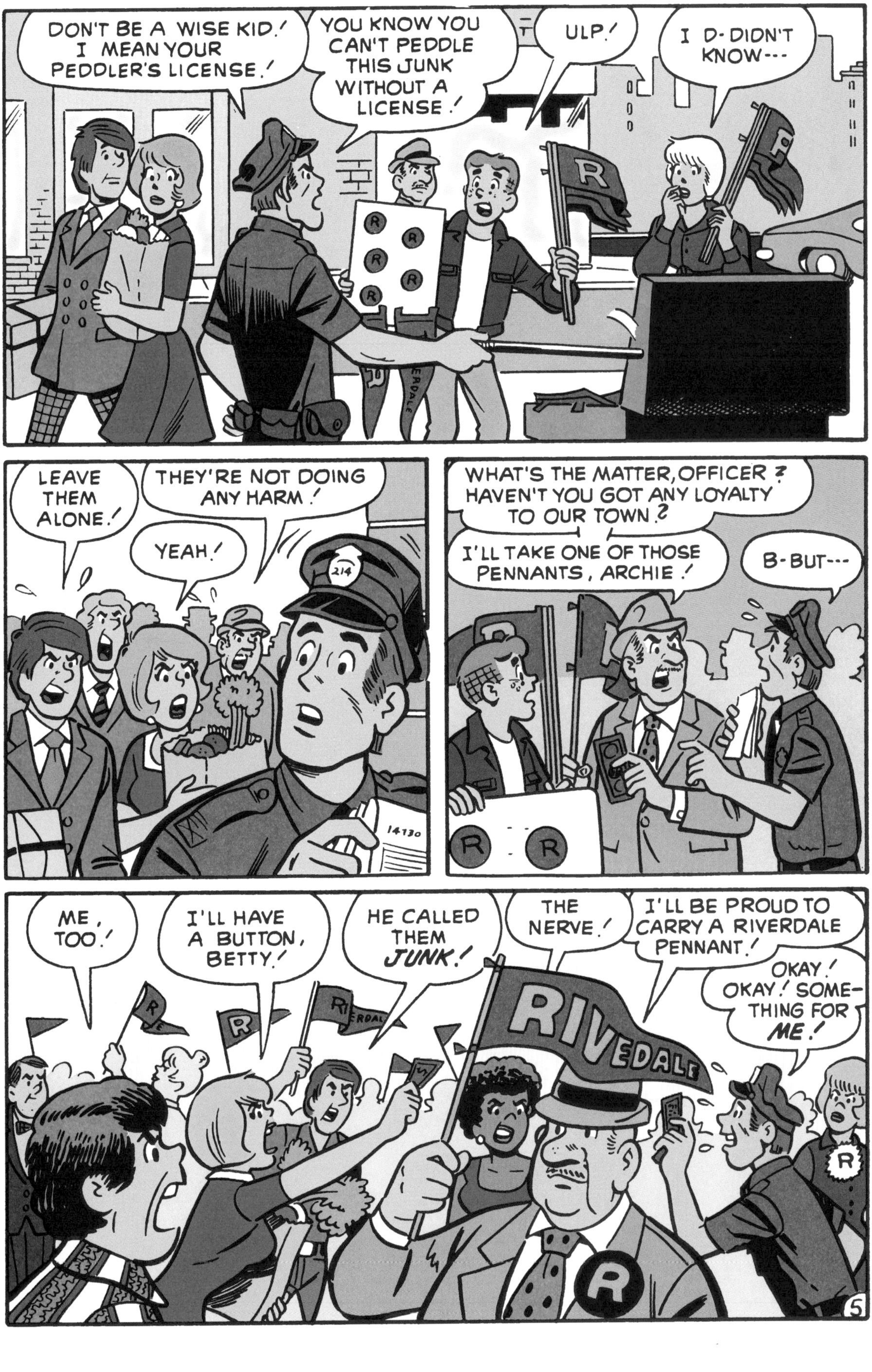
DON'T BE A WISE KID! I MEAN YOUR PEDDLER'S LICENSE!
YOU KNOW YOU CAN'T PEDDLE THIS JUNK WITHOUT A LICENSE!
ULP!
I D-DIDN'T KNOW---
LEAVE THEM ALONE!
THEY'RE NOT DOING ANY HARM!
YEAH!
214
14130
WHAT'S THE MATTER, OFFICER? HAVEN'T YOU GOT ANY LOYALTY TO OUR TOWN?
I'LL TAKE ONE OF THOSE PENNANTS, ARCHIE!
B-BUT---
ME, TOO!
I'LL HAVE A BUTTON, BETTY!
HE CALLED THEM *JUNK*!
THE NERVE!
I'LL BE PROUD TO CARRY A RIVERDALE PENNANT!
OKAY! OKAY! SOMETHING FOR *ME*!
RIVEDALE
5

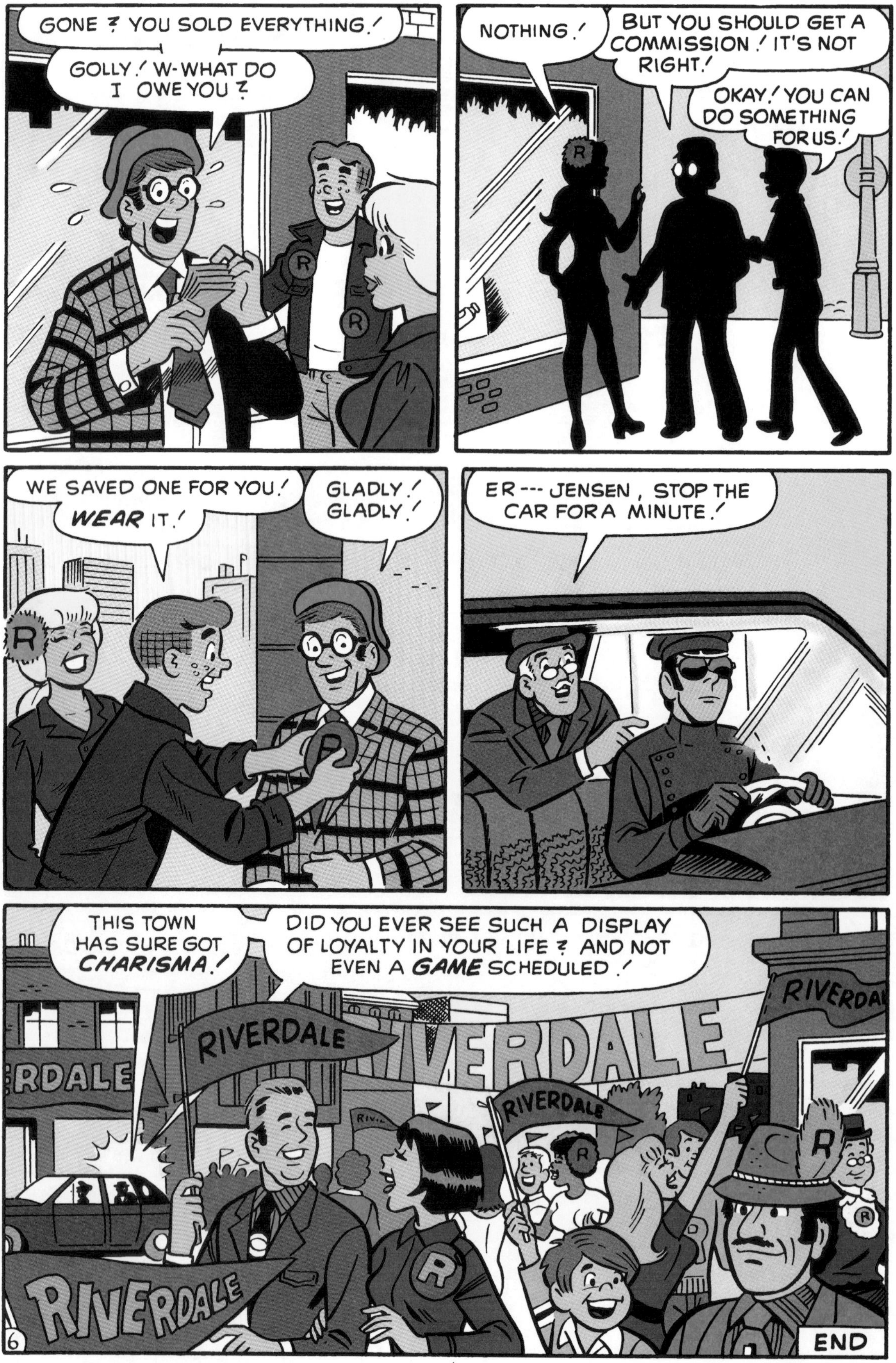
GONE ? YOU SOLD EVERYTHING !
GOLLY ! W-WHAT DO I OWE YOU ?
NOTHING !
BUT YOU SHOULD GET A COMMISSION ! IT'S NOT RIGHT !
OKAY ! YOU CAN DO SOMETHING FOR US !
WE SAVED ONE FOR YOU ! WEAR IT !
GLADLY ! GLADLY !
ER --- JENSEN , STOP THE CAR FOR A MINUTE !
THIS TOWN HAS SURE GOT CHARISMA !
DID YOU EVER SEE SUCH A DISPLAY OF LOYALTY IN YOUR LIFE ? AND NOT EVEN A GAME SCHEDULED !
RIVERDALE
VERDALE
RDALE
RIVERDALE
RIVERDALE
RIVERDALE
6
END

Archie in "No Fuel Like an Old Fuel"

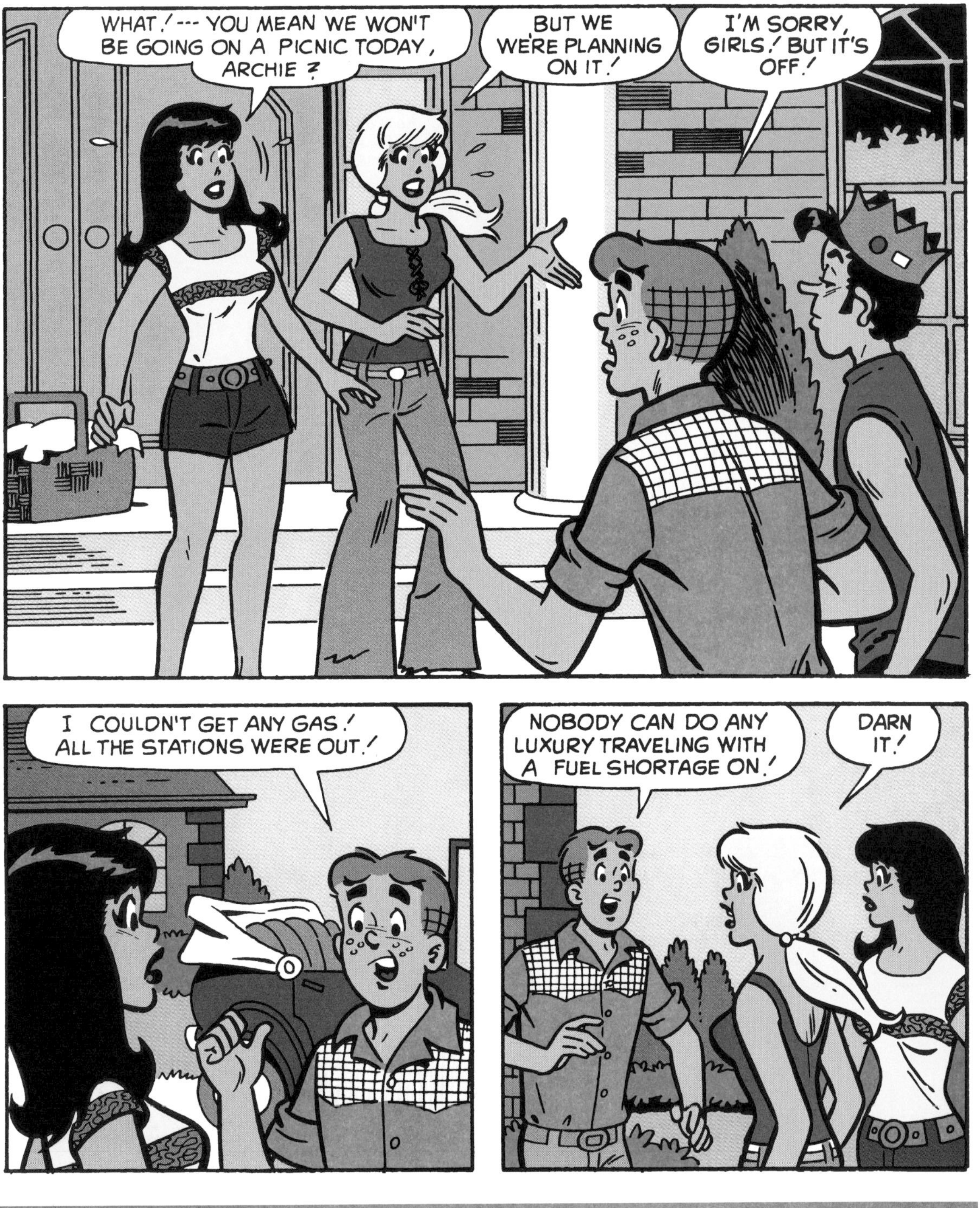
WHAT!--- YOU MEAN WE WON'T BE GOING ON A PICNIC TODAY, ARCHIE?
BUT WE WE'RE PLANNING ON IT!
I'M SORRY, GIRLS! BUT IT'S OFF!
I COULDN'T GET ANY GAS! ALL THE STATIONS WERE OUT!
NOBODY CAN DO ANY LUXURY TRAVELING WITH A FUEL SHORTAGE ON!
DARN IT!

Originally presented in PEP #296, December, 1974

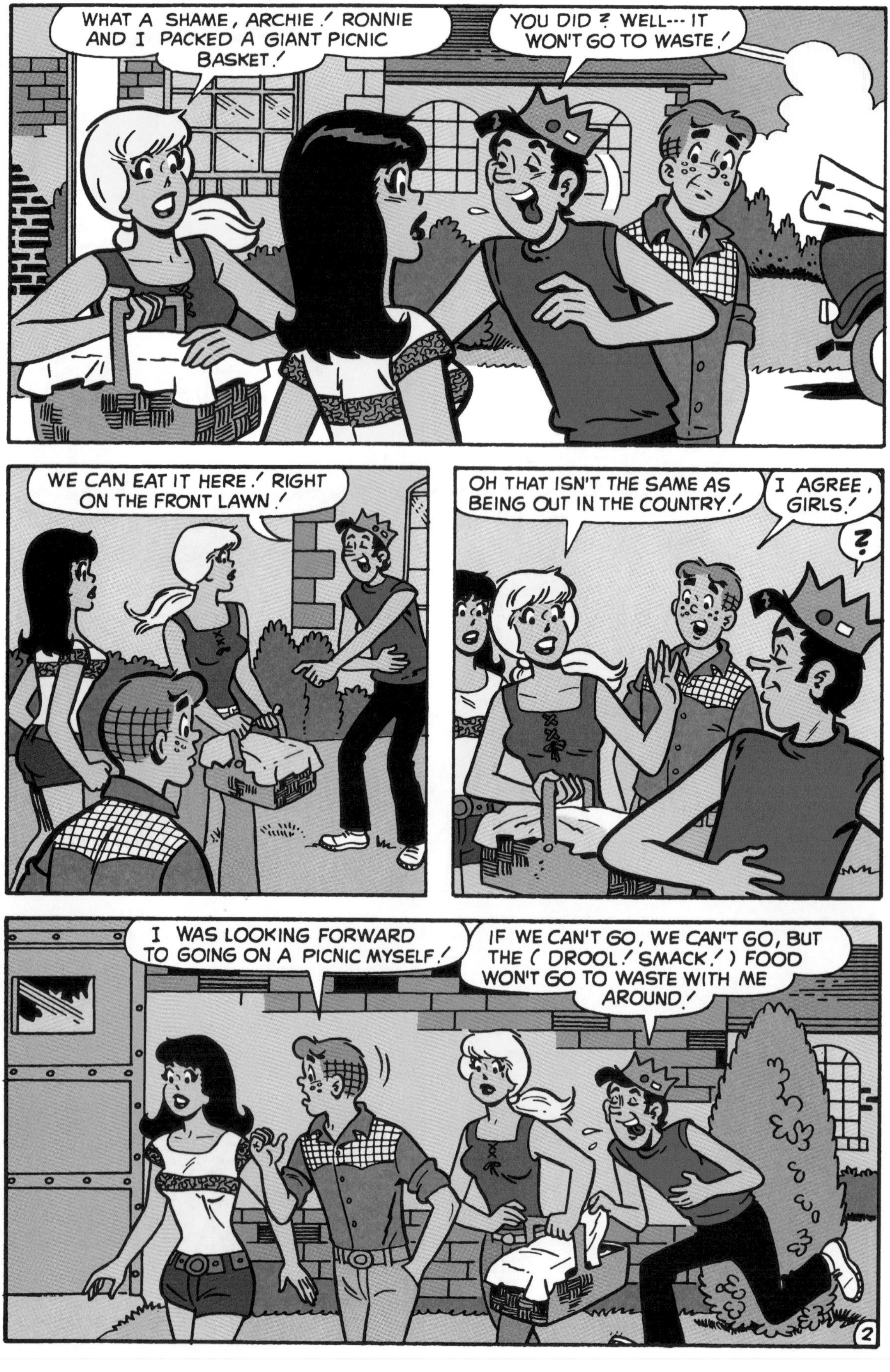
WHAT A SHAME, ARCHIE! RONNIE AND I PACKED A GIANT PICNIC BASKET!
YOU DID? WELL--- IT WON'T GO TO WASTE!
WE CAN EAT IT HERE! RIGHT ON THE FRONT LAWN!
OH THAT ISN'T THE SAME AS BEING OUT IN THE COUNTRY!
I AGREE, GIRLS!
?
I WAS LOOKING FORWARD TO GOING ON A PICNIC MYSELF!
IF WE CAN'T GO, WE CAN'T GO, BUT THE (DROOL! SMACK!) FOOD WON'T GO TO WASTE WITH ME AROUND!
2

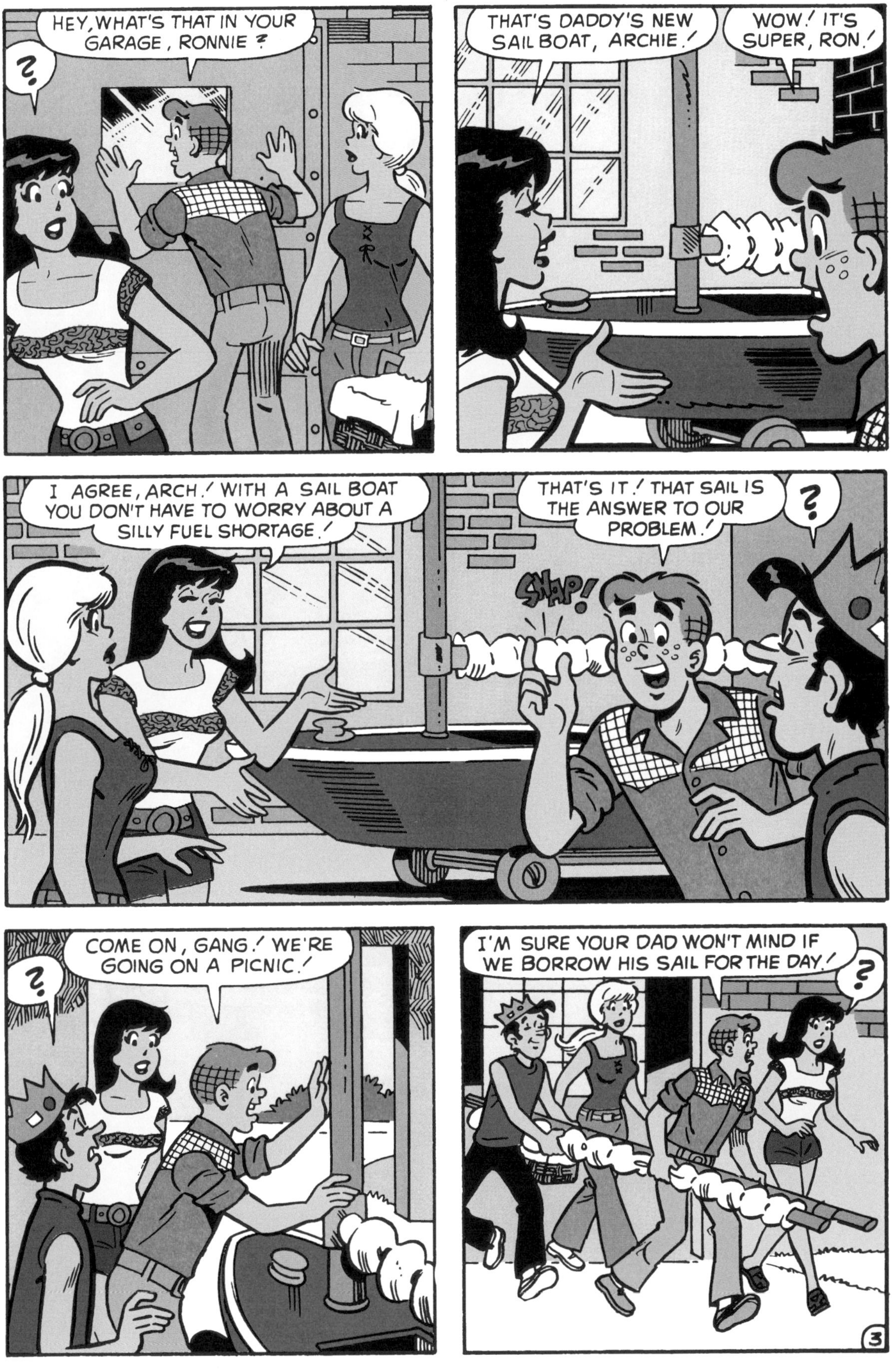
HEY, WHAT'S THAT IN YOUR GARAGE, RONNIE ?
?
THAT'S DADDY'S NEW SAIL BOAT, ARCHIE!
WOW! IT'S SUPER, RON!
I AGREE, ARCH! WITH A SAIL BOAT YOU DON'T HAVE TO WORRY ABOUT A SILLY FUEL SHORTAGE!
SNAP!
THAT'S IT! THAT SAIL IS THE ANSWER TO OUR PROBLEM!
?
COME ON, GANG! WE'RE GOING ON A PICNIC!
?
I'M SURE YOUR DAD WON'T MIND IF WE BORROW HIS SAIL FOR THE DAY!
?
3

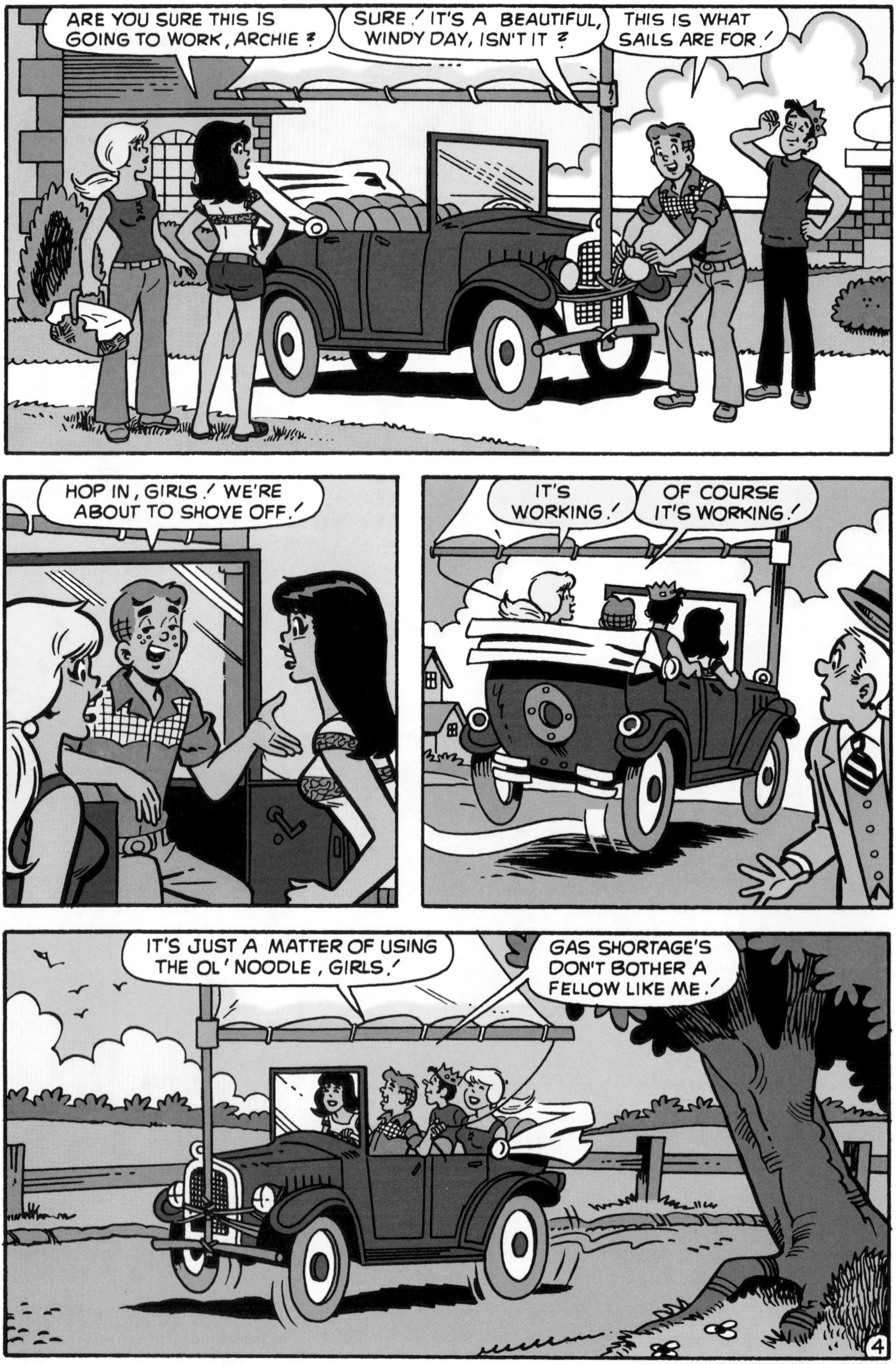
ARE YOU SURE THIS IS GOING TO WORK, ARCHIE ?
SURE! IT'S A BEAUTIFUL, WINDY DAY, ISN'T IT ?
THIS IS WHAT SAILS ARE FOR!
HOP IN, GIRLS! WE'RE ABOUT TO SHOVE OFF!
IT'S WORKING!
OF COURSE IT'S WORKING!
IT'S JUST A MATTER OF USING THE OL' NOODLE, GIRLS!
GAS SHORTAGE'S DON'T BOTHER A FELLOW LIKE ME!
4

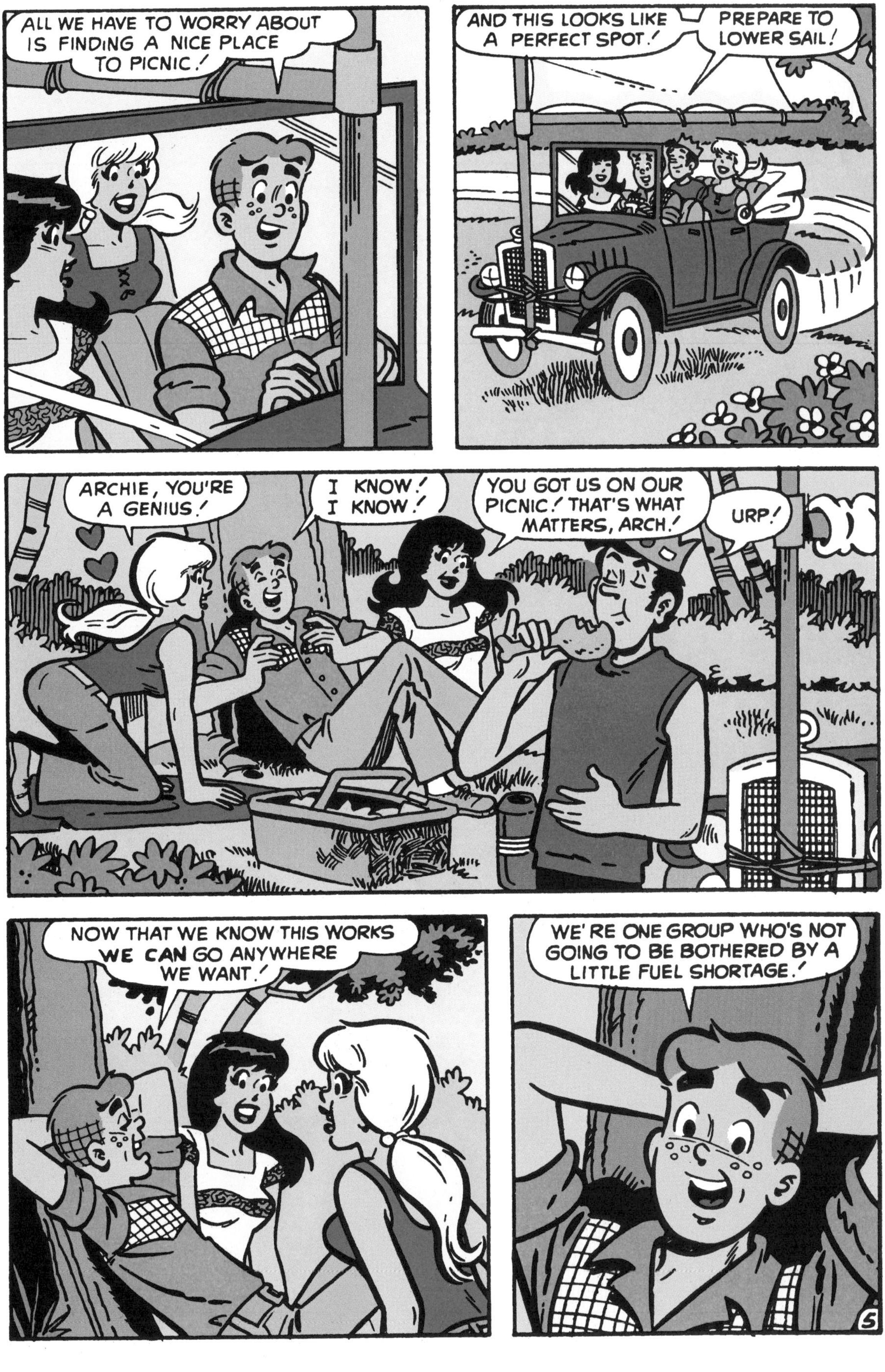
ALL WE HAVE TO WORRY ABOUT IS FINDING A NICE PLACE TO PICNIC!
AND THIS LOOKS LIKE A PERFECT SPOT!
PREPARE TO LOWER SAIL!
ARCHIE, YOU'RE A GENIUS!
I KNOW! I KNOW!
YOU GOT US ON OUR PICNIC! THAT'S WHAT MATTERS, ARCH!
URP!
NOW THAT WE KNOW THIS WORKS WE CAN GO ANYWHERE WE WANT!
WE'RE ONE GROUP WHO'S NOT GOING TO BE BOTHERED BY A LITTLE FUEL SHORTAGE!
5

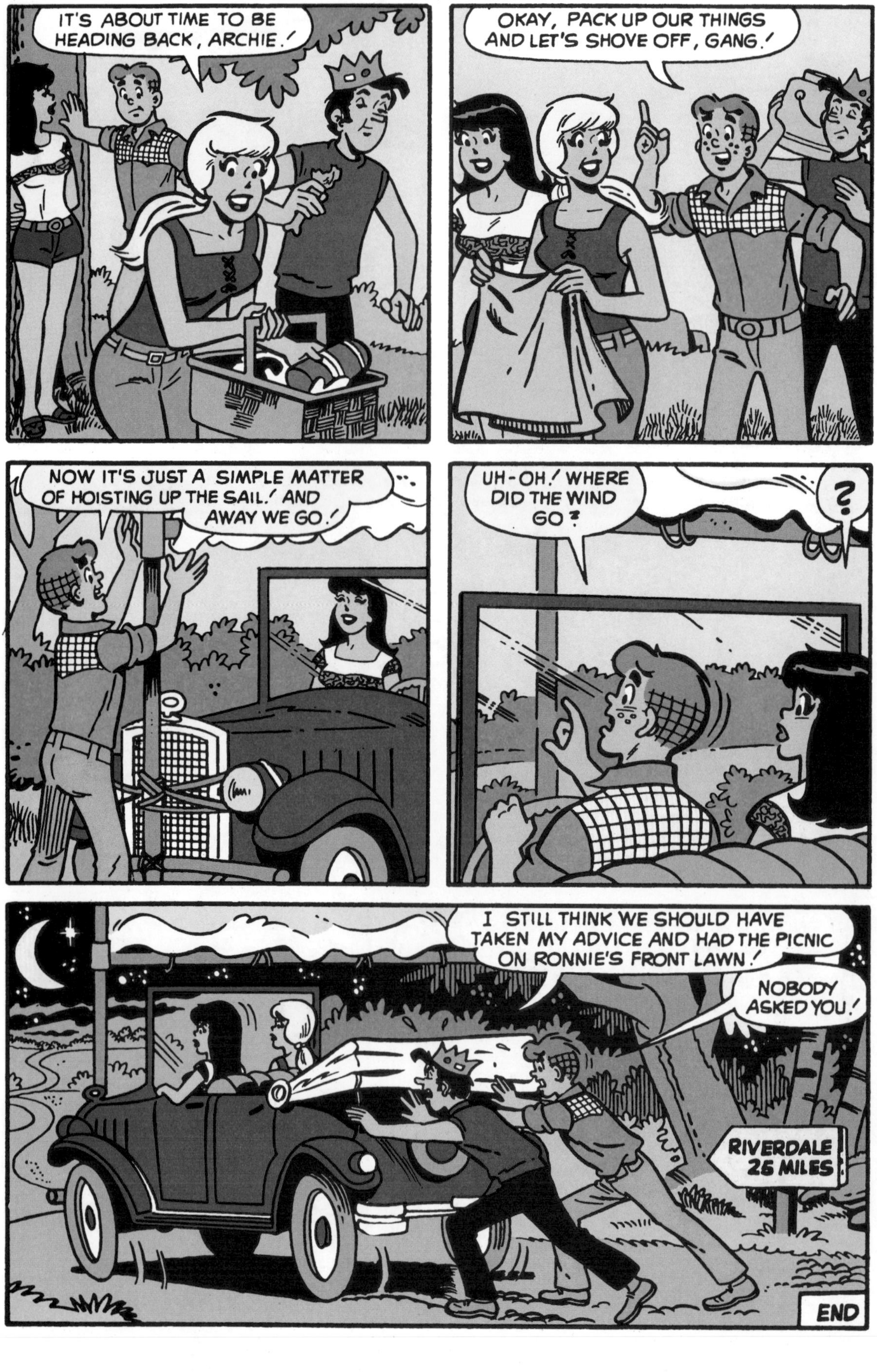
IT'S ABOUT TIME TO BE HEADING BACK, ARCHIE!
OKAY, PACK UP OUR THINGS AND LET'S SHOVE OFF, GANG!
NOW IT'S JUST A SIMPLE MATTER OF HOISTING UP THE SAIL! AND AWAY WE GO!
UH-OH! WHERE DID THE WIND GO?
?
I STILL THINK WE SHOULD HAVE TAKEN MY ADVICE AND HAD THE PICNIC ON RONNIE'S FRONT LAWN!
NOBODY ASKED YOU!
RIVERDALE 25 MILES
END

Betty and Veronica in "YOU CAME A LONG WAY, BABY.."

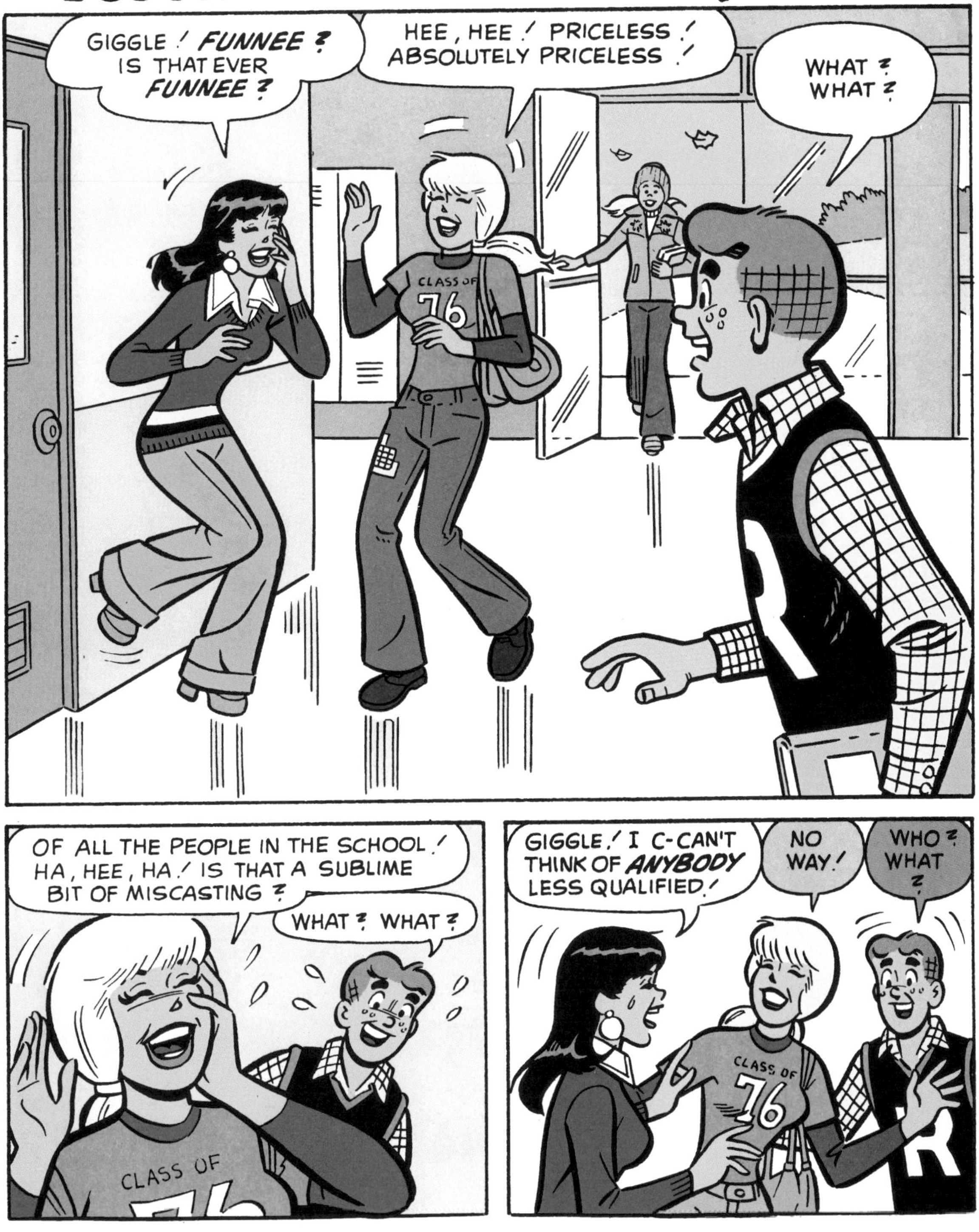
GIGGLE! FUNNEE? IS THAT EVER FUNNEE?
HEE, HEE! PRICELESS! ABSOLUTELY PRICELESS!
WHAT? WHAT?
CLASS OF 76
OF ALL THE PEOPLE IN THE SCHOOL! HA, HEE, HA! IS THAT A SUBLIME BIT OF MISCASTING?
WHAT? WHAT?
GIGGLE! I C-CAN'T THINK OF ANYBODY LESS QUALIFIED!
NO WAY!
WHO? WHAT?

Originally presented in BETTY & VERONICA #233, May, 1975

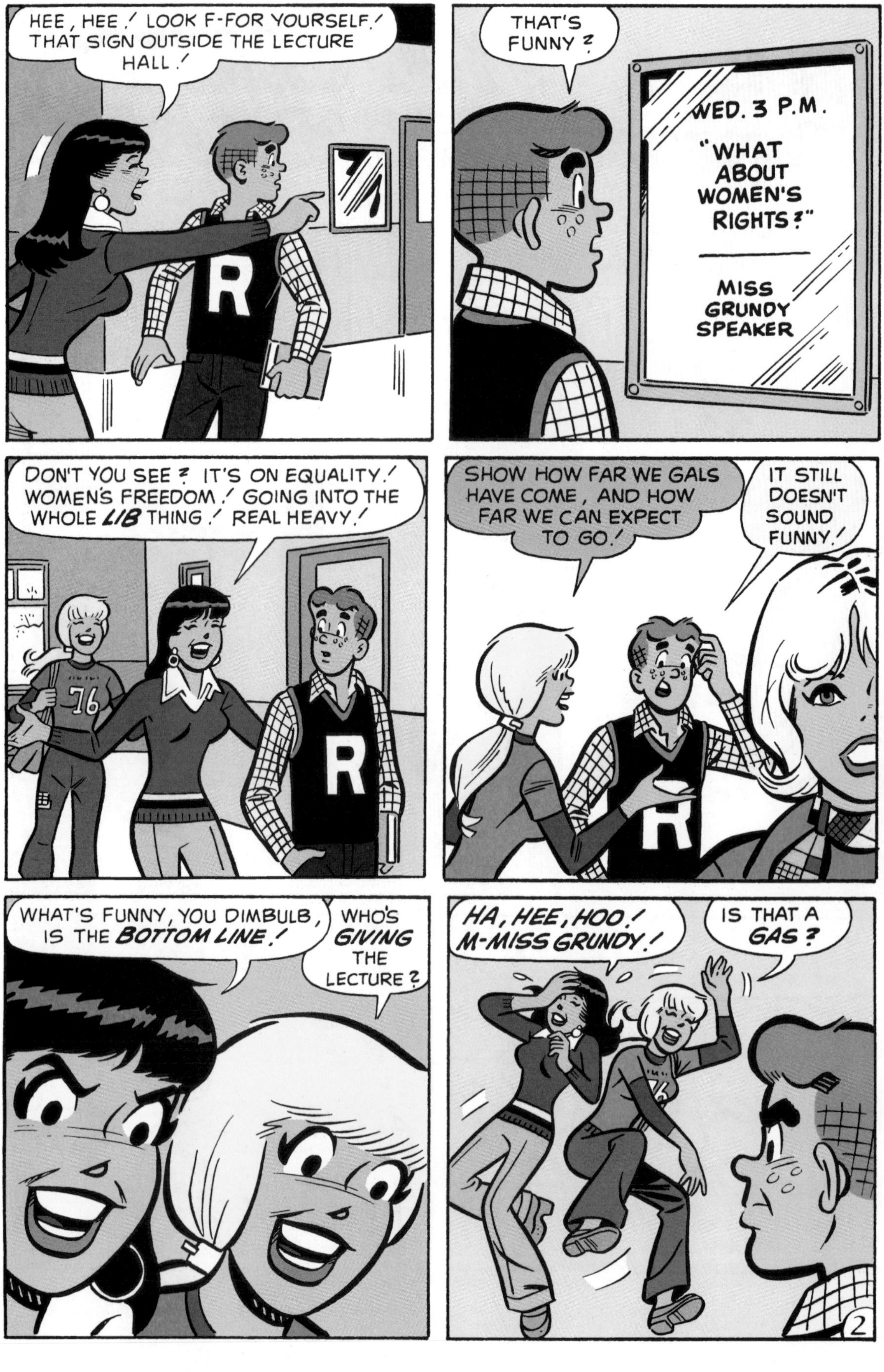
HEE, HEE! LOOK F-FOR YOURSELF! THAT SIGN OUTSIDE THE LECTURE HALL!
THAT'S FUNNY?
WED. 3 P.M.
"WHAT ABOUT WOMEN'S RIGHTS?"
MISS GRUNDY SPEAKER
DON'T YOU SEE? IT'S ON EQUALITY! WOMEN'S FREEDOM! GOING INTO THE WHOLE LIB THING! REAL HEAVY!
76
SHOW HOW FAR WE GALS HAVE COME, AND HOW FAR WE CAN EXPECT TO GO!
IT STILL DOESN'T SOUND FUNNY!
WHAT'S FUNNY, YOU DIMBULB, IS THE BOTTOM LINE!
WHO'S GIVING THE LECTURE?
HA, HEE, HOO! M-MISS GRUNDY!
IS THAT A GAS?
2

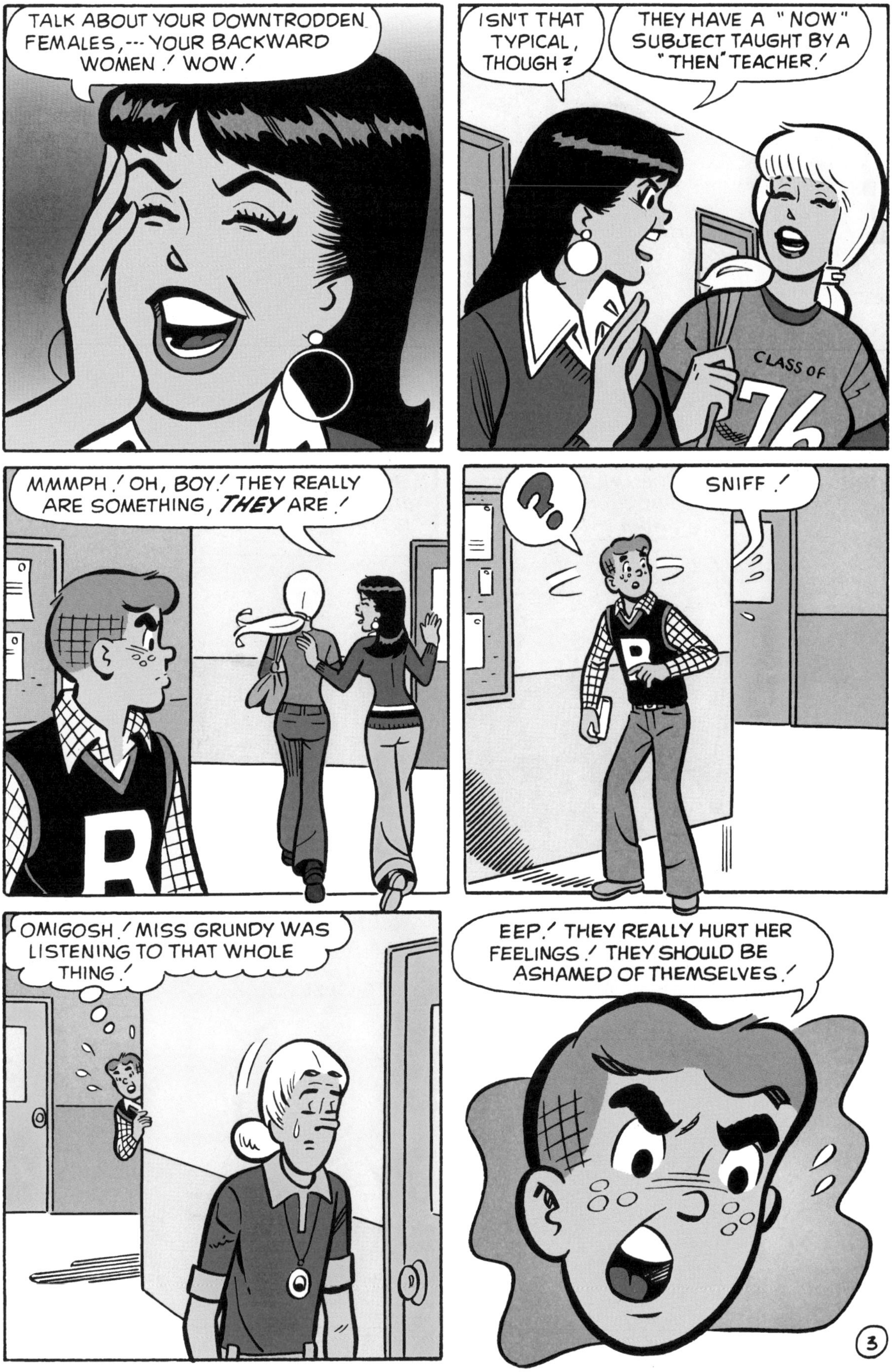
TALK ABOUT YOUR DOWNTRODDEN FEMALES,--- YOUR BACKWARD WOMEN! WOW!
ISN'T THAT TYPICAL, THOUGH?
THEY HAVE A "NOW" SUBJECT TAUGHT BY A "THEN" TEACHER!
CLASS OF 76
MMMPH! OH, BOY! THEY REALLY ARE SOMETHING, THEY ARE!
?
SNIFF!
OMIGOSH! MISS GRUNDY WAS LISTENING TO THAT WHOLE THING!
EEP! THEY REALLY HURT HER FEELINGS! THEY SHOULD BE ASHAMED OF THEMSELVES!
3

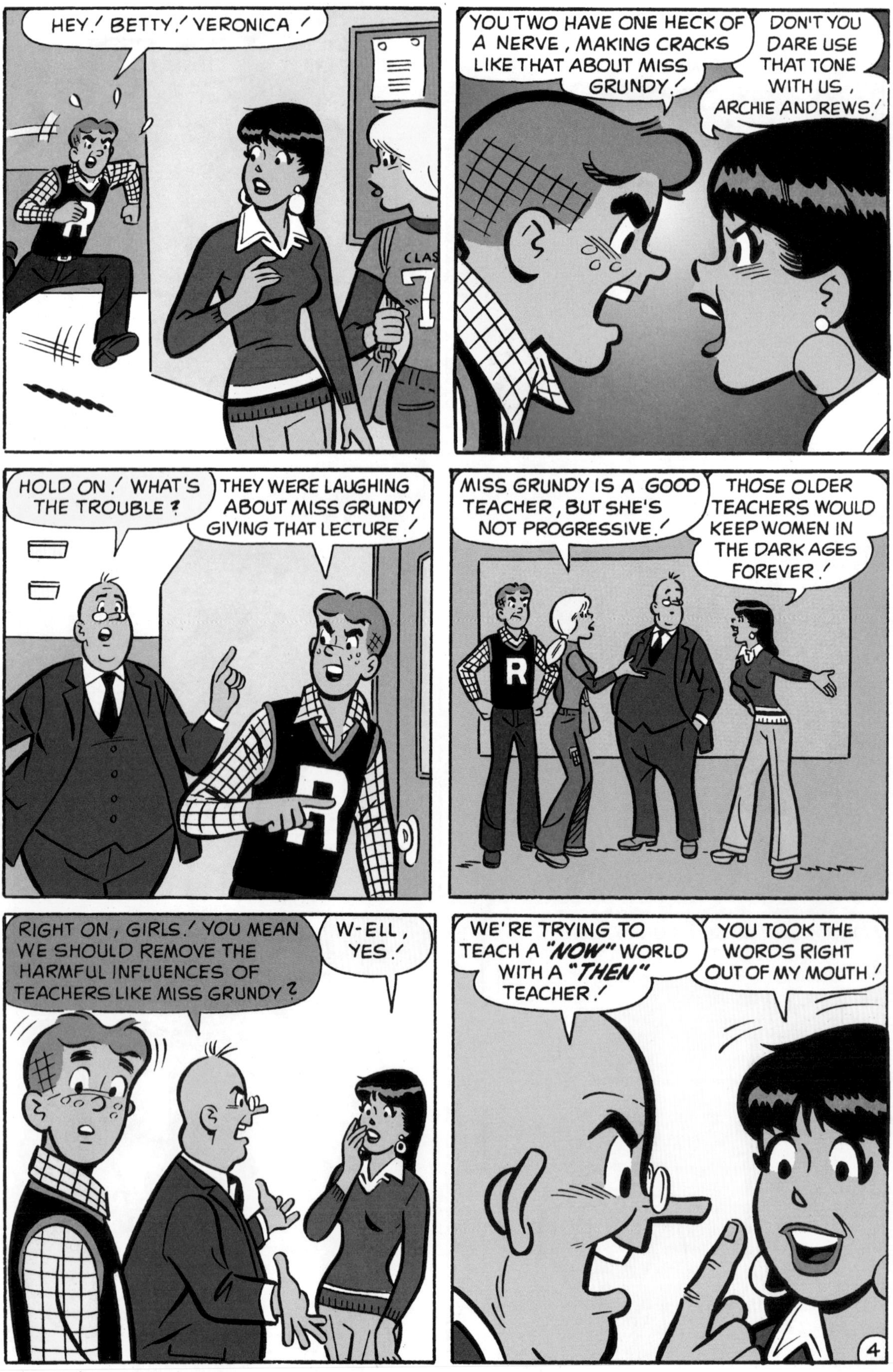
HEY! BETTY! VERONICA!
YOU TWO HAVE ONE HECK OF A NERVE, MAKING CRACKS LIKE THAT ABOUT MISS GRUNDY!
DON'T YOU DARE USE THAT TONE WITH US, ARCHIE ANDREWS!
HOLD ON! WHAT'S THE TROUBLE?
THEY WERE LAUGHING ABOUT MISS GRUNDY GIVING THAT LECTURE!
MISS GRUNDY IS A GOOD TEACHER, BUT SHE'S NOT PROGRESSIVE!
THOSE OLDER TEACHERS WOULD KEEP WOMEN IN THE DARK AGES FOREVER!
RIGHT ON, GIRLS! YOU MEAN WE SHOULD REMOVE THE HARMFUL INFLUENCES OF TEACHERS LIKE MISS GRUNDY?
W-ELL, YES!
WE'RE TRYING TO TEACH A "NOW" WORLD WITH A "THEN" TEACHER!
YOU TOOK THE WORDS RIGHT OUT OF MY MOUTH!
4

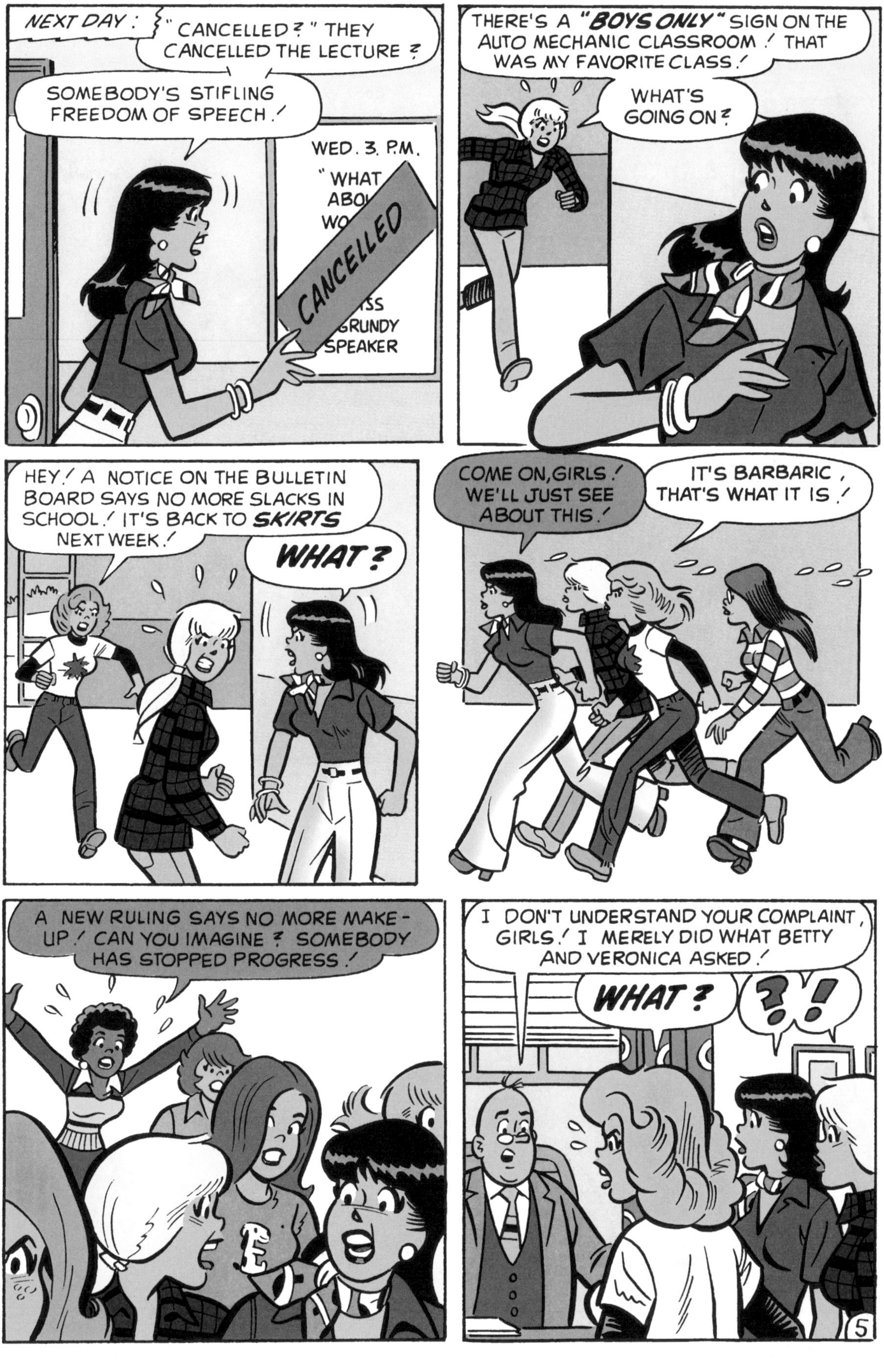
NEXT DAY :
"CANCELLED ?" THEY CANCELLED THE LECTURE ?
SOMEBODY'S STIFLING FREEDOM OF SPEECH !
WED. 3. P.M.
CANCELLED
SPEAKER
THERE'S A "BOYS ONLY" SIGN ON THE AUTO MECHANIC CLASSROOM ! THAT WAS MY FAVORITE CLASS !
WHAT'S GOING ON ?
HEY ! A NOTICE ON THE BULLETIN BOARD SAYS NO MORE SLACKS IN SCHOOL ! IT'S BACK TO SKIRTS NEXT WEEK !
WHAT ?
COME ON, GIRLS ! WE'LL JUST SEE ABOUT THIS !
IT'S BARBARIC , THAT'S WHAT IT IS !
A NEW RULING SAYS NO MORE MAKE-UP ! CAN YOU IMAGINE ? SOMEBODY HAS STOPPED PROGRESS !
I DON'T UNDERSTAND YOUR COMPLAINT, GIRLS ! I MERELY DID WHAT BETTY AND VERONICA ASKED !
WHAT ?
?!
5

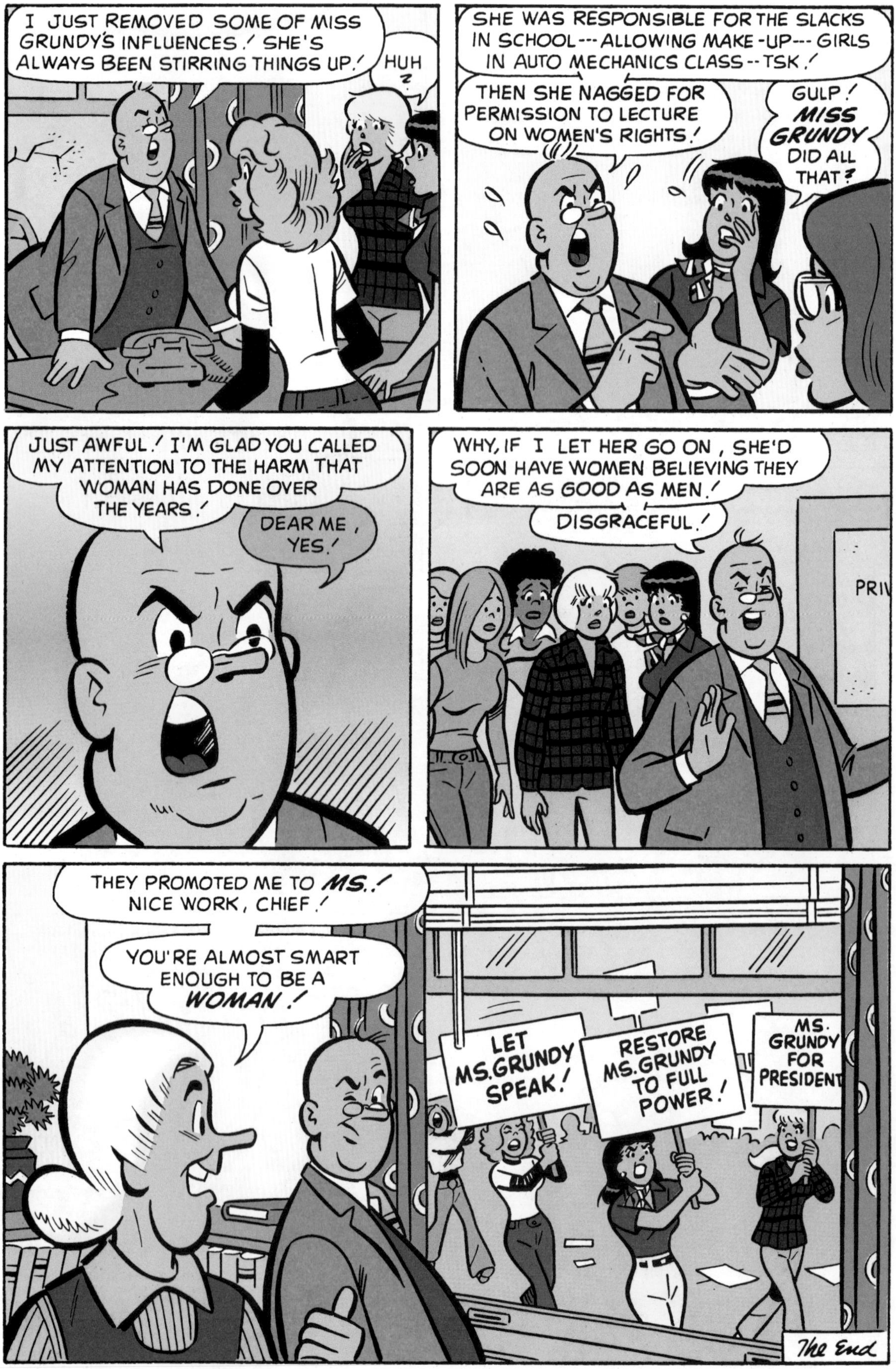

I JUST REMOVED SOME OF MISS GRUNDY'S INFLUENCES! SHE'S ALWAYS BEEN STIRRING THINGS UP!
HUH?
SHE WAS RESPONSIBLE FOR THE SLACKS IN SCHOOL--- ALLOWING MAKE-UP--- GIRLS IN AUTO MECHANICS CLASS--TSK!
THEN SHE NAGGED FOR PERMISSION TO LECTURE ON WOMEN'S RIGHTS!
GULP! MISS GRUNDY DID ALL THAT?
JUST AWFUL! I'M GLAD YOU CALLED MY ATTENTION TO THE HARM THAT WOMAN HAS DONE OVER THE YEARS!
DEAR ME, YES!
WHY, IF I LET HER GO ON, SHE'D SOON HAVE WOMEN BELIEVING THEY ARE AS GOOD AS MEN!
DISGRACEFUL!
PRIV
THEY PROMOTED ME TO MS.! NICE WORK, CHIEF!
YOU'RE ALMOST SMART ENOUGH TO BE A WOMAN!
LET MS. GRUNDY SPEAK!
RESTORE MS. GRUNDY TO FULL POWER!
MS. GRUNDY FOR PRESIDENT
The End

Archie AND THE GANG in "BICENTENNIAL BANTER"

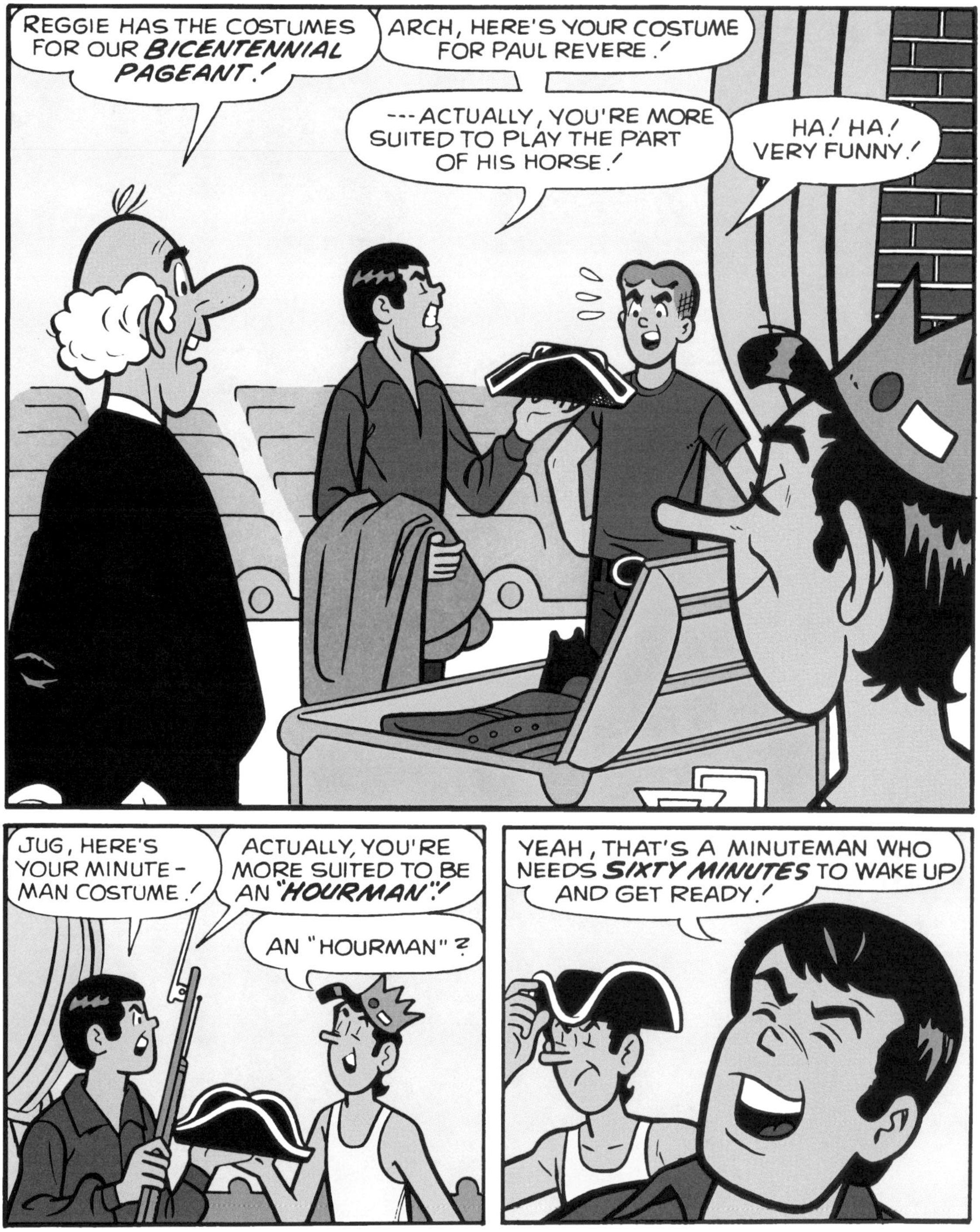
REGGIE HAS THE COSTUMES FOR OUR BICENTENNIAL PAGEANT!
ARCH, HERE'S YOUR COSTUME FOR PAUL REVERE!
---ACTUALLY, YOU'RE MORE SUITED TO PLAY THE PART OF HIS HORSE!
HA! HA! VERY FUNNY!
JUG, HERE'S YOUR MINUTE-MAN COSTUME!
ACTUALLY, YOU'RE MORE SUITED TO BE AN "HOURMAN"!
AN "HOURMAN"?
YEAH, THAT'S A MINUTEMAN WHO NEEDS SIXTY MINUTES TO WAKE UP AND GET READY!

Originally presented in ARCHIE'S TV LAUGHOUT #36, December, 1975

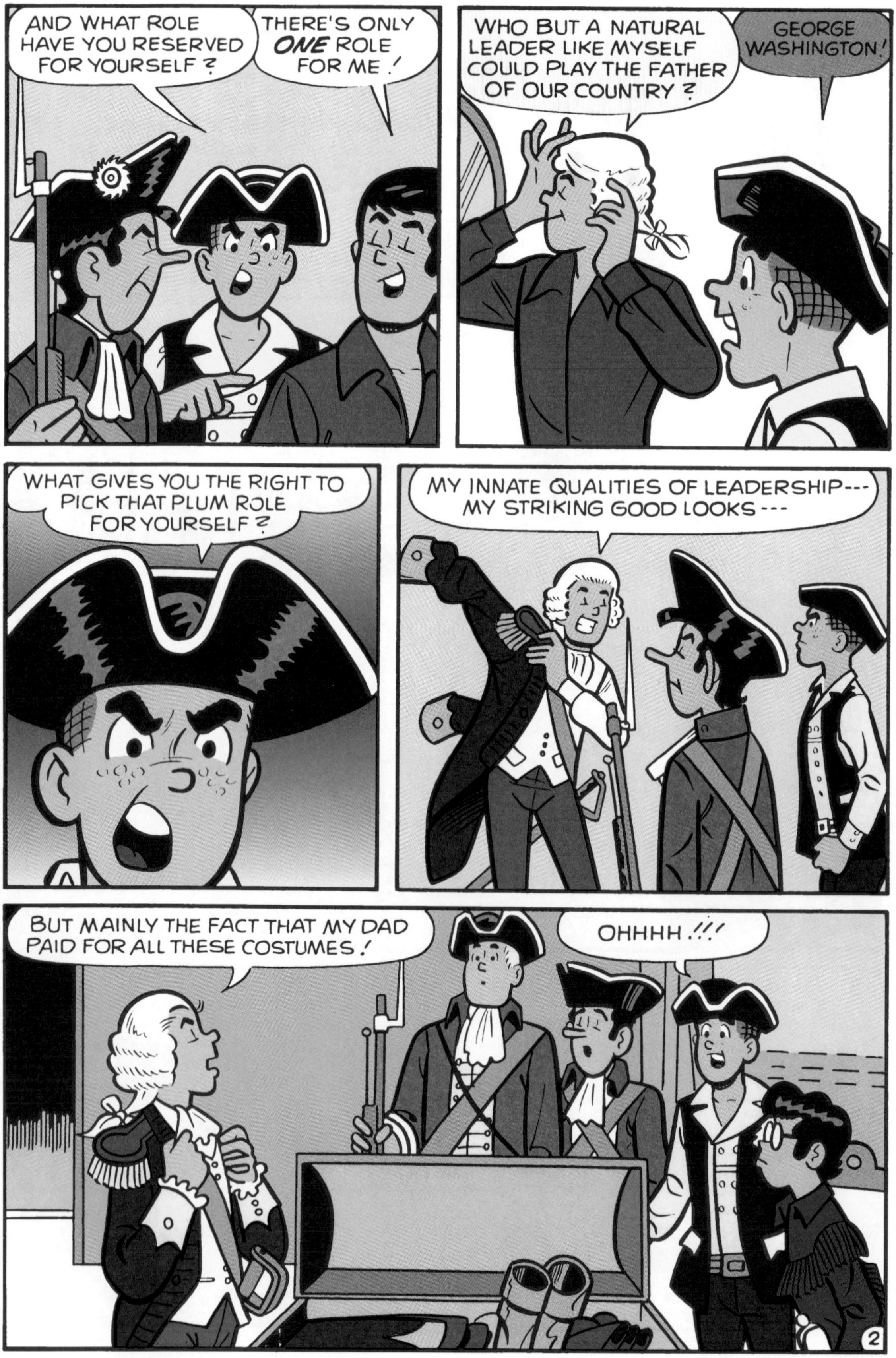
AND WHAT ROLE HAVE YOU RESERVED FOR YOURSELF ?
THERE'S ONLY ONE ROLE FOR ME !
WHO BUT A NATURAL LEADER LIKE MYSELF COULD PLAY THE FATHER OF OUR COUNTRY ?
GEORGE WASHINGTON !
WHAT GIVES YOU THE RIGHT TO PICK THAT PLUM ROLE FOR YOURSELF ?
MY INNATE QUALITIES OF LEADERSHIP--- MY STRIKING GOOD LOOKS ---
BUT MAINLY THE FACT THAT MY DAD PAID FOR ALL THESE COSTUMES !
OHHHH !!!
2

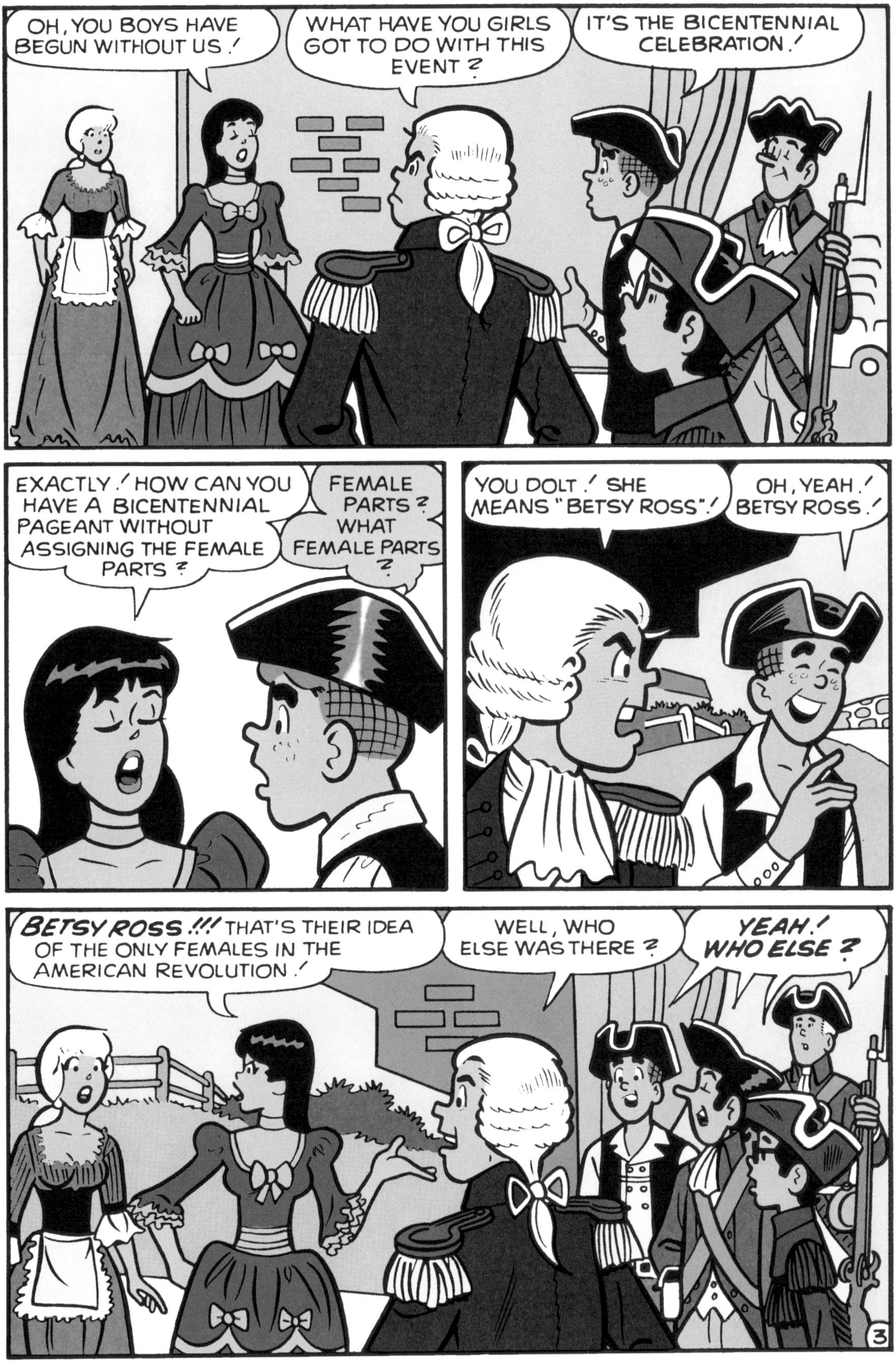
OH, YOU BOYS HAVE BEGUN WITHOUT US!
WHAT HAVE YOU GIRLS GOT TO DO WITH THIS EVENT?
IT'S THE BICENTENNIAL CELEBRATION!
EXACTLY! HOW CAN YOU HAVE A BICENTENNIAL PAGEANT WITHOUT ASSIGNING THE FEMALE PARTS?
FEMALE PARTS? WHAT FEMALE PARTS?
YOU DOLT! SHE MEANS "BETSY ROSS"!
OH, YEAH! BETSY ROSS!
BETSY ROSS!!! THAT'S THEIR IDEA OF THE ONLY FEMALES IN THE AMERICAN REVOLUTION!
WELL, WHO ELSE WAS THERE?
YEAH! WHO ELSE?
3

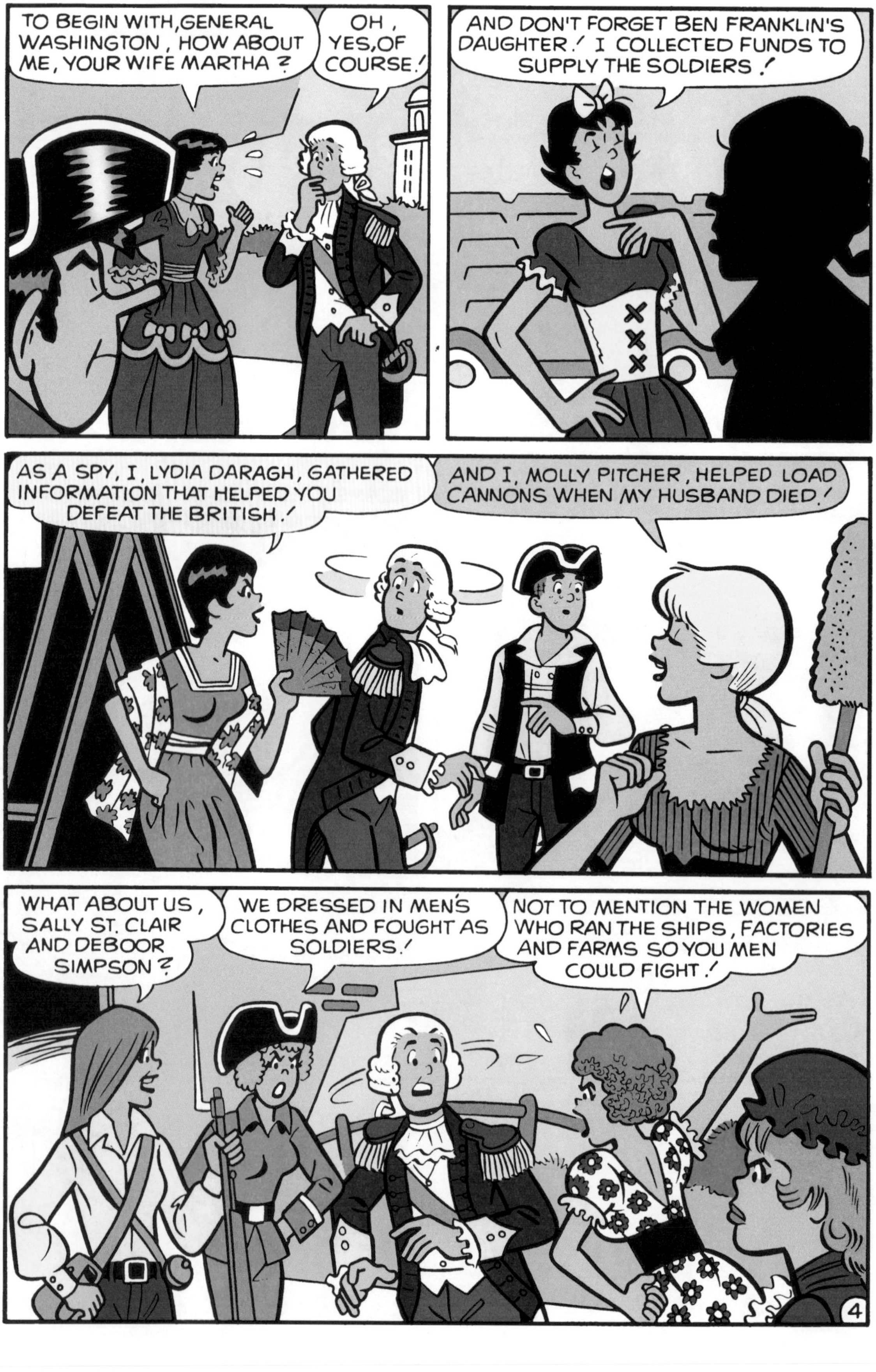
TO BEGIN WITH, GENERAL WASHINGTON, HOW ABOUT ME, YOUR WIFE MARTHA?
OH, YES, OF COURSE!
AND DON'T FORGET BEN FRANKLIN'S DAUGHTER! I COLLECTED FUNDS TO SUPPLY THE SOLDIERS!
AS A SPY, I, LYDIA DARAGH, GATHERED INFORMATION THAT HELPED YOU DEFEAT THE BRITISH!
AND I, MOLLY PITCHER, HELPED LOAD CANNONS WHEN MY HUSBAND DIED!
WHAT ABOUT US, SALLY ST. CLAIR AND DEBOOR SIMPSON?
WE DRESSED IN MEN'S CLOTHES AND FOUGHT AS SOLDIERS!
NOT TO MENTION THE WOMEN WHO RAN THE SHIPS, FACTORIES AND FARMS SO YOU MEN COULD FIGHT!
4

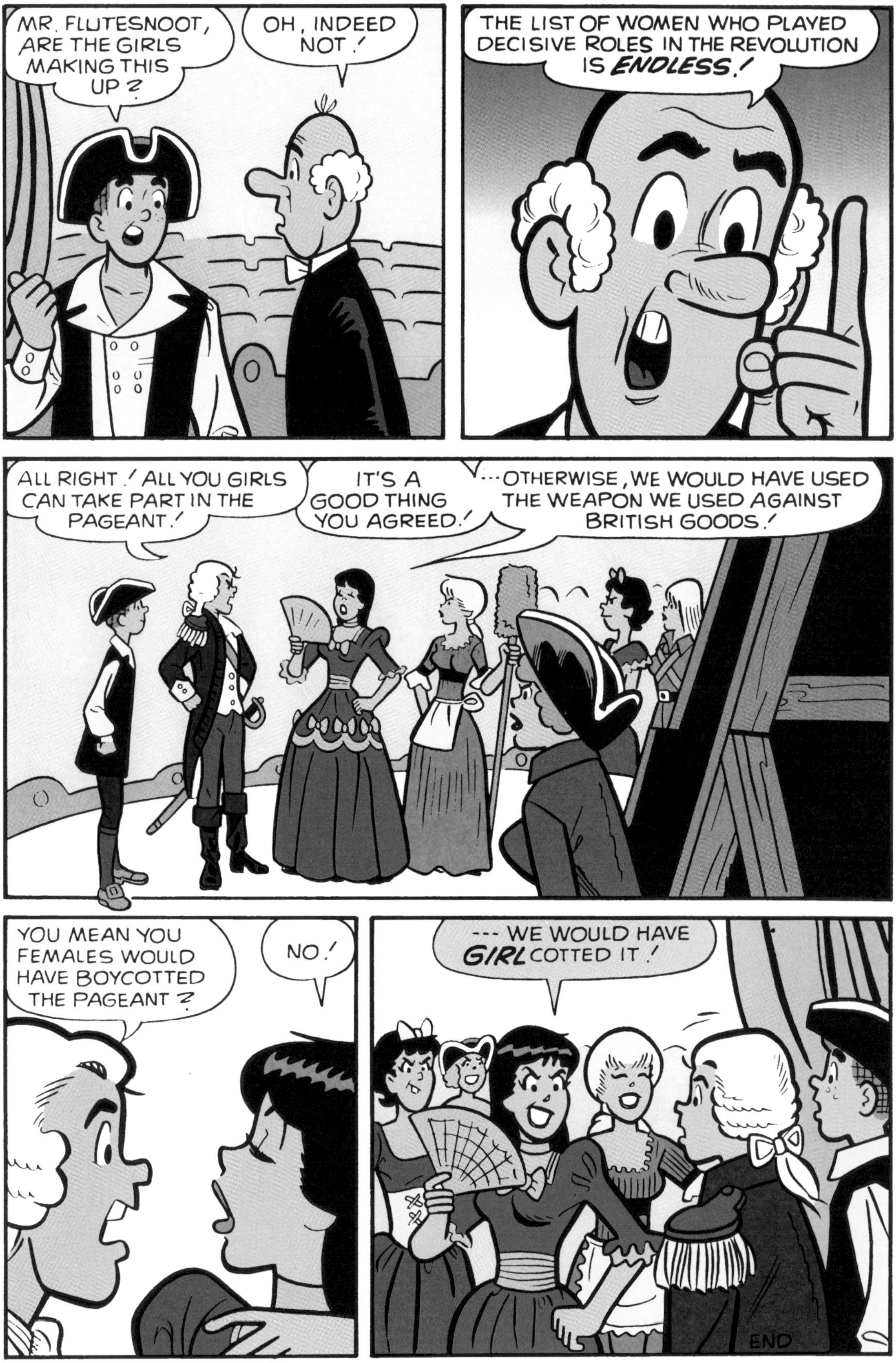
MR. FLUTESNOOT, ARE THE GIRLS MAKING THIS UP?
OH, INDEED NOT!
THE LIST OF WOMEN WHO PLAYED DECISIVE ROLES IN THE REVOLUTION IS ENDLESS!
ALL RIGHT! ALL YOU GIRLS CAN TAKE PART IN THE PAGEANT!
IT'S A GOOD THING YOU AGREED!
---OTHERWISE, WE WOULD HAVE USED THE WEAPON WE USED AGAINST BRITISH GOODS!
YOU MEAN YOU FEMALES WOULD HAVE BOYCOTTED THE PAGEANT?
NO!
--- WE WOULD HAVE GIRLCOTTED IT!
END

Archie in OVER and OUT

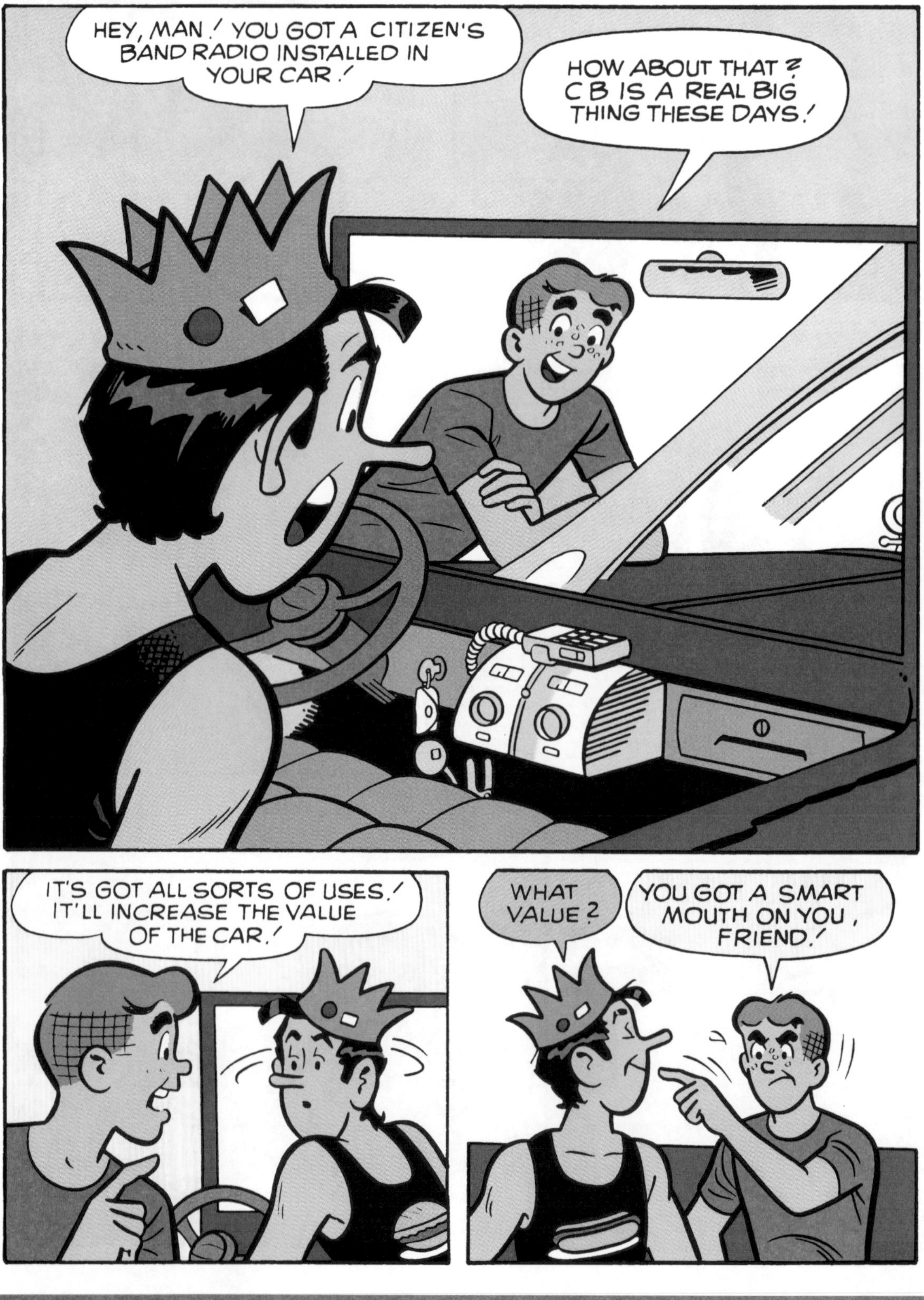
HEY, MAN! YOU GOT A CITIZEN'S BAND RADIO INSTALLED IN YOUR CAR!
HOW ABOUT THAT? CB IS A REAL BIG THING THESE DAYS!
IT'S GOT ALL SORTS OF USES! IT'LL INCREASE THE VALUE OF THE CAR!
WHAT VALUE?
YOU GOT A SMART MOUTH ON YOU, FRIEND!

Originally presented in ARCHIE #256, September, 1976

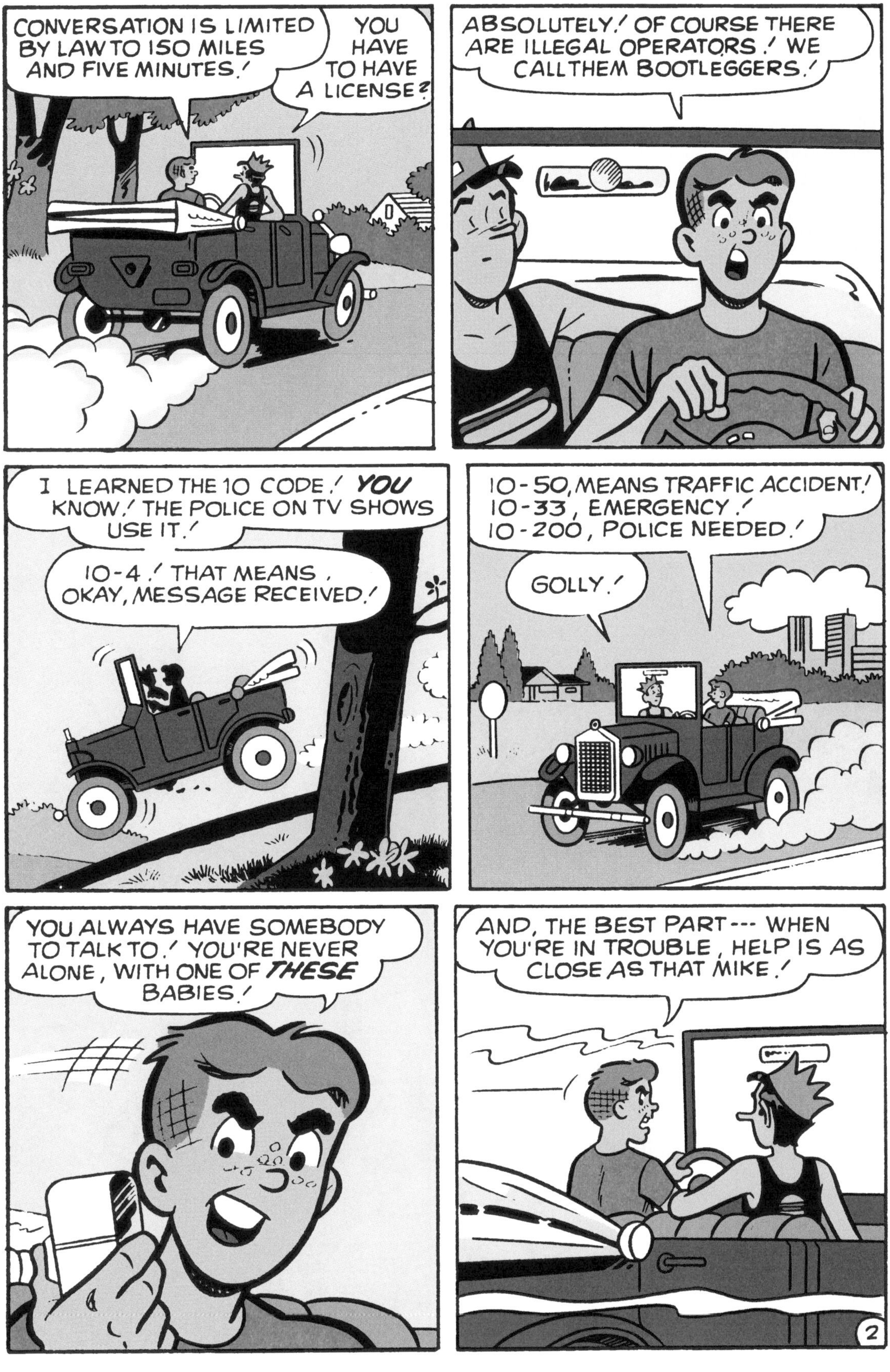
CONVERSATION IS LIMITED BY LAW TO 150 MILES AND FIVE MINUTES!
YOU HAVE TO HAVE A LICENSE?
ABSOLUTELY! OF COURSE THERE ARE ILLEGAL OPERATORS! WE CALL THEM BOOTLEGGERS!
I LEARNED THE 10 CODE! YOU KNOW! THE POLICE ON TV SHOWS USE IT!
10-4! THAT MEANS, OKAY, MESSAGE RECEIVED!
10-50, MEANS TRAFFIC ACCIDENT! 10-33, EMERGENCY! 10-200, POLICE NEEDED!
GOLLY!
YOU ALWAYS HAVE SOMEBODY TO TALK TO! YOU'RE NEVER ALONE, WITH ONE OF THESE BABIES!
AND, THE BEST PART--- WHEN YOU'RE IN TROUBLE, HELP IS AS CLOSE AS THAT MIKE!
2

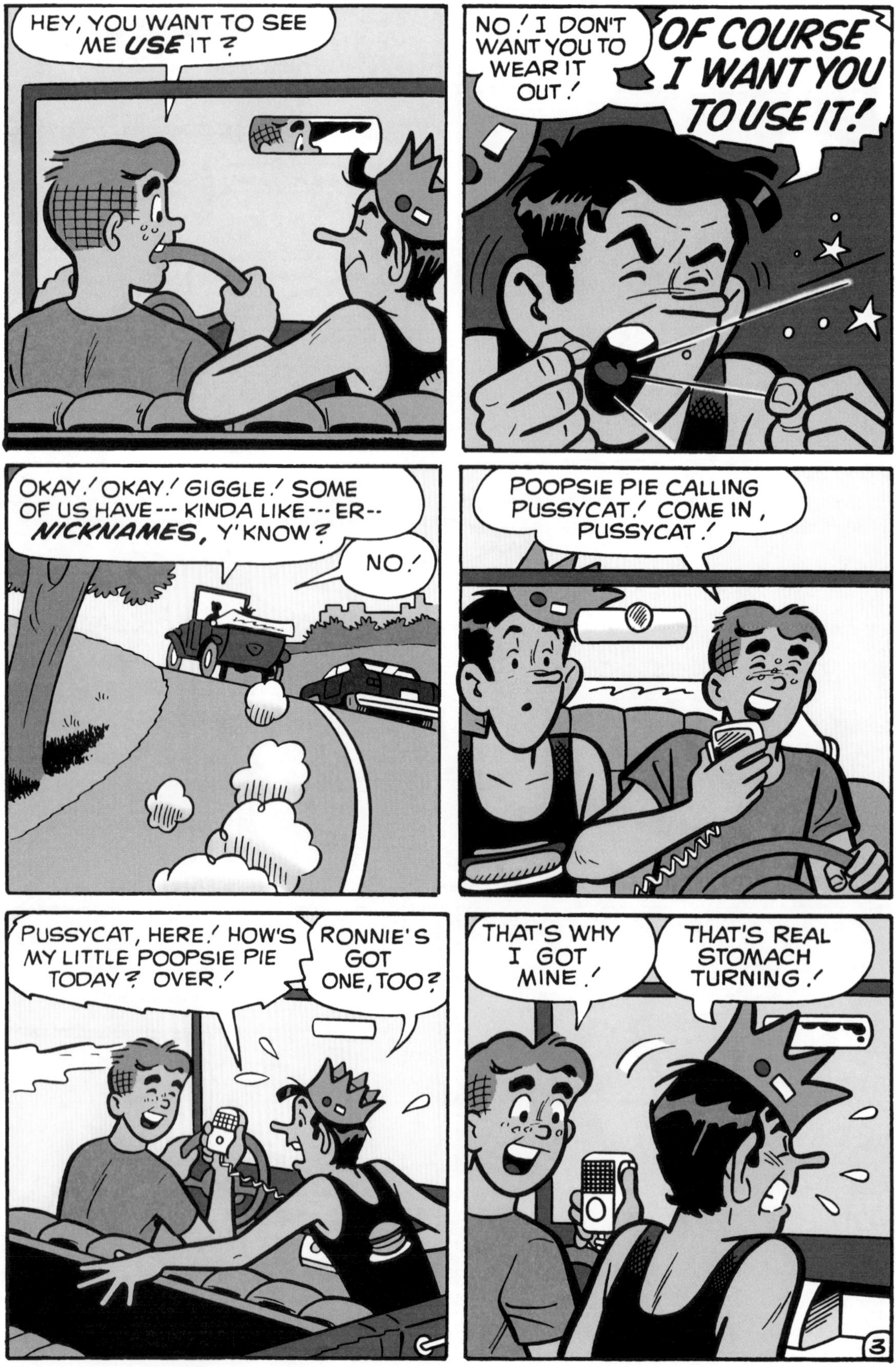
HEY, YOU WANT TO SEE ME *USE* IT ?
NO! I DON'T WANT YOU TO WEAR IT OUT!
OF COURSE I WANT YOU TO USE IT!
OKAY! OKAY! GIGGLE! SOME OF US HAVE--- KINDA LIKE--- ER-- *NICKNAMES*, Y'KNOW?
NO!
POOPSIE PIE CALLING PUSSYCAT! COME IN, PUSSYCAT!
PUSSYCAT, HERE! HOW'S MY LITTLE POOPSIE PIE TODAY? OVER!
RONNIE'S GOT ONE, TOO?
THAT'S WHY I GOT MINE!
THAT'S REAL STOMACH TURNING!
3

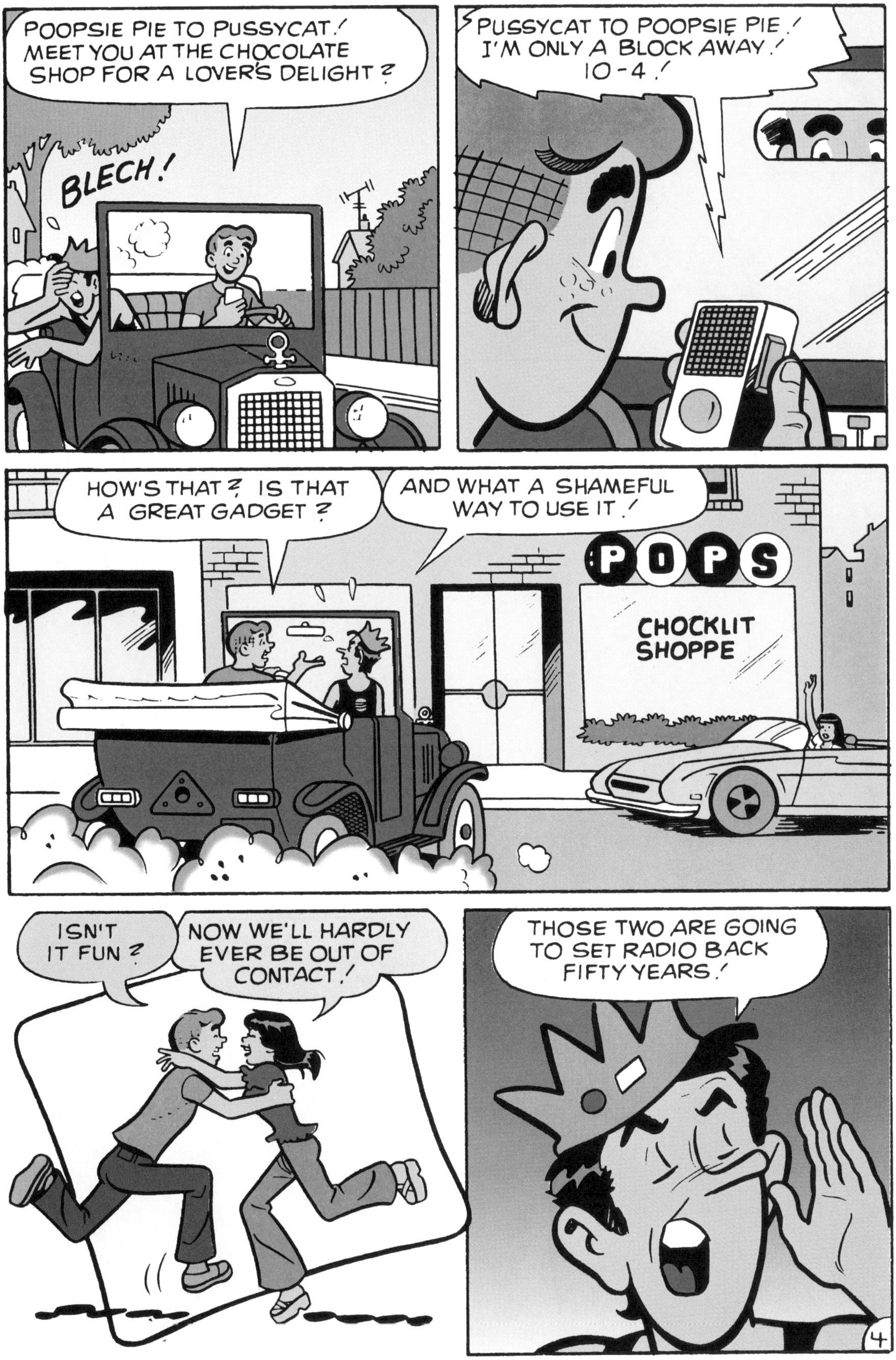
POOPSIE PIE TO PUSSYCAT! MEET YOU AT THE CHOCOLATE SHOP FOR A LOVER'S DELIGHT?
BLECH!
PUSSYCAT TO POOPSIE PIE! I'M ONLY A BLOCK AWAY! 10-4!
HOW'S THAT? IS THAT A GREAT GADGET?
AND WHAT A SHAMEFUL WAY TO USE IT!
POPS
CHOCKLIT SHOPPE
ISN'T IT FUN?
NOW WE'LL HARDLY EVER BE OUT OF CONTACT!
THOSE TWO ARE GOING TO SET RADIO BACK FIFTY YEARS!

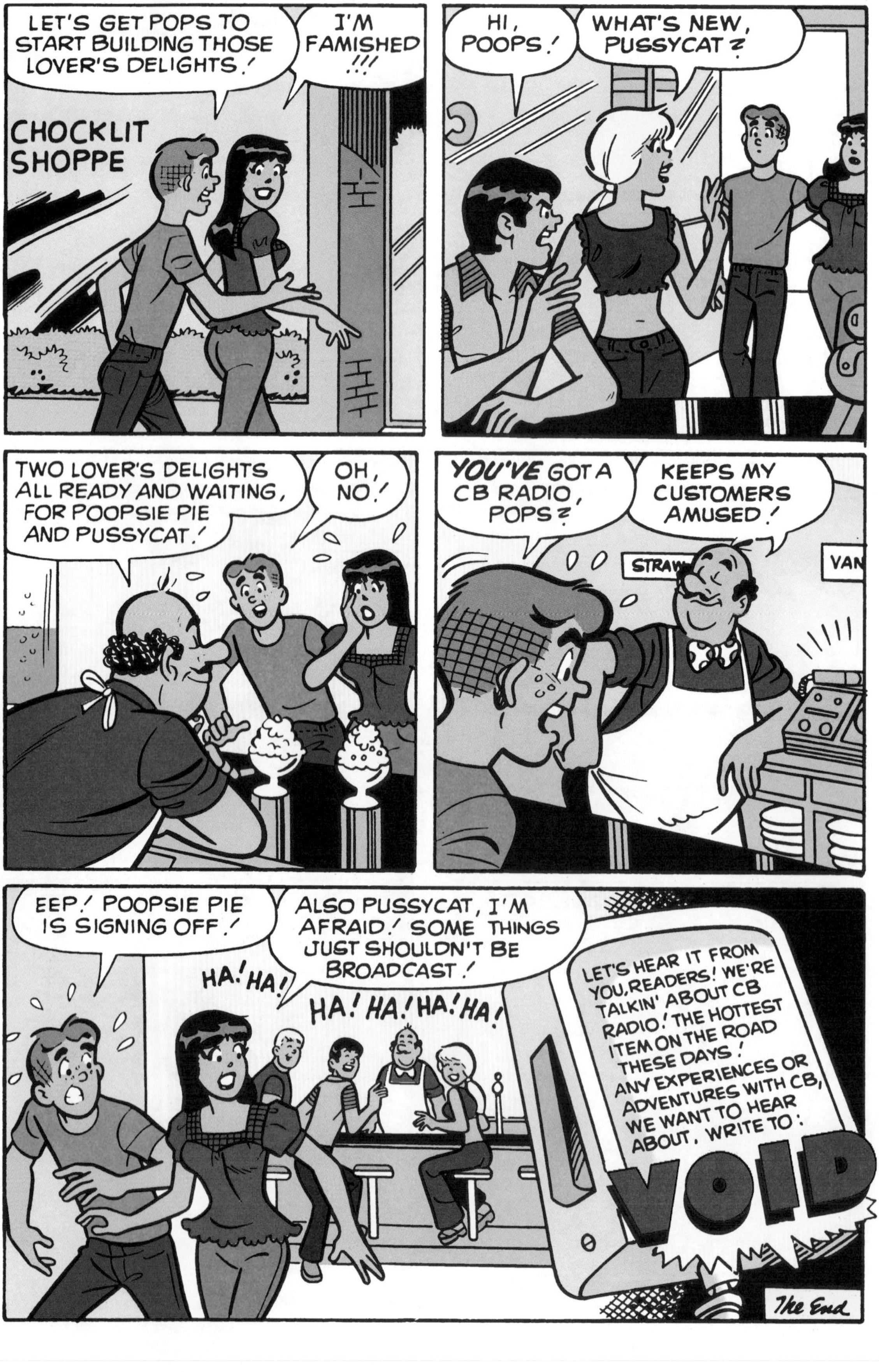
LET'S GET POPS TO START BUILDING THOSE LOVER'S DELIGHTS!
I'M FAMISHED!!!
CHOCKLIT SHOPPE
HI, POOPS!
WHAT'S NEW, PUSSYCAT?
TWO LOVER'S DELIGHTS ALL READY AND WAITING, FOR POOPSIE PIE AND PUSSYCAT!
OH, NO!
YOU'VE GOT A CB RADIO, POPS?
KEEPS MY CUSTOMERS AMUSED!
STRAW
VAN
EEP! POOPSIE PIE IS SIGNING OFF!
ALSO PUSSYCAT, I'M AFRAID! SOME THINGS JUST SHOULDN'T BE BROADCAST!
HA! HA!
HA! HA! HA! HA!
LET'S HEAR IT FROM YOU, READERS! WE'RE TALKIN' ABOUT CB RADIO! THE HOTTEST ITEM ON THE ROAD THESE DAYS! ANY EXPERIENCES OR ADVENTURES WITH CB, WE WANT TO HEAR ABOUT, WRITE TO:
VOID
The End

A GALLERY OF CLASSIC 1970s COVERS

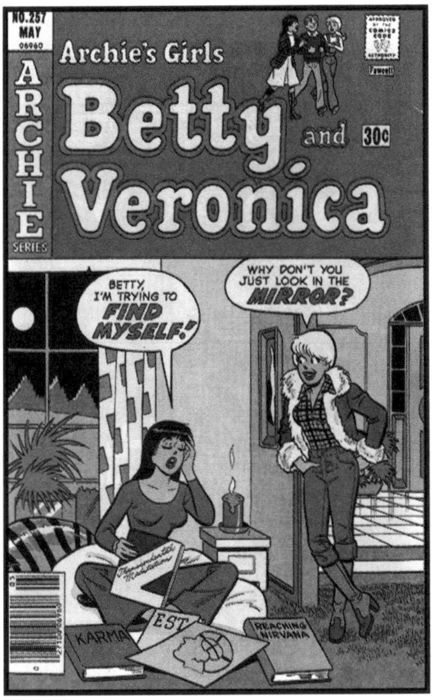
NO.257
MAY
06960
Archie's Girls
Betty and Veronica
30¢
ARCHIE SERIES
BETTY, I'M TRYING TO FIND MYSELF!
WHY DON'T YOU JUST LOOK IN THE MIRROR?
KARMA
EST
REACHING NIRVANA

BETTY & VERONICA #257
(May, 1977)

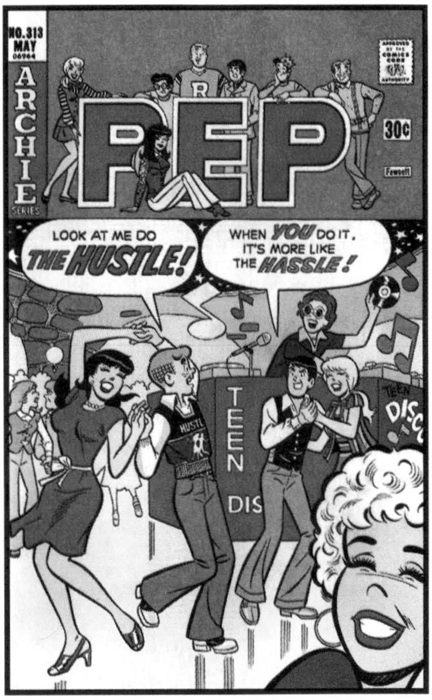
NO.313
MAY
06964
ARCHIE SERIES
PEP
30¢
LOOK AT ME DO THE HUSTLE!
WHEN YOU DO IT, IT'S MORE LIKE THE HASSLE!

PEP #313
(May, 1976)

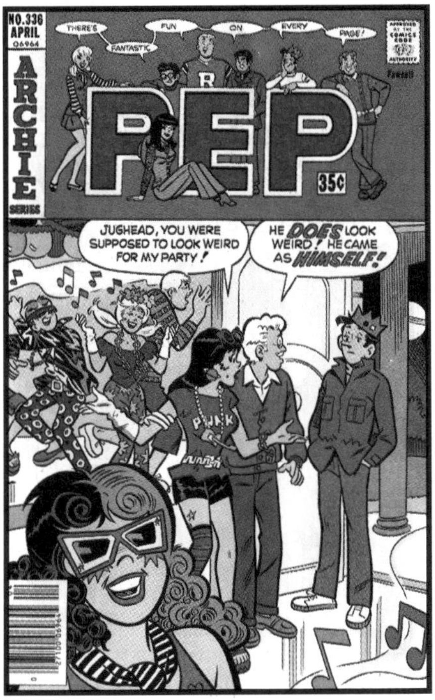
NO.336
APRIL
06964
ARCHIE SERIES
THERE'S FANTASTIC FUN ON EVERY PAGE!
PEP
35¢
JUGHEAD, YOU WERE SUPPOSED TO LOOK WEIRD FOR MY PARTY!
HE DOES LOOK WEIRD! HE CAME AS HIMSELF!

PEP #336
(April, 1978)

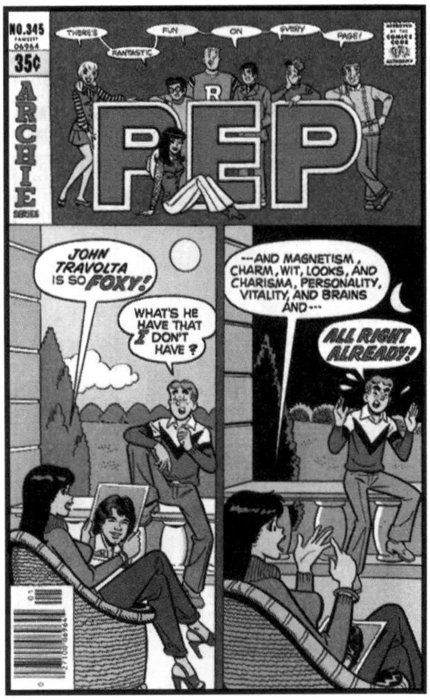
NO.345
06964
35¢
ARCHIE SERIES
THERE'S FANTASTIC FUN ON EVERY PAGE!
PEP
JOHN TRAVOLTA IS SO FOXY!
WHAT'S HE HAVE THAT I DON'T HAVE?
---AND MAGNETISM, CHARM, WIT, LOOKS, AND CHARISMA, PERSONALITY, VITALITY, AND BRAINS AND---
ALL RIGHT ALREADY!

PEP #345
(January, 1979)

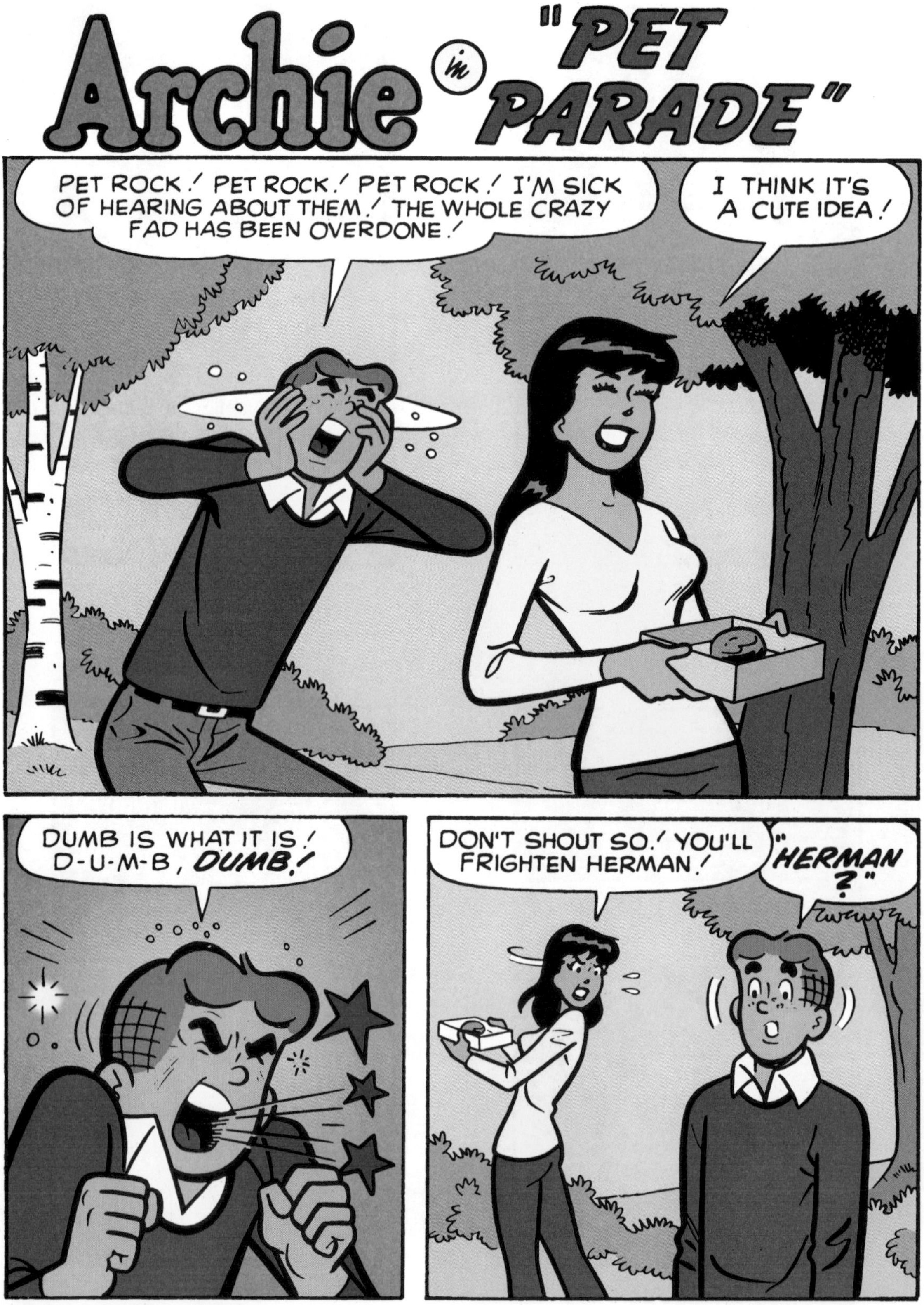
Archie in "PET PARADE"
PET ROCK! PET ROCK! PET ROCK! I'M SICK OF HEARING ABOUT THEM! THE WHOLE CRAZY FAD HAS BEEN OVERDONE!
I THINK IT'S A CUTE IDEA!
DUMB IS WHAT IT IS! D-U-M-B, DUMB!
DON'T SHOUT SO! YOU'LL FRIGHTEN HERMAN!
"HERMAN?"

Originally presented in EVERYTHING'S ARCHIE #57, June, 1977

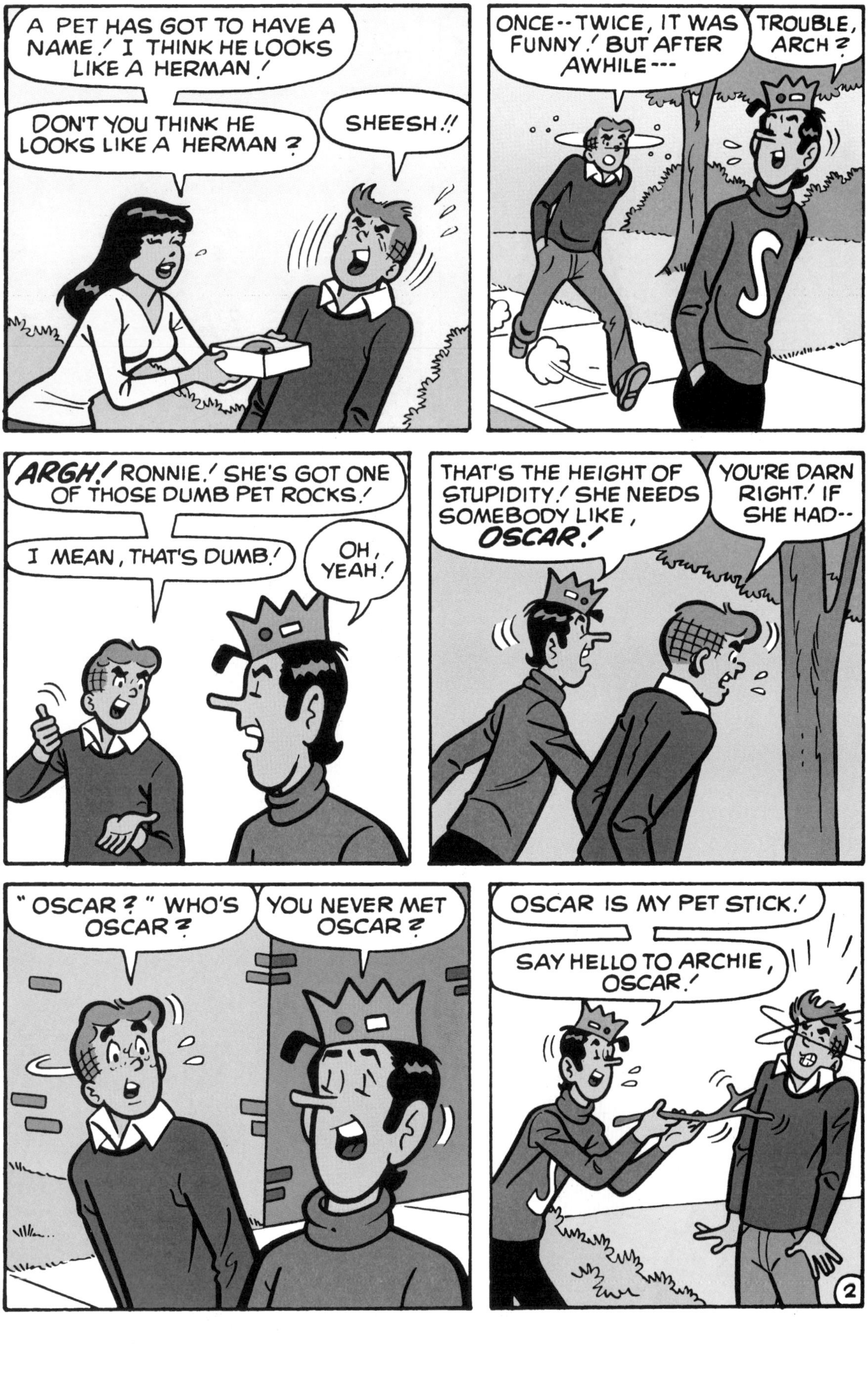
A PET HAS GOT TO HAVE A NAME! I THINK HE LOOKS LIKE A HERMAN!
DON'T YOU THINK HE LOOKS LIKE A HERMAN?
SHEESH!!
ONCE--TWICE, IT WAS FUNNY! BUT AFTER AWHILE---
TROUBLE, ARCH?
ARGH! RONNIE! SHE'S GOT ONE OF THOSE DUMB PET ROCKS!
I MEAN, THAT'S DUMB!
OH, YEAH!
THAT'S THE HEIGHT OF STUPIDITY! SHE NEEDS SOMEBODY LIKE, OSCAR!
YOU'RE DARN RIGHT! IF SHE HAD--
"OSCAR?" WHO'S OSCAR?
YOU NEVER MET OSCAR?
OSCAR IS MY PET STICK!
SAY HELLO TO ARCHIE, OSCAR!
2

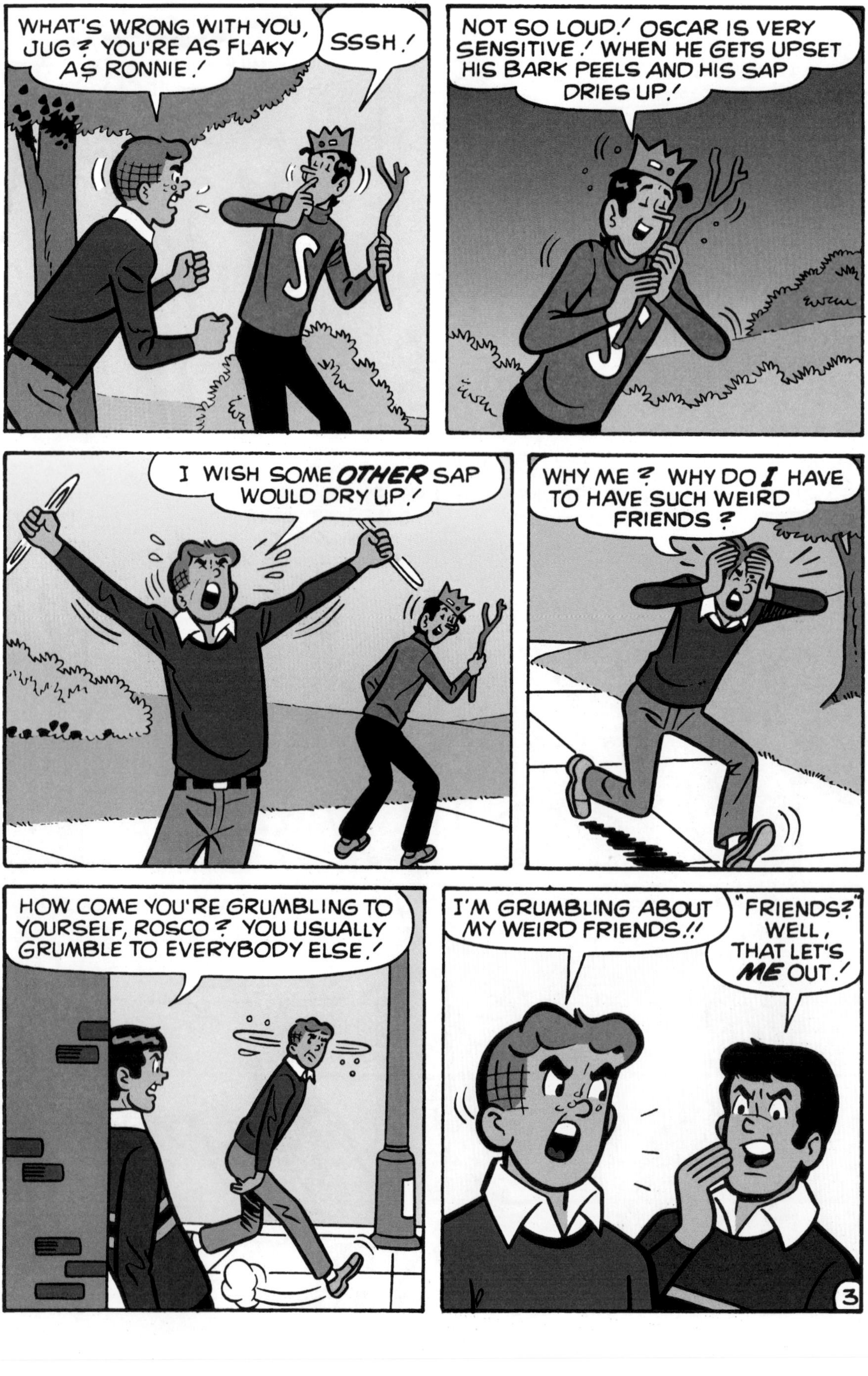
WHAT'S WRONG WITH YOU, JUG? YOU'RE AS FLAKY AS RONNIE!
SSSH!
NOT SO LOUD! OSCAR IS VERY SENSITIVE! WHEN HE GETS UPSET HIS BARK PEELS AND HIS SAP DRIES UP!
I WISH SOME OTHER SAP WOULD DRY UP!
WHY ME? WHY DO I HAVE TO HAVE SUCH WEIRD FRIENDS?
HOW COME YOU'RE GRUMBLING TO YOURSELF, ROSCO? YOU USUALLY GRUMBLE TO EVERYBODY ELSE!
I'M GRUMBLING ABOUT MY WEIRD FRIENDS!!
"FRIENDS?" WELL, THAT LET'S ME OUT!
3

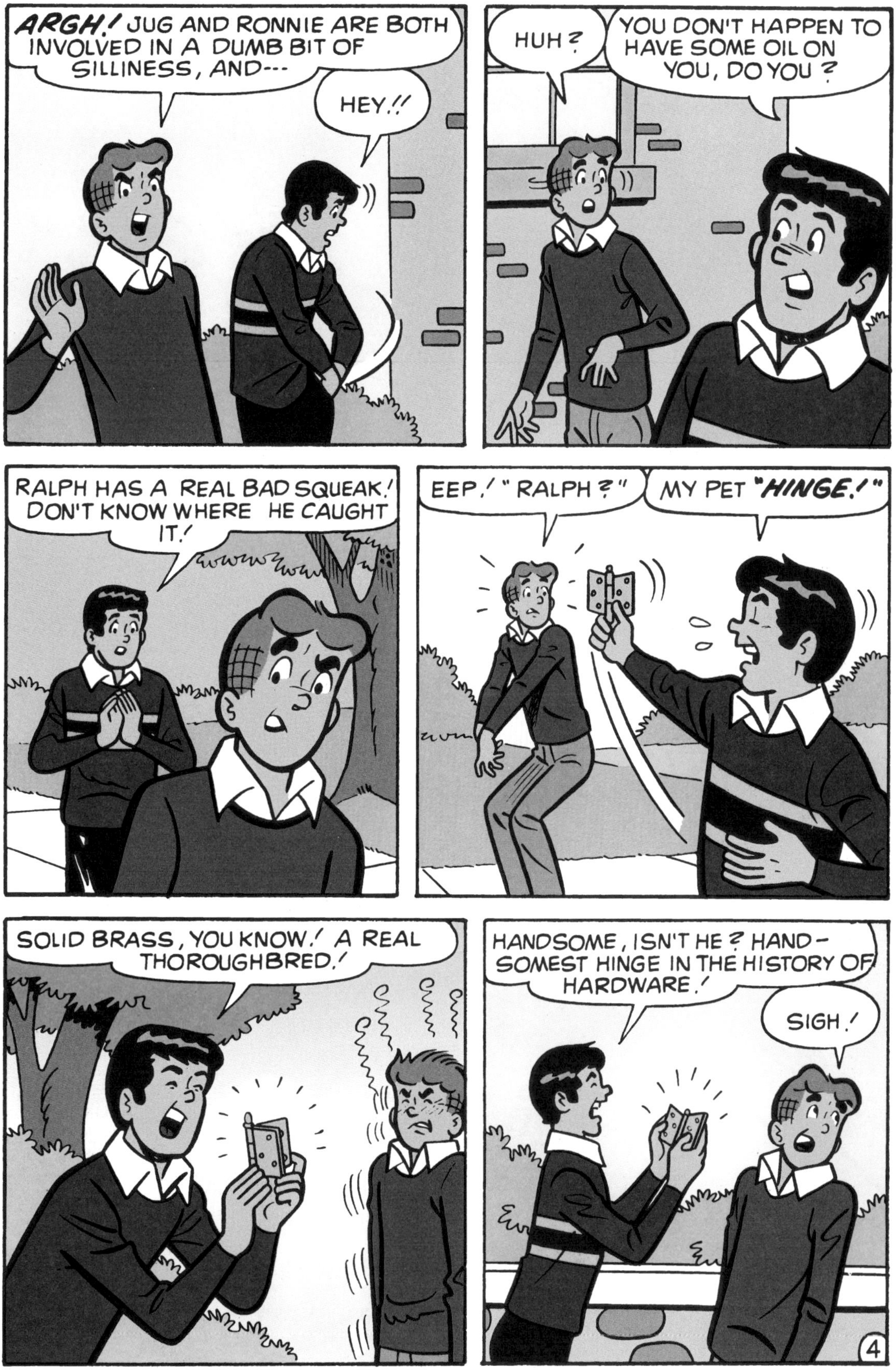
ARGH! JUG AND RONNIE ARE BOTH INVOLVED IN A DUMB BIT OF SILLINESS, AND---
HEY!!
HUH?
YOU DON'T HAPPEN TO HAVE SOME OIL ON YOU, DO YOU?
RALPH HAS A REAL BAD SQUEAK! DON'T KNOW WHERE HE CAUGHT IT!
EEP! "RALPH?"
MY PET "HINGE!"
SOLID BRASS, YOU KNOW! A REAL THOROUGHBRED!
HANDSOME, ISN'T HE? HANDSOMEST HINGE IN THE HISTORY OF HARDWARE!
SIGH!
4

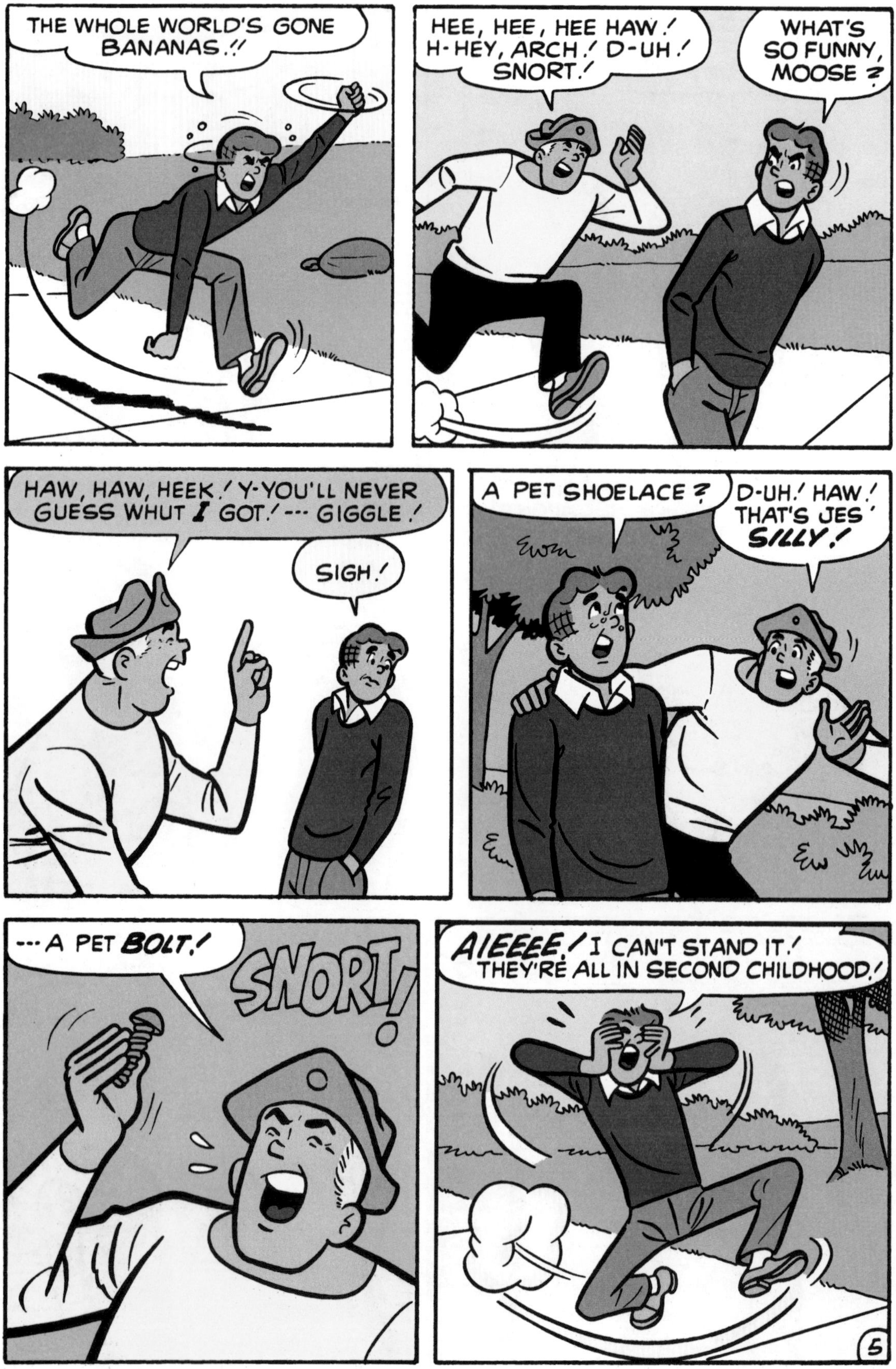
THE WHOLE WORLD'S GONE BANANAS.!!
HEE, HEE, HEE HAW! H-HEY, ARCH! D-UH! SNORT!
WHAT'S SO FUNNY, MOOSE?
HAW, HAW, HEEK! Y-YOU'LL NEVER GUESS WHUT I GOT! --- GIGGLE!
SIGH!
A PET SHOELACE?
D-UH! HAW! THAT'S JES SILLY!
--- A PET BOLT!
SNORT!
AIEEEE! I CAN'T STAND IT! THEY'RE ALL IN SECOND CHILDHOOD!
5

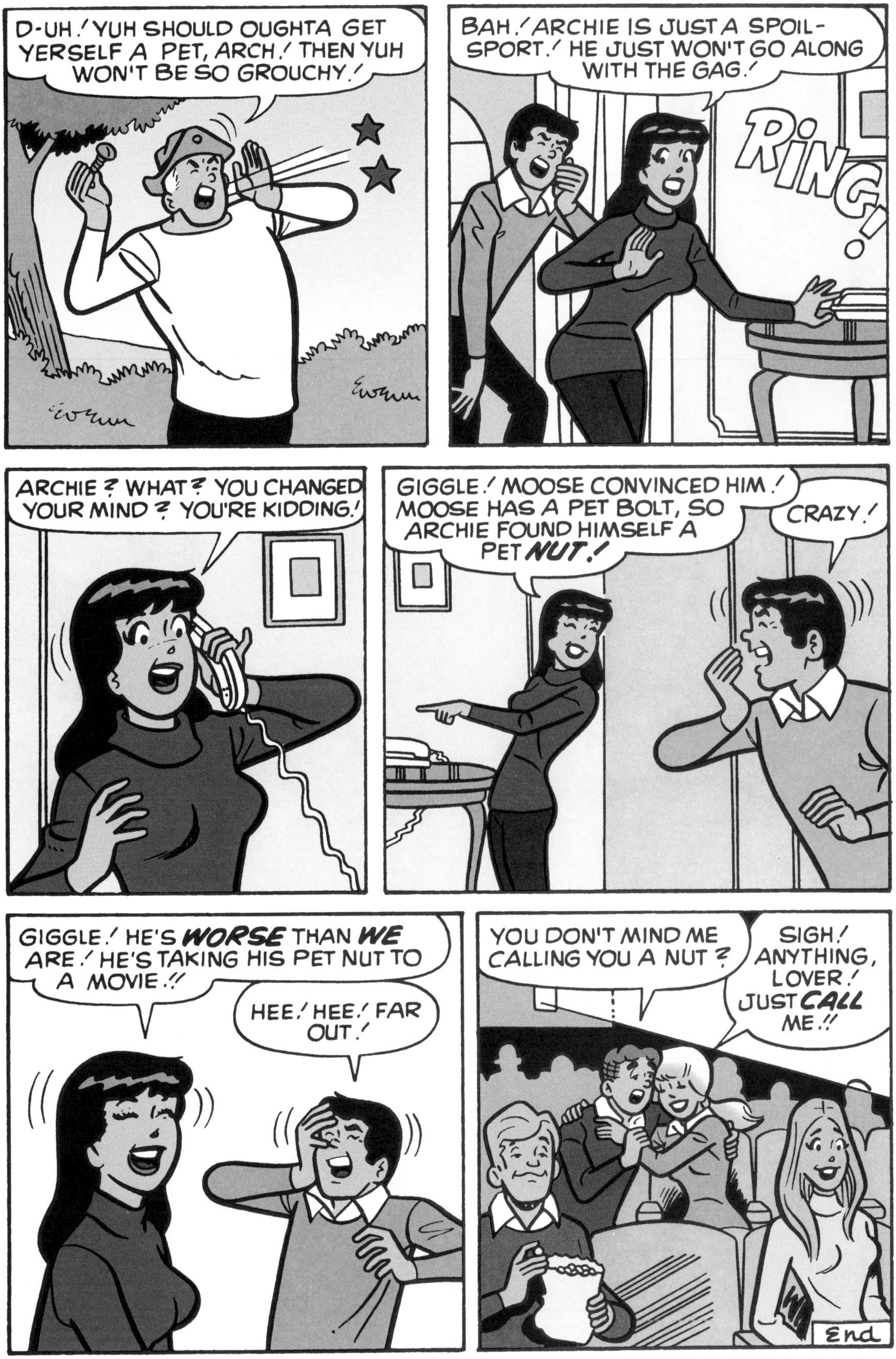
D-UH.! YUH SHOULD OUGHTA GET YERSELF A PET, ARCH! THEN YUH WON'T BE SO GROUCHY!
BAH.! ARCHIE IS JUST A SPOIL-SPORT.! HE JUST WON'T GO ALONG WITH THE GAG.!
RING!
ARCHIE? WHAT? YOU CHANGED YOUR MIND? YOU'RE KIDDING!
GIGGLE.! MOOSE CONVINCED HIM.! MOOSE HAS A PET BOLT, SO ARCHIE FOUND HIMSELF A PET NUT.!
CRAZY.!
GIGGLE.! HE'S WORSE THAN WE ARE.! HE'S TAKING HIS PET NUT TO A MOVIE.!!
HEE.! HEE.! FAR OUT.!
YOU DON'T MIND ME CALLING YOU A NUT?
SIGH.! ANYTHING, LOVER.! JUST CALL ME.!!
End

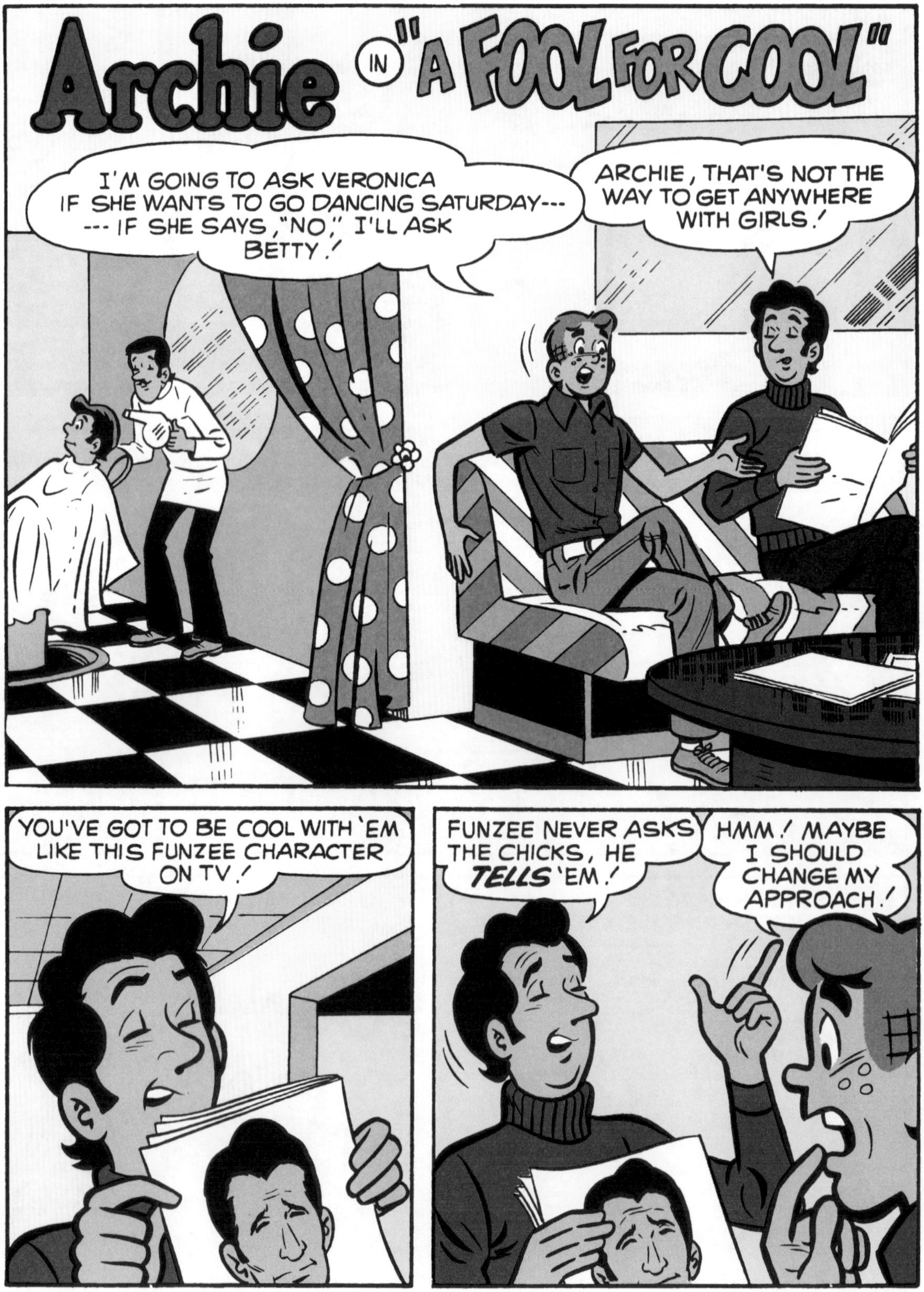
Archie IN "A FOOL FOR COOL"
I'M GOING TO ASK VERONICA IF SHE WANTS TO GO DANCING SATURDAY--- --- IF SHE SAYS, "NO," I'LL ASK BETTY!
ARCHIE, THAT'S NOT THE WAY TO GET ANYWHERE WITH GIRLS!
YOU'VE GOT TO BE COOL WITH 'EM LIKE THIS FUNZEE CHARACTER ON TV!
FUNZEE NEVER ASKS THE CHICKS, HE *TELLS* 'EM!
HMM! MAYBE I SHOULD CHANGE MY APPROACH!

Originally presented in ARCHIE GIANT SERIES #461 (WORLD OF ARCHIE) #461, September, 1977

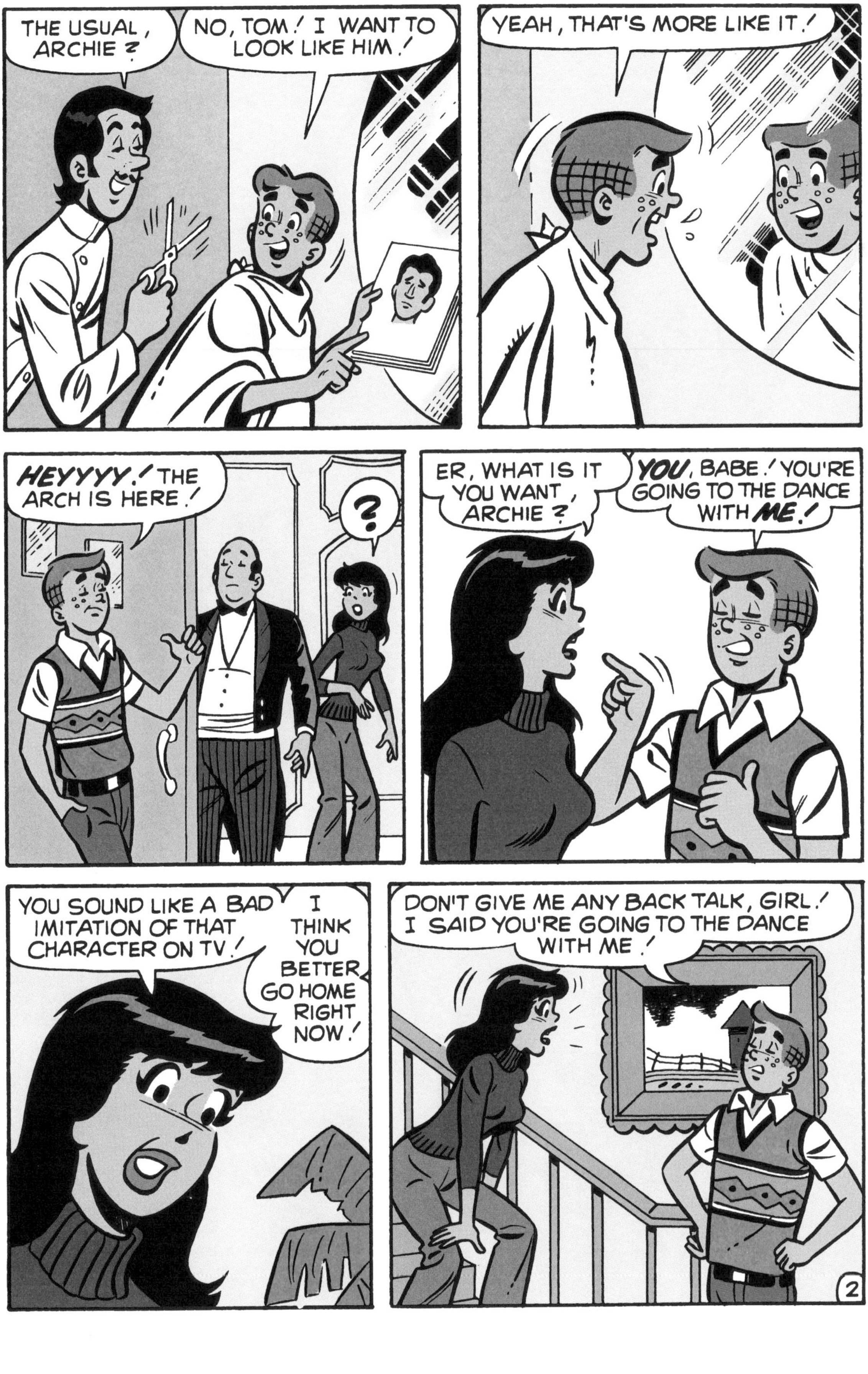
THE USUAL, ARCHIE?
NO, TOM! I WANT TO LOOK LIKE HIM!
YEAH, THAT'S MORE LIKE IT!
HEYYYY! THE ARCH IS HERE!
?
ER, WHAT IS IT YOU WANT, ARCHIE?
YOU, BABE! YOU'RE GOING TO THE DANCE WITH ME!
YOU SOUND LIKE A BAD IMITATION OF THAT CHARACTER ON TV!
I THINK YOU BETTER GO HOME RIGHT NOW!
DON'T GIVE ME ANY BACK TALK, GIRL! I SAID YOU'RE GOING TO THE DANCE WITH ME!
2

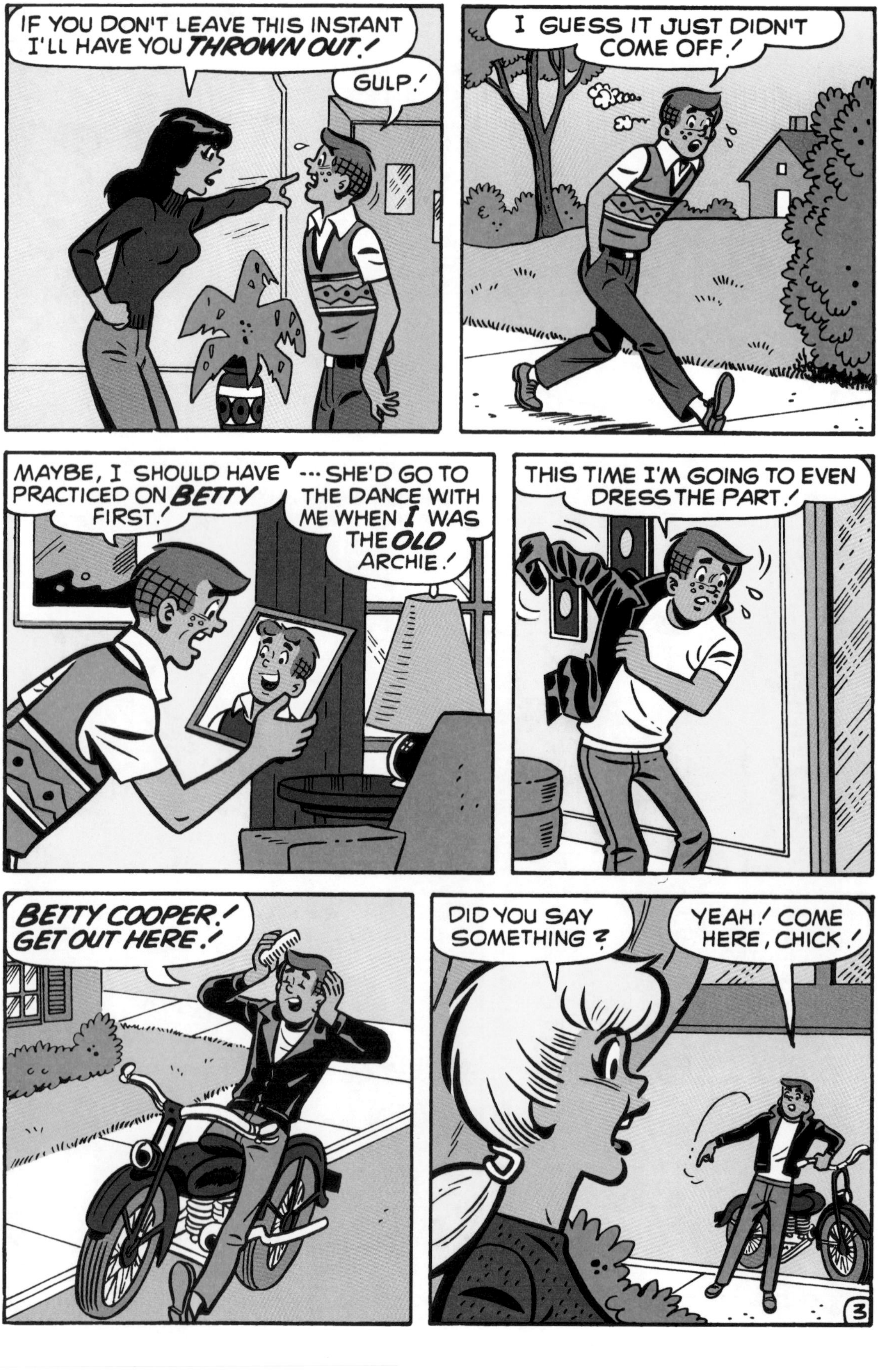
IF YOU DON'T LEAVE THIS INSTANT I'LL HAVE YOU THROWN OUT!
GULP!
I GUESS IT JUST DIDN'T COME OFF!
MAYBE, I SHOULD HAVE PRACTICED ON BETTY FIRST!
--- SHE'D GO TO THE DANCE WITH ME WHEN I WAS THE OLD ARCHIE!
THIS TIME I'M GOING TO EVEN DRESS THE PART!
BETTY COOPER! GET OUT HERE!
DID YOU SAY SOMETHING?
YEAH! COME HERE, CHICK!
3

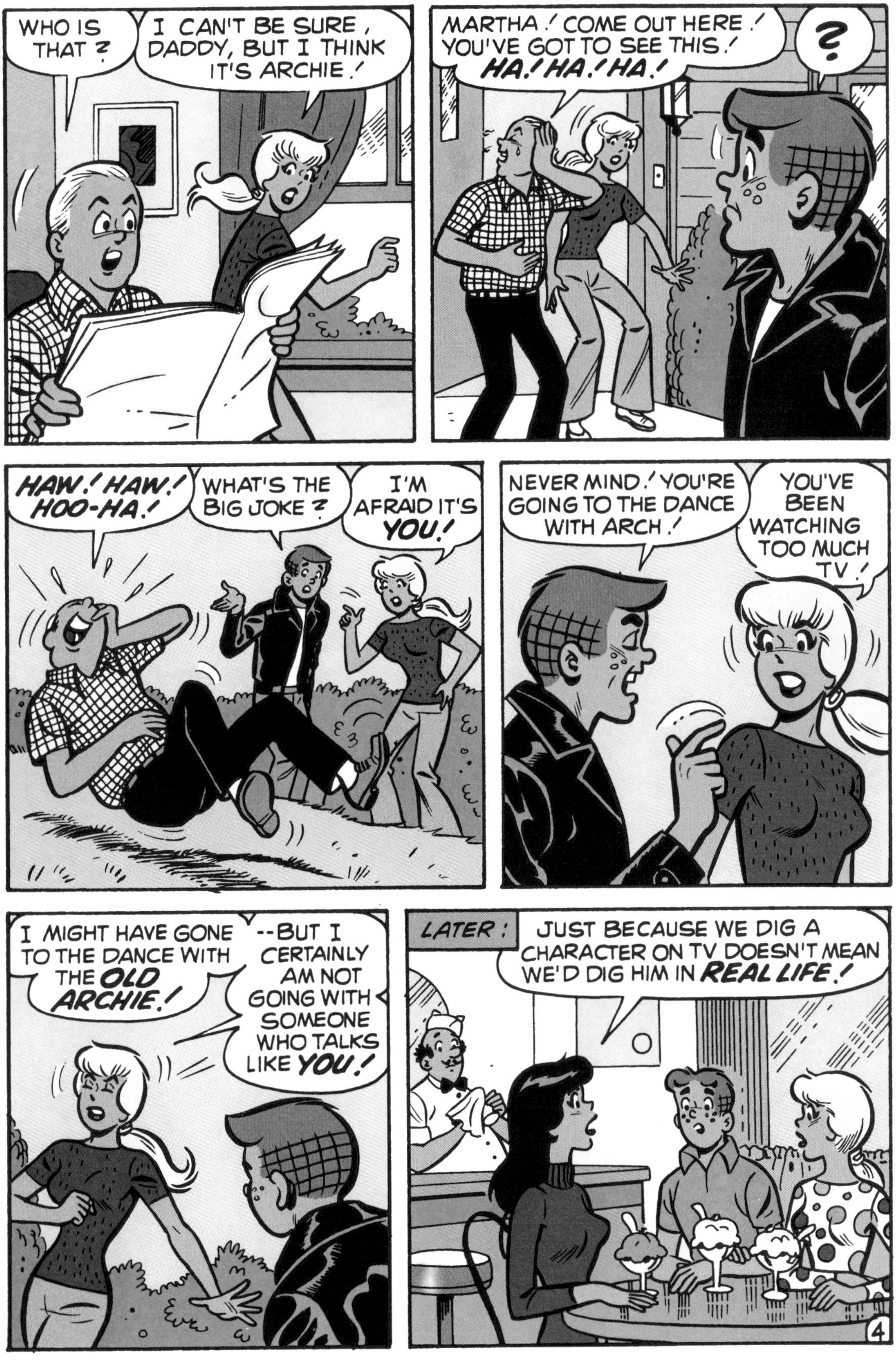
WHO IS THAT ?
I CAN'T BE SURE, DADDY, BUT I THINK IT'S ARCHIE!
MARTHA! COME OUT HERE! YOU'VE GOT TO SEE THIS! HA! HA! HA!
?
HAW! HAW! HOO-HA!
WHAT'S THE BIG JOKE ?
I'M AFRAID IT'S YOU!
NEVER MIND! YOU'RE GOING TO THE DANCE WITH ARCH!
YOU'VE BEEN WATCHING TOO MUCH TV!
I MIGHT HAVE GONE TO THE DANCE WITH THE OLD ARCHIE!
--BUT I CERTAINLY AM NOT GOING WITH SOMEONE WHO TALKS LIKE YOU!
LATER:
JUST BECAUSE WE DIG A CHARACTER ON TV DOESN'T MEAN WE'D DIG HIM IN REAL LIFE!
4

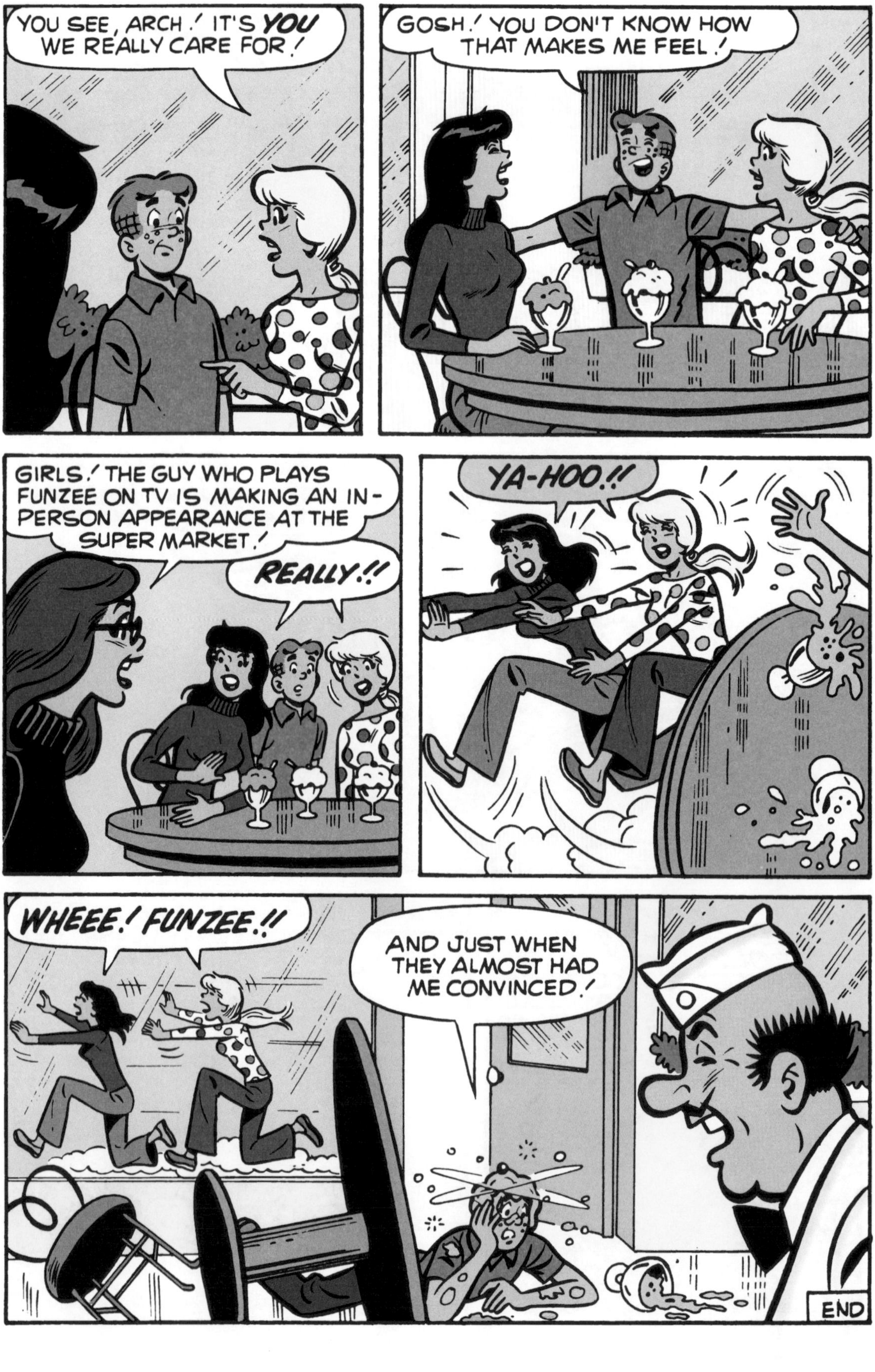
YOU SEE, ARCH! IT'S YOU WE REALLY CARE FOR!
GOSH! YOU DON'T KNOW HOW THAT MAKES ME FEEL!
GIRLS! THE GUY WHO PLAYS FUNZEE ON TV IS MAKING AN IN-PERSON APPEARANCE AT THE SUPER MARKET!
REALLY!!
YA-HOO!!
WHEEE! FUNZEE!!
AND JUST WHEN THEY ALMOST HAD ME CONVINCED!
END

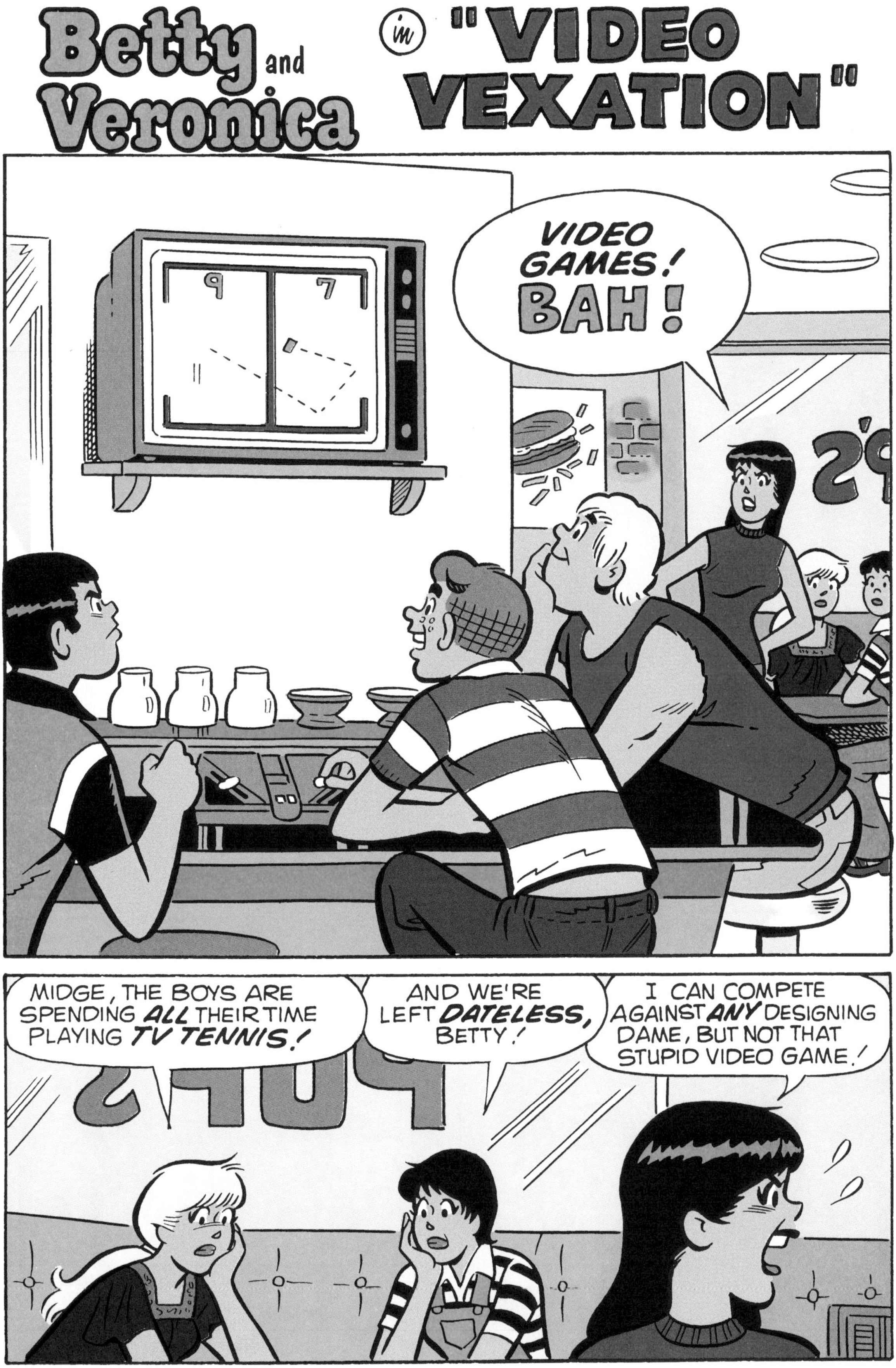
Betty and Veronica
in "VIDEO VEXATION"
VIDEO GAMES! BAH!
MIDGE, THE BOYS ARE SPENDING ALL THEIR TIME PLAYING TV TENNIS!
AND WE'RE LEFT DATELESS, BETTY!
I CAN COMPETE AGAINST ANY DESIGNING DAME, BUT NOT THAT STUPID VIDEO GAME!

Originally presented in BETTY & VERONICA #263, November, 1977

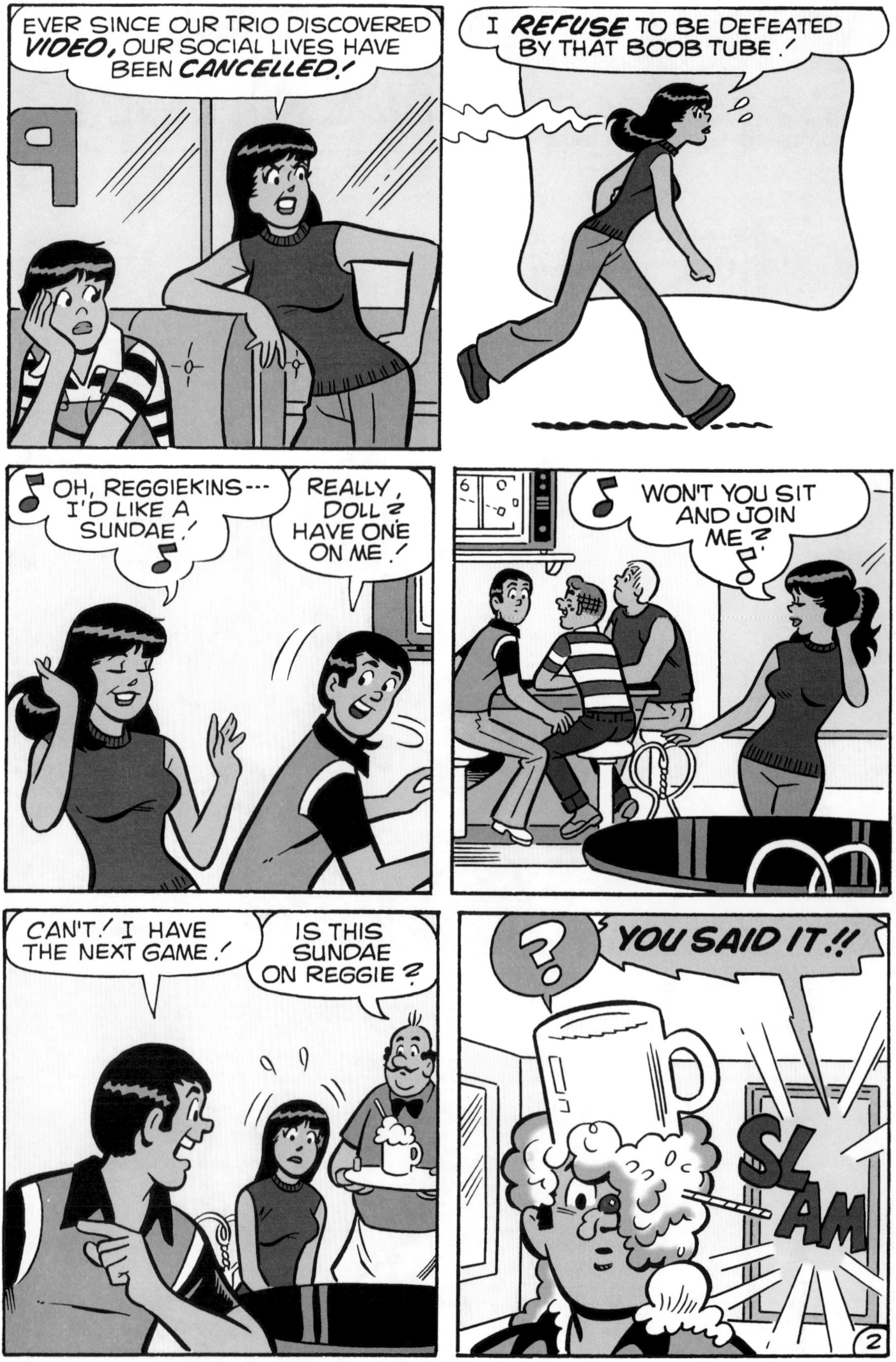
EVER SINCE OUR TRIO DISCOVERED VIDEO, OUR SOCIAL LIVES HAVE BEEN CANCELLED!
I REFUSE TO BE DEFEATED BY THAT BOOB TUBE!
OH, REGGIEKINS--- I'D LIKE A SUNDAE!
REALLY, DOLL? HAVE ONE ON ME!
WON'T YOU SIT AND JOIN ME?
CAN'T! I HAVE THE NEXT GAME!
IS THIS SUNDAE ON REGGIE?
YOU SAID IT!!
SLAM
2

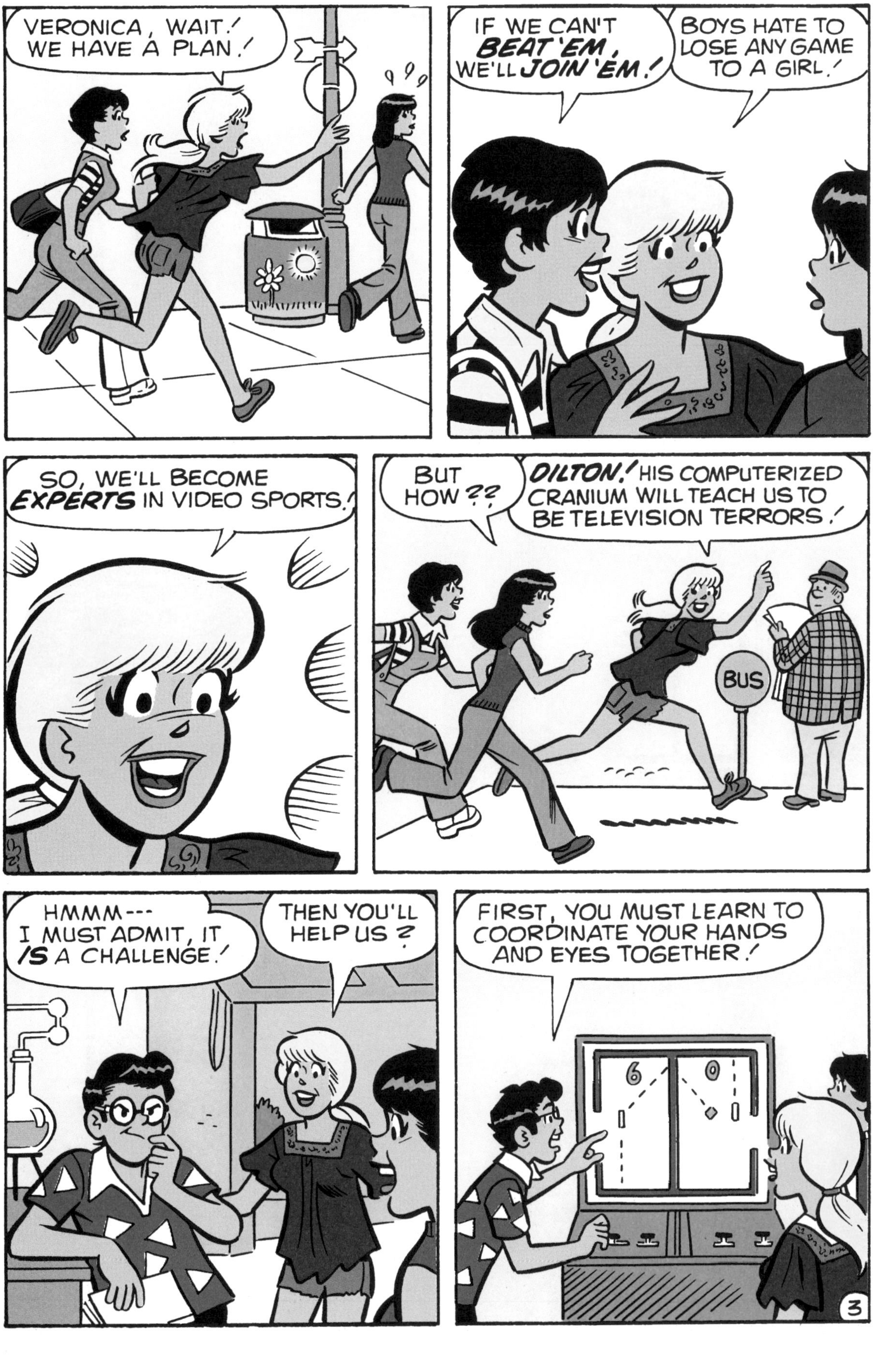
VERONICA, WAIT! WE HAVE A PLAN!
IF WE CAN'T BEAT 'EM, WE'LL JOIN 'EM!
BOYS HATE TO LOSE ANY GAME TO A GIRL!
SO, WE'LL BECOME EXPERTS IN VIDEO SPORTS!
BUT HOW??
DILTON! HIS COMPUTERIZED CRANIUM WILL TEACH US TO BE TELEVISION TERRORS!
BUS
HMMM--- I MUST ADMIT, IT IS A CHALLENGE!
THEN YOU'LL HELP US?
FIRST, YOU MUST LEARN TO COORDINATE YOUR HANDS AND EYES TOGETHER!
6
0
3

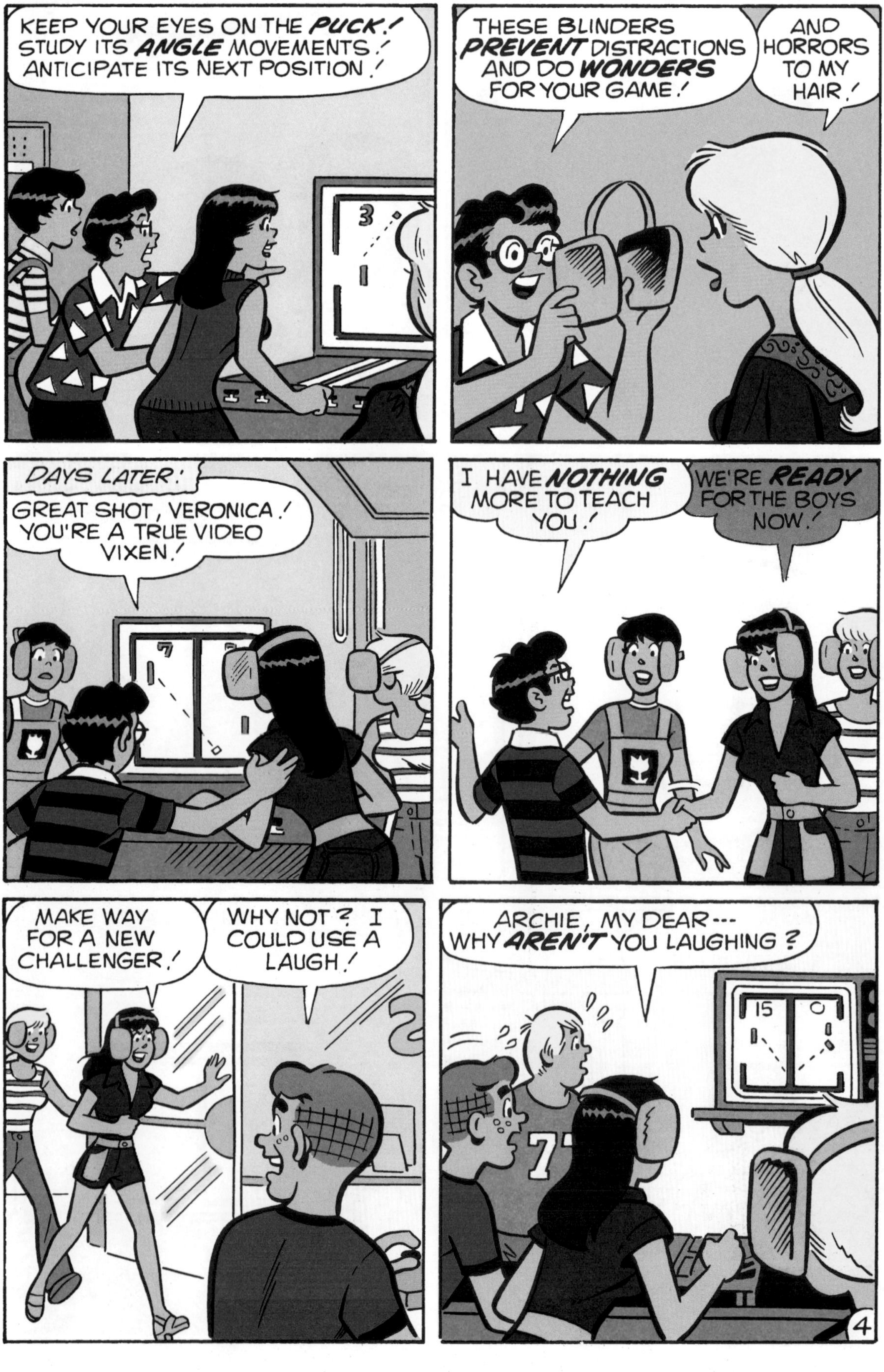

KEEP YOUR EYES ON THE PUCK! STUDY ITS ANGLE MOVEMENTS! ANTICIPATE ITS NEXT POSITION!
3
THESE BLINDERS PREVENT DISTRACTIONS AND DO WONDERS FOR YOUR GAME!
AND HORRORS TO MY HAIR!
DAYS LATER:
GREAT SHOT, VERONICA! YOU'RE A TRUE VIDEO VIXEN!
7
I HAVE NOTHING MORE TO TEACH YOU!
WE'RE READY FOR THE BOYS NOW!
MAKE WAY FOR A NEW CHALLENGER!
WHY NOT? I COULD USE A LAUGH!
ARCHIE, MY DEAR--- WHY AREN'T YOU LAUGHING?
15
0
7
4

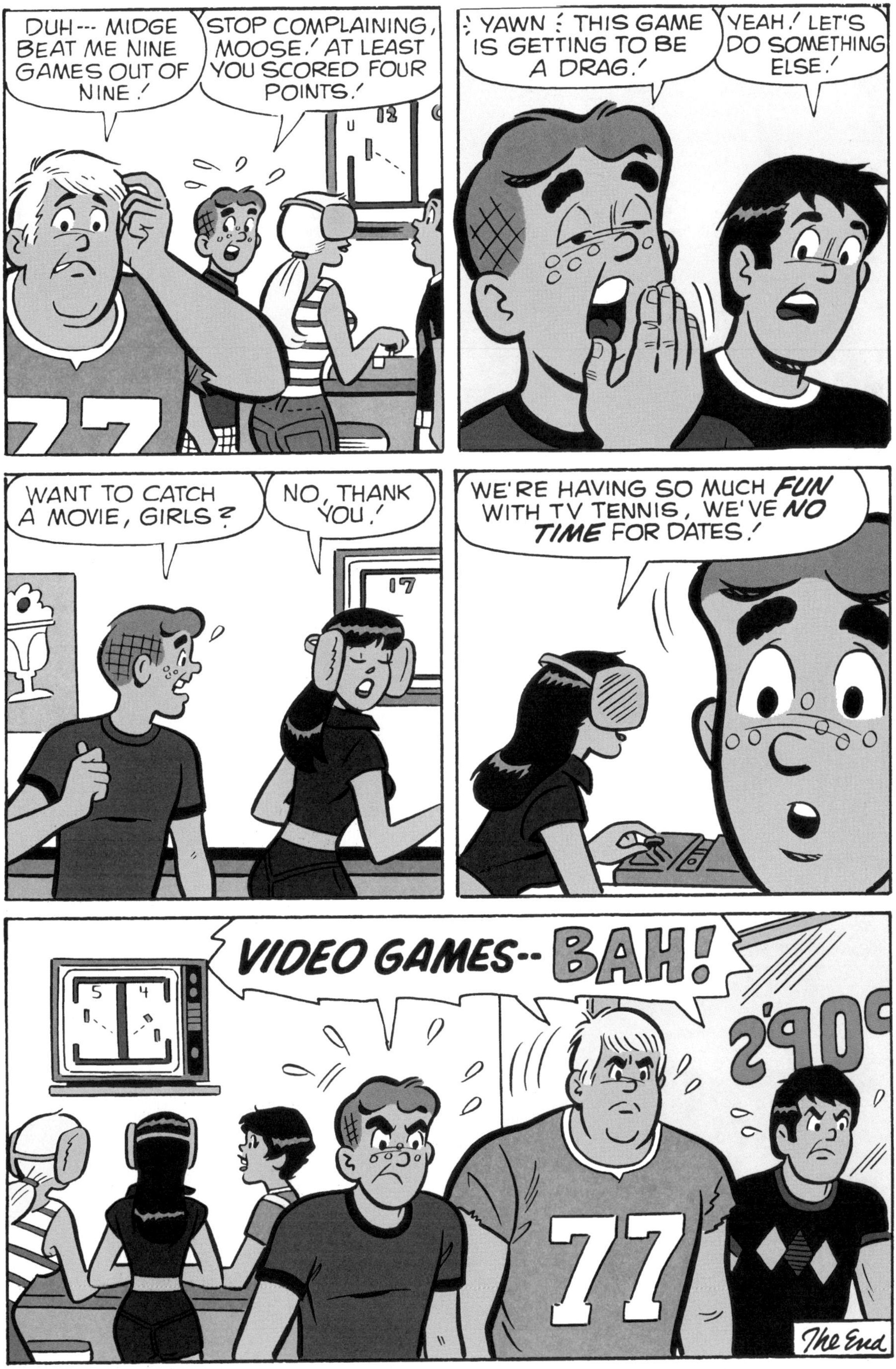
DUH--- MIDGE BEAT ME NINE GAMES OUT OF NINE!
STOP COMPLAINING, MOOSE! AT LEAST YOU SCORED FOUR POINTS!
YAWN! THIS GAME IS GETTING TO BE A DRAG!
YEAH! LET'S DO SOMETHING ELSE!
WANT TO CATCH A MOVIE, GIRLS?
NO, THANK YOU!
WE'RE HAVING SO MUCH FUN WITH TV TENNIS, WE'VE NO TIME FOR DATES!
VIDEO GAMES-- BAH!
POP'S
The End

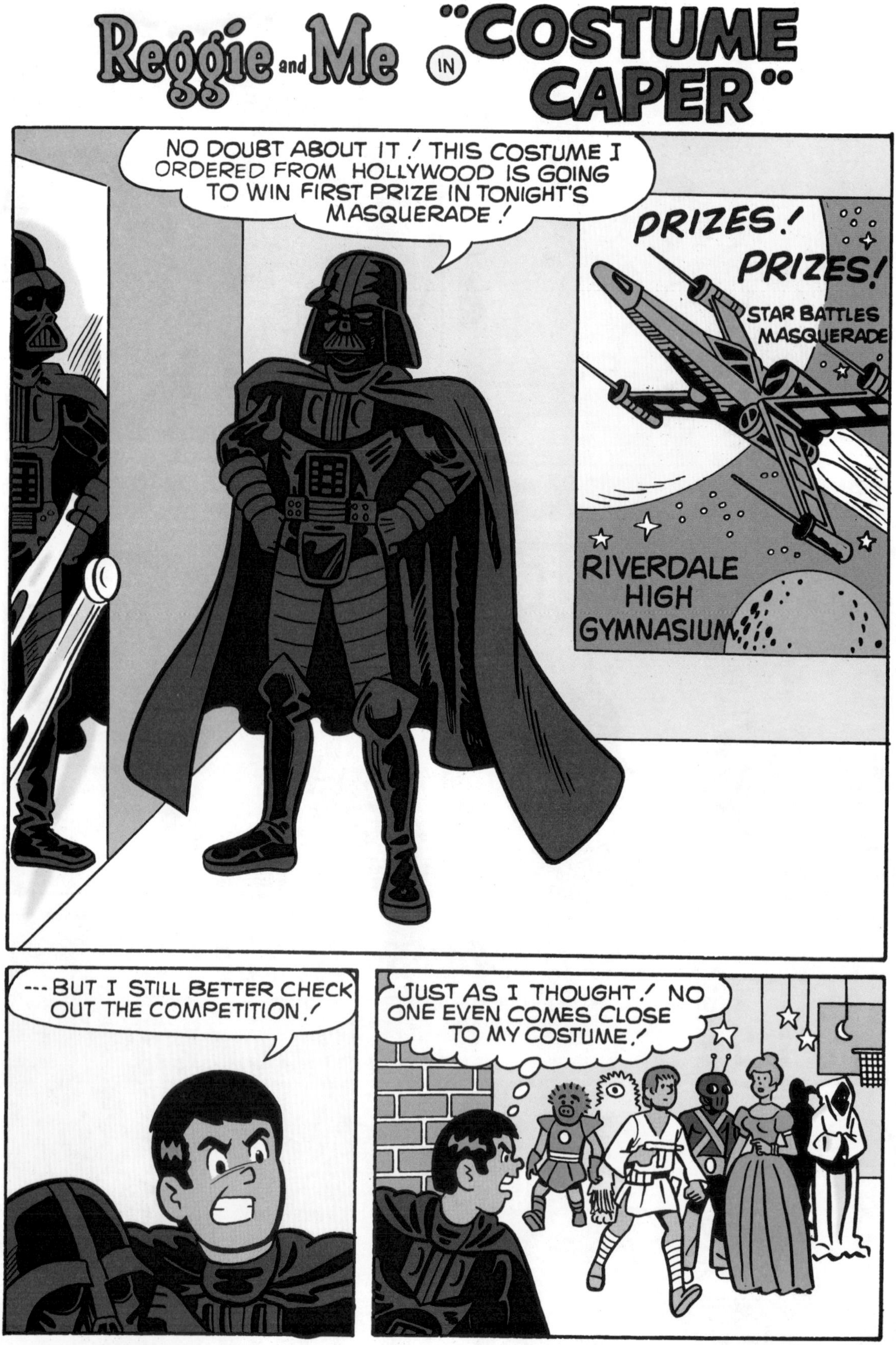
Reggie and Me
IN
"COSTUME CAPER"
NO DOUBT ABOUT IT! THIS COSTUME I ORDERED FROM HOLLYWOOD IS GOING TO WIN FIRST PRIZE IN TONIGHT'S MASQUERADE!
PRIZES! PRIZES!
STAR BATTLES MASQUERADE
RIVERDALE HIGH GYMNASIUM
---BUT I STILL BETTER CHECK OUT THE COMPETITION!
JUST AS I THOUGHT! NO ONE EVEN COMES CLOSE TO MY COSTUME!

Originally presented in REGGIE AND ME #104, April, 1978

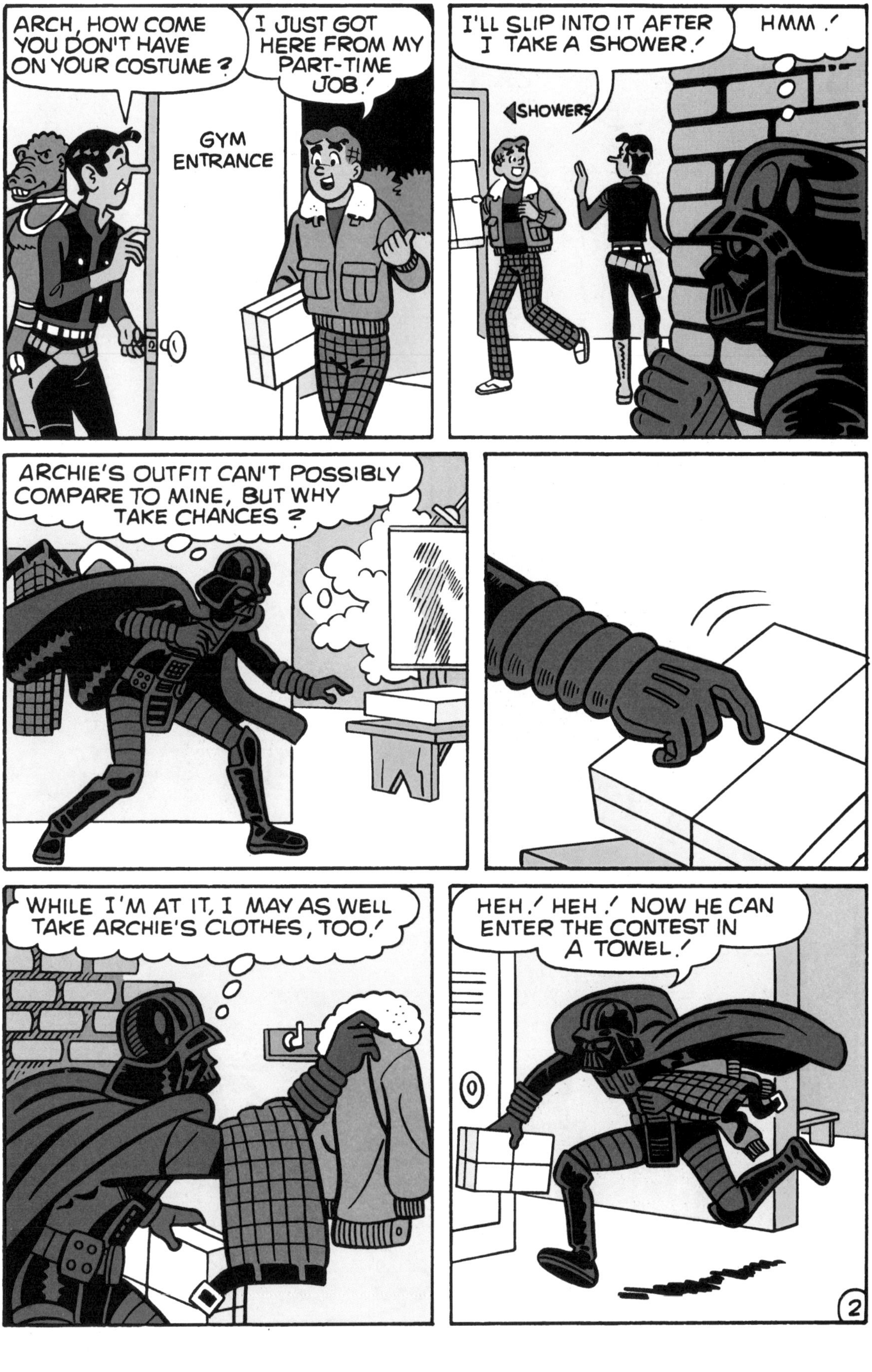
ARCH, HOW COME YOU DON'T HAVE ON YOUR COSTUME ?
I JUST GOT HERE FROM MY PART-TIME JOB!
GYM ENTRANCE
I'LL SLIP INTO IT AFTER I TAKE A SHOWER!
HMM!
SHOWERS
ARCHIE'S OUTFIT CAN'T POSSIBLY COMPARE TO MINE, BUT WHY TAKE CHANCES ?
WHILE I'M AT IT, I MAY AS WELL TAKE ARCHIE'S CLOTHES, TOO!
HEH! HEH! NOW HE CAN ENTER THE CONTEST IN A TOWEL!
2

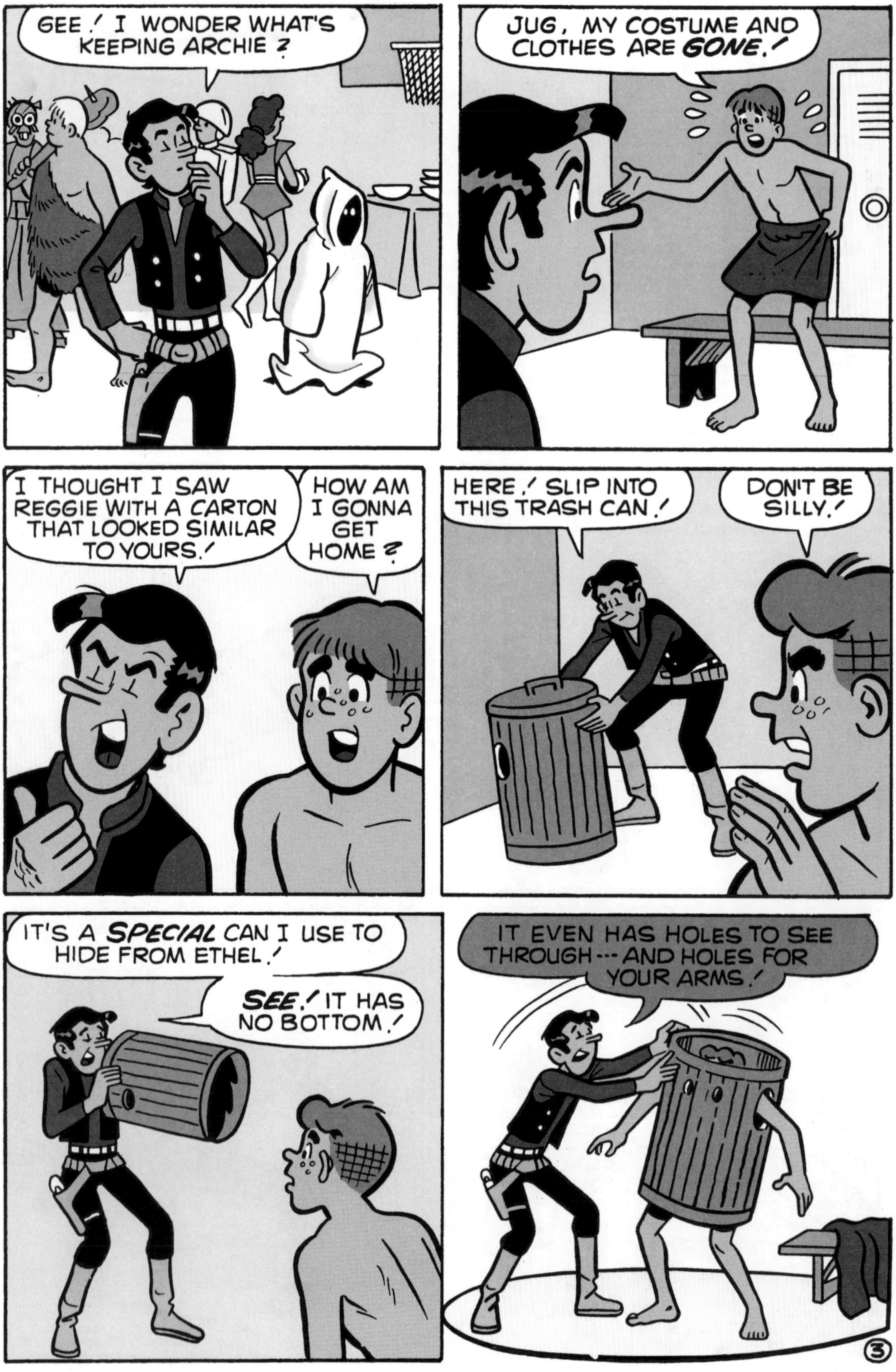
GEE! I WONDER WHAT'S KEEPING ARCHIE?
JUG, MY COSTUME AND CLOTHES ARE GONE!
I THOUGHT I SAW REGGIE WITH A CARTON THAT LOOKED SIMILAR TO YOURS!
HOW AM I GONNA GET HOME?
HERE! SLIP INTO THIS TRASH CAN!
DON'T BE SILLY!
IT'S A SPECIAL CAN I USE TO HIDE FROM ETHEL!
SEE! IT HAS NO BOTTOM!
IT EVEN HAS HOLES TO SEE THROUGH --- AND HOLES FOR YOUR ARMS!
3

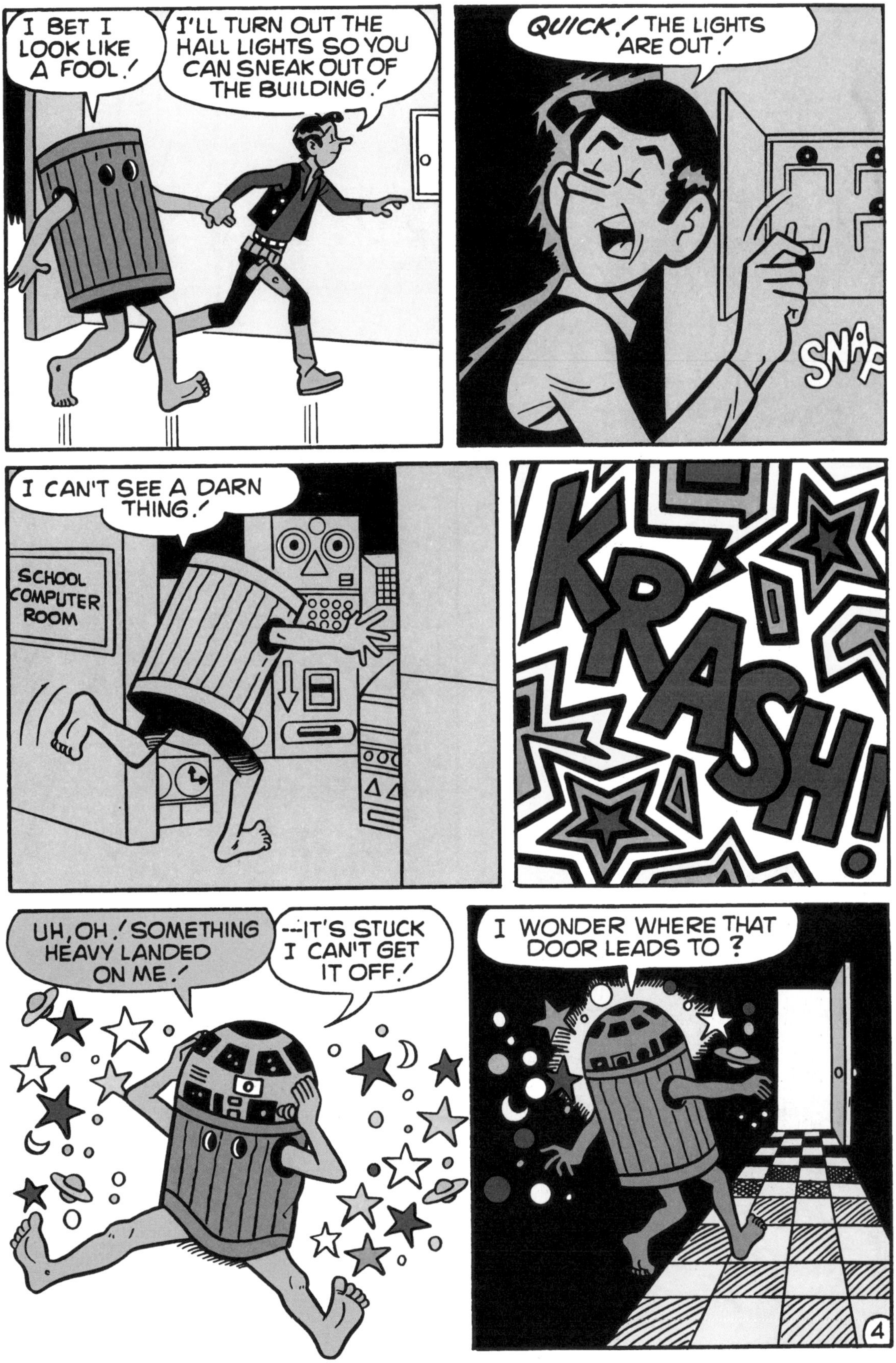
I BET I LOOK LIKE A FOOL!
I'LL TURN OUT THE HALL LIGHTS SO YOU CAN SNEAK OUT OF THE BUILDING!
QUICK! THE LIGHTS ARE OUT!
SNAP
I CAN'T SEE A DARN THING!
SCHOOL COMPUTER ROOM
KRASH!
UH, OH! SOMETHING HEAVY LANDED ON ME!
--IT'S STUCK I CAN'T GET IT OFF!
I WONDER WHERE THAT DOOR LEADS TO ?
4

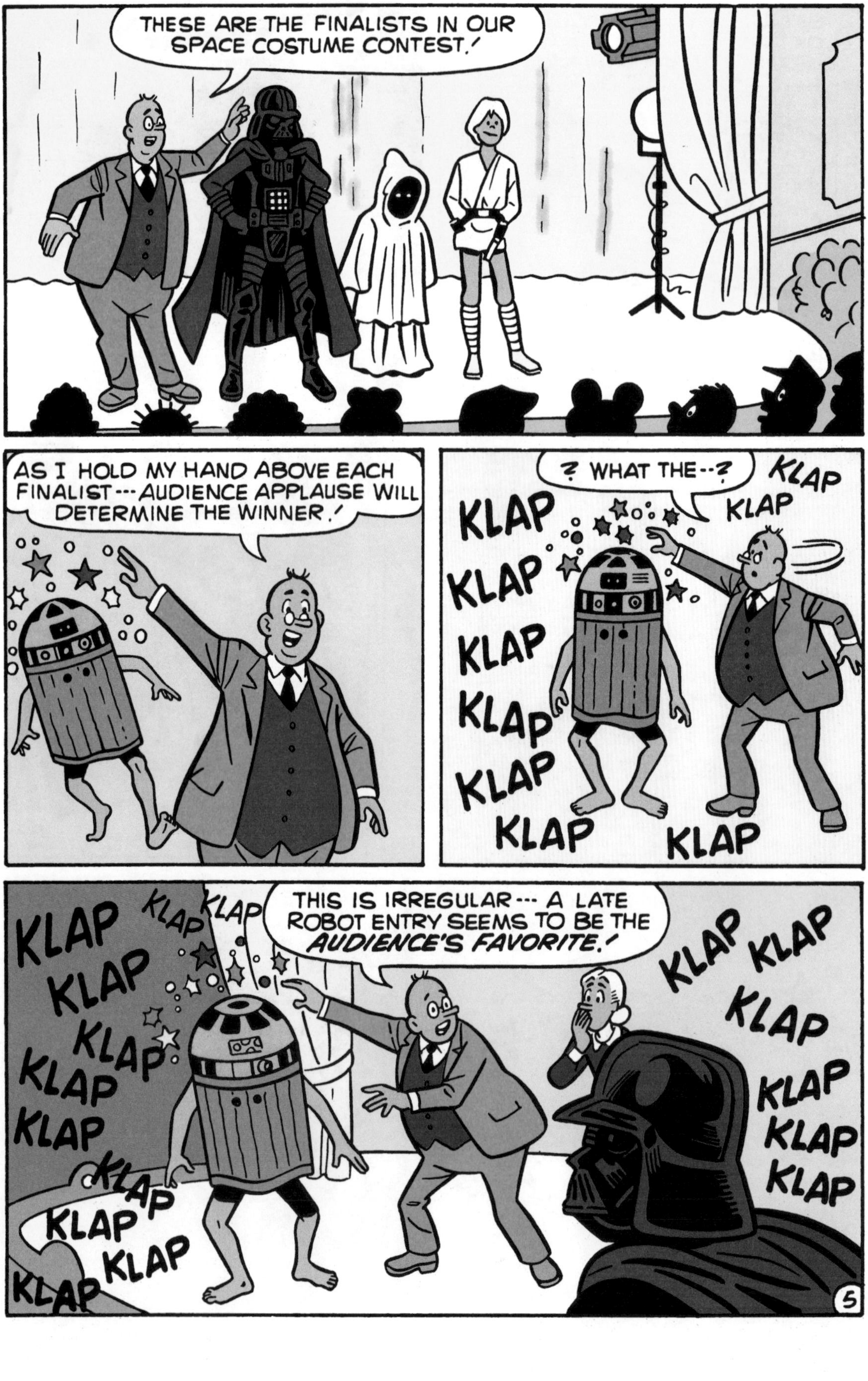
THESE ARE THE FINALISTS IN OUR SPACE COSTUME CONTEST.!
AS I HOLD MY HAND ABOVE EACH FINALIST--- AUDIENCE APPLAUSE WILL DETERMINE THE WINNER.!
? WHAT THE--?
KLAP KLAP KLAP KLAP KLAP KLAP KLAP KLAP KLAP KLAP
THIS IS IRREGULAR--- A LATE ROBOT ENTRY SEEMS TO BE THE *AUDIENCE'S FAVORITE*.!
KLAP KLAP KLAP KLAP KLAP KLAP KLAP KLAP KLAP KLAP KLAP KLAP KLAP KLAP KLAP KLAP KLAP KLAP
5

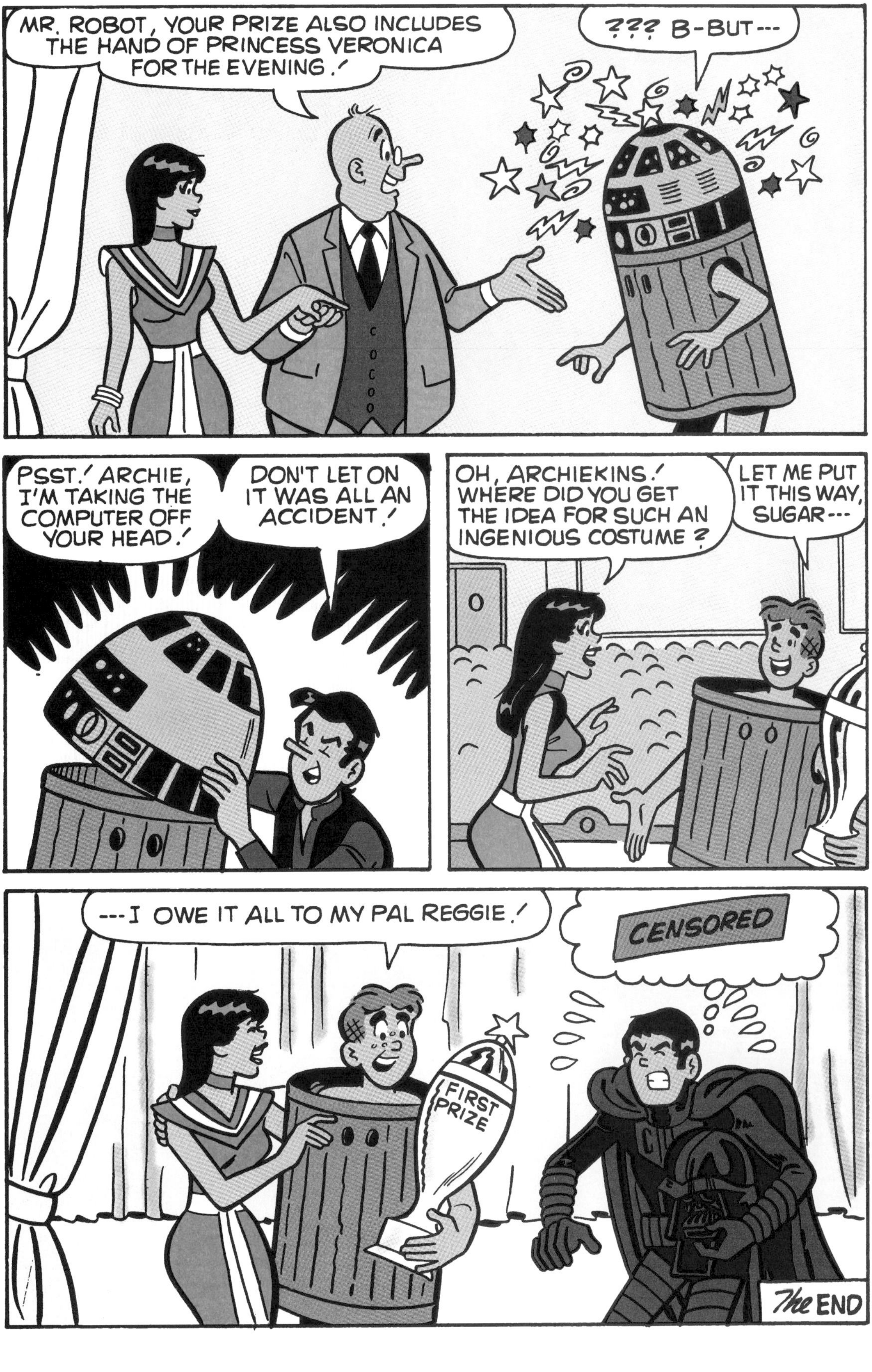
MR. ROBOT, YOUR PRIZE ALSO INCLUDES THE HAND OF PRINCESS VERONICA FOR THE EVENING!
??? B-BUT---
PSST! ARCHIE, I'M TAKING THE COMPUTER OFF YOUR HEAD!
DON'T LET ON IT WAS ALL AN ACCIDENT!
OH, ARCHIEKINS! WHERE DID YOU GET THE IDEA FOR SUCH AN INGENIOUS COSTUME?
LET ME PUT IT THIS WAY, SUGAR---
---I OWE IT ALL TO MY PAL REGGIE!
CENSORED
FIRST PRIZE
The END

Betty and Veronica in "MELVIN'S ANGELS"

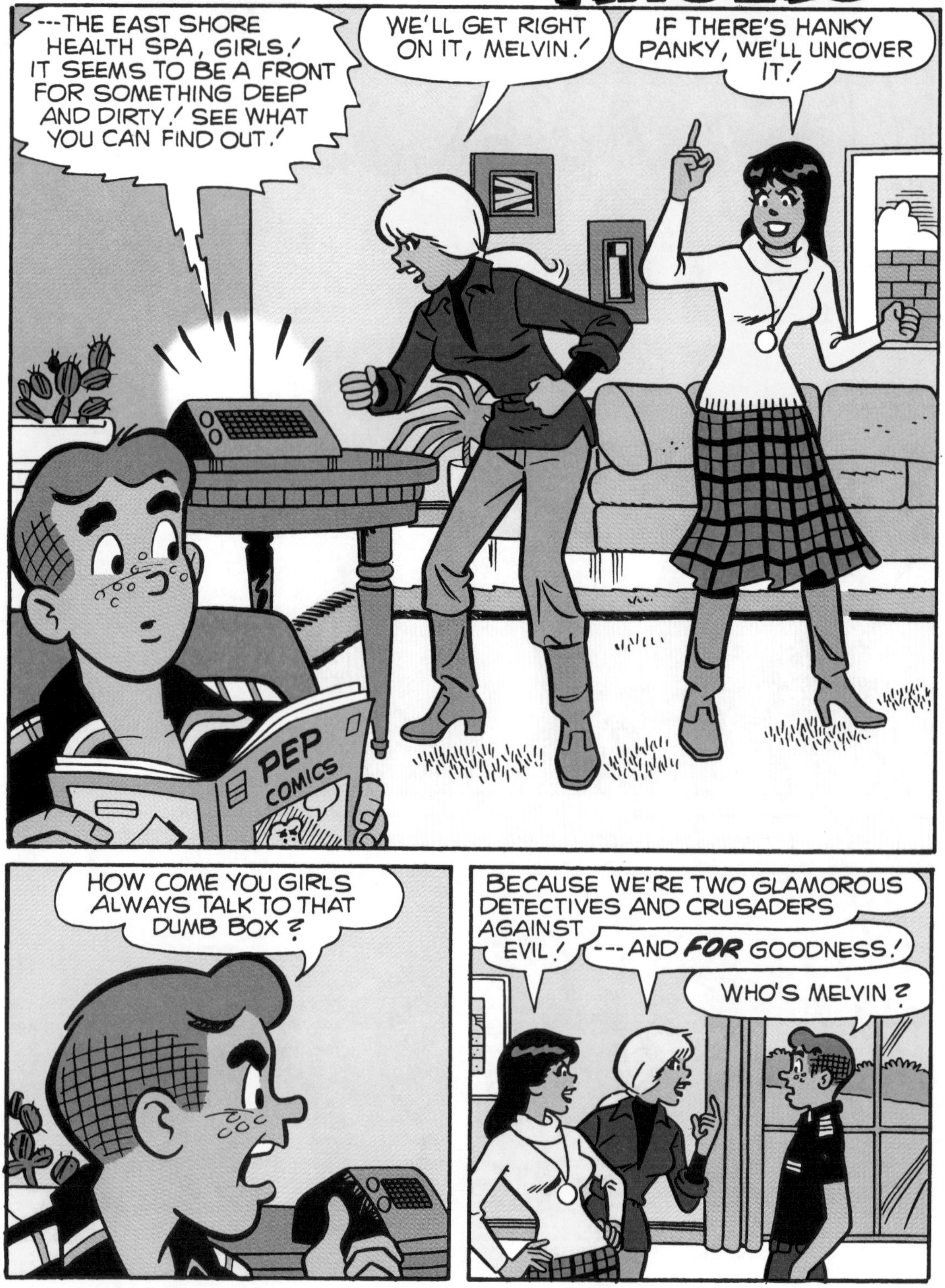
---THE EAST SHORE HEALTH SPA, GIRLS! IT SEEMS TO BE A FRONT FOR SOMETHING DEEP AND DIRTY! SEE WHAT YOU CAN FIND OUT!
WE'LL GET RIGHT ON IT, MELVIN!
IF THERE'S HANKY PANKY, WE'LL UNCOVER IT!
PEP COMICS
HOW COME YOU GIRLS ALWAYS TALK TO THAT DUMB BOX?
BECAUSE WE'RE TWO GLAMOROUS DETECTIVES AND CRUSADERS AGAINST EVIL!
---AND FOR GOODNESS!
WHO'S MELVIN?

Originally presented in BETTY & VERONICA #277, January, 1979

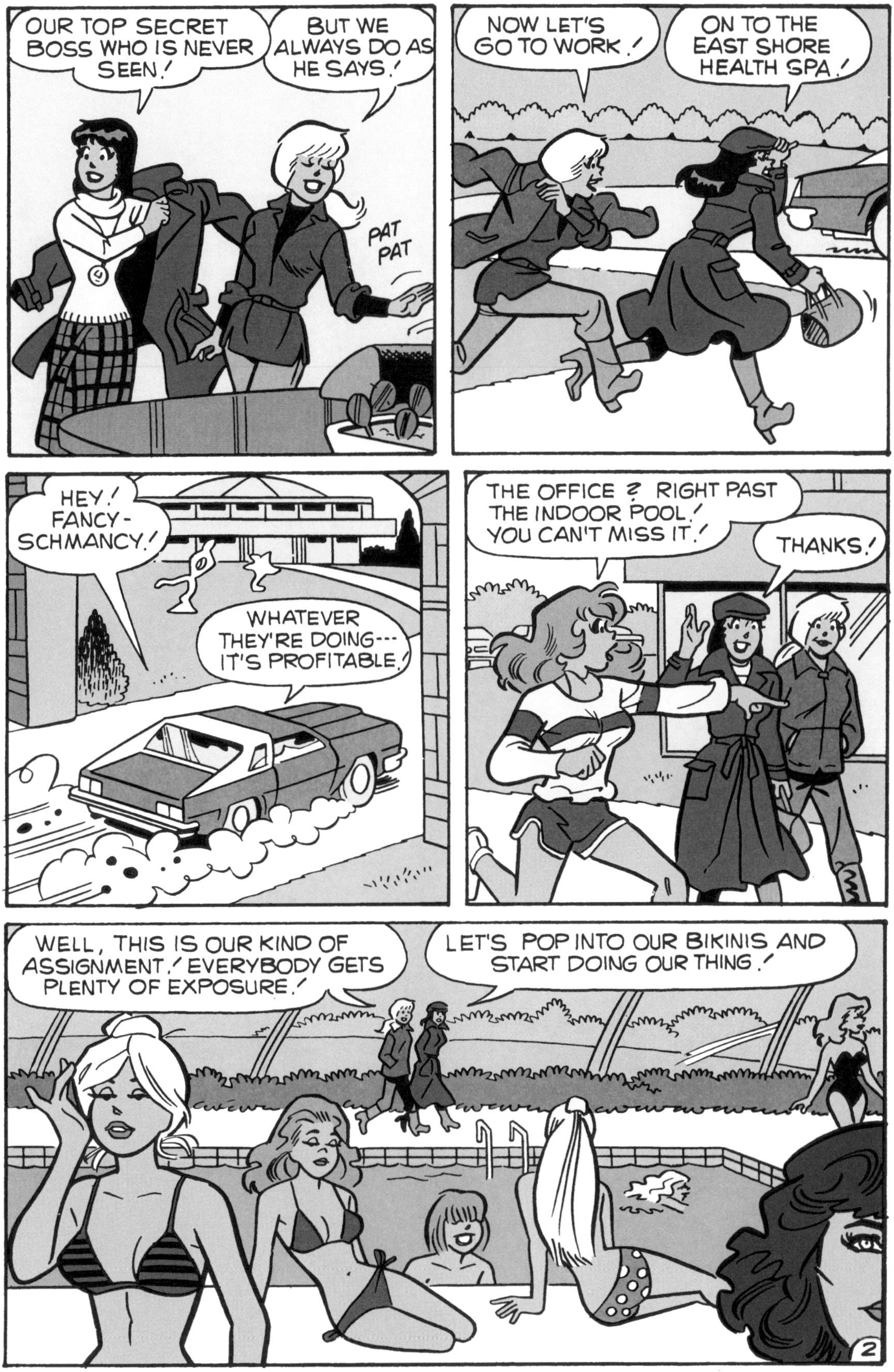
OUR TOP SECRET BOSS WHO IS NEVER SEEN!
BUT WE ALWAYS DO AS HE SAYS!
PAT PAT
NOW LET'S GO TO WORK!
ON TO THE EAST SHORE HEALTH SPA!
HEY! FANCY-SCHMANCY!
WHATEVER THEY'RE DOING--- IT'S PROFITABLE!
THE OFFICE? RIGHT PAST THE INDOOR POOL! YOU CAN'T MISS IT!
THANKS!
WELL, THIS IS OUR KIND OF ASSIGNMENT! EVERYBODY GETS PLENTY OF EXPOSURE!
LET'S POP INTO OUR BIKINIS AND START DOING OUR THING!
2

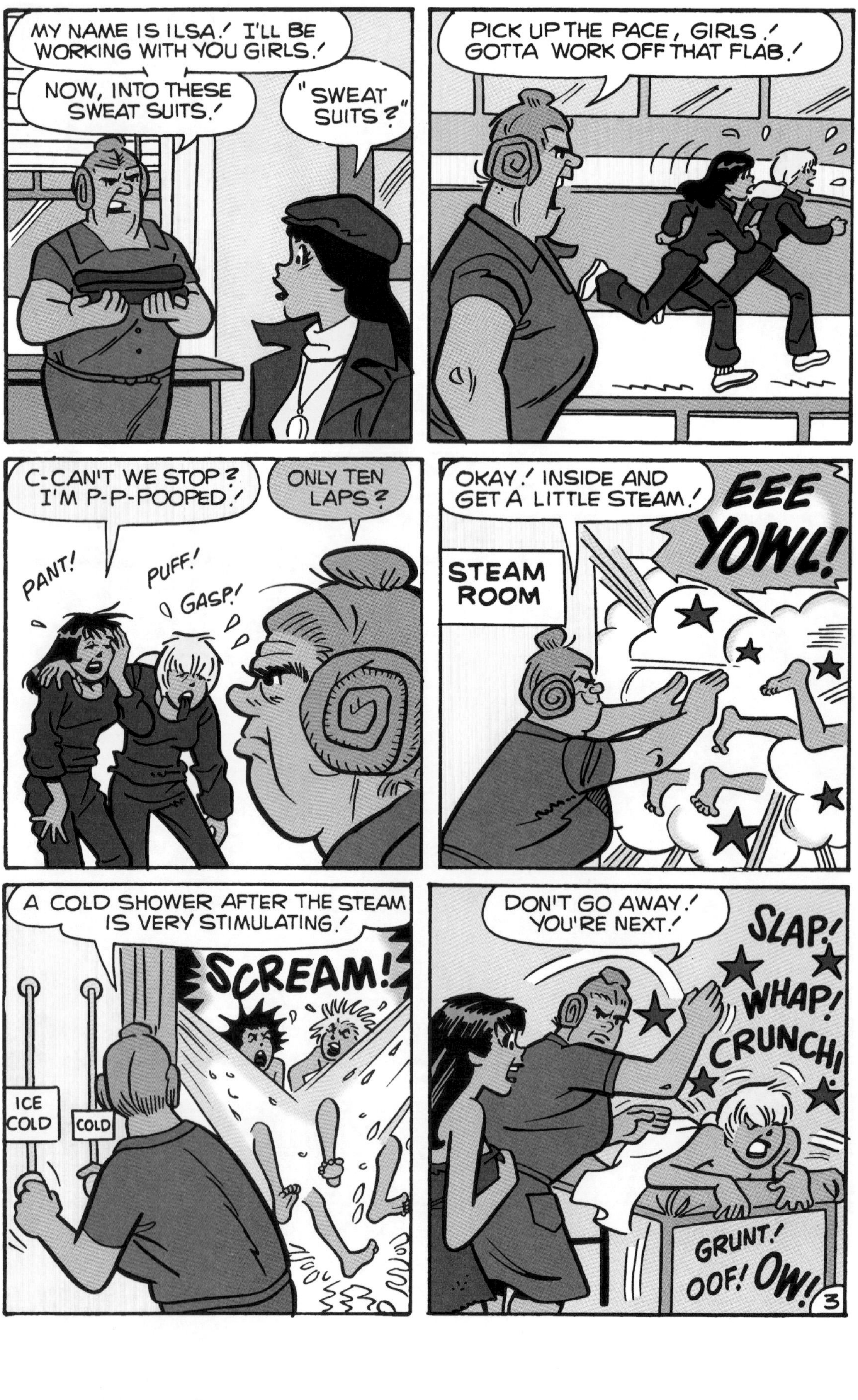
MY NAME IS ILSA! I'LL BE WORKING WITH YOU GIRLS!
NOW, INTO THESE SWEAT SUITS!
"SWEAT SUITS?"
PICK UP THE PACE, GIRLS! GOTTA WORK OFF THAT FLAB!
C-CAN'T WE STOP? I'M P-P-POOPED!
ONLY TEN LAPS?
PANT!
PUFF!
GASP!
OKAY! INSIDE AND GET A LITTLE STEAM!
STEAM ROOM
EEE YOWL!
A COLD SHOWER AFTER THE STEAM IS VERY STIMULATING!
SCREAM!
ICE COLD
COLD
DON'T GO AWAY! YOU'RE NEXT!
SLAP!
WHAP!
CRUNCH!
GRUNT!
OOF! OW!
3

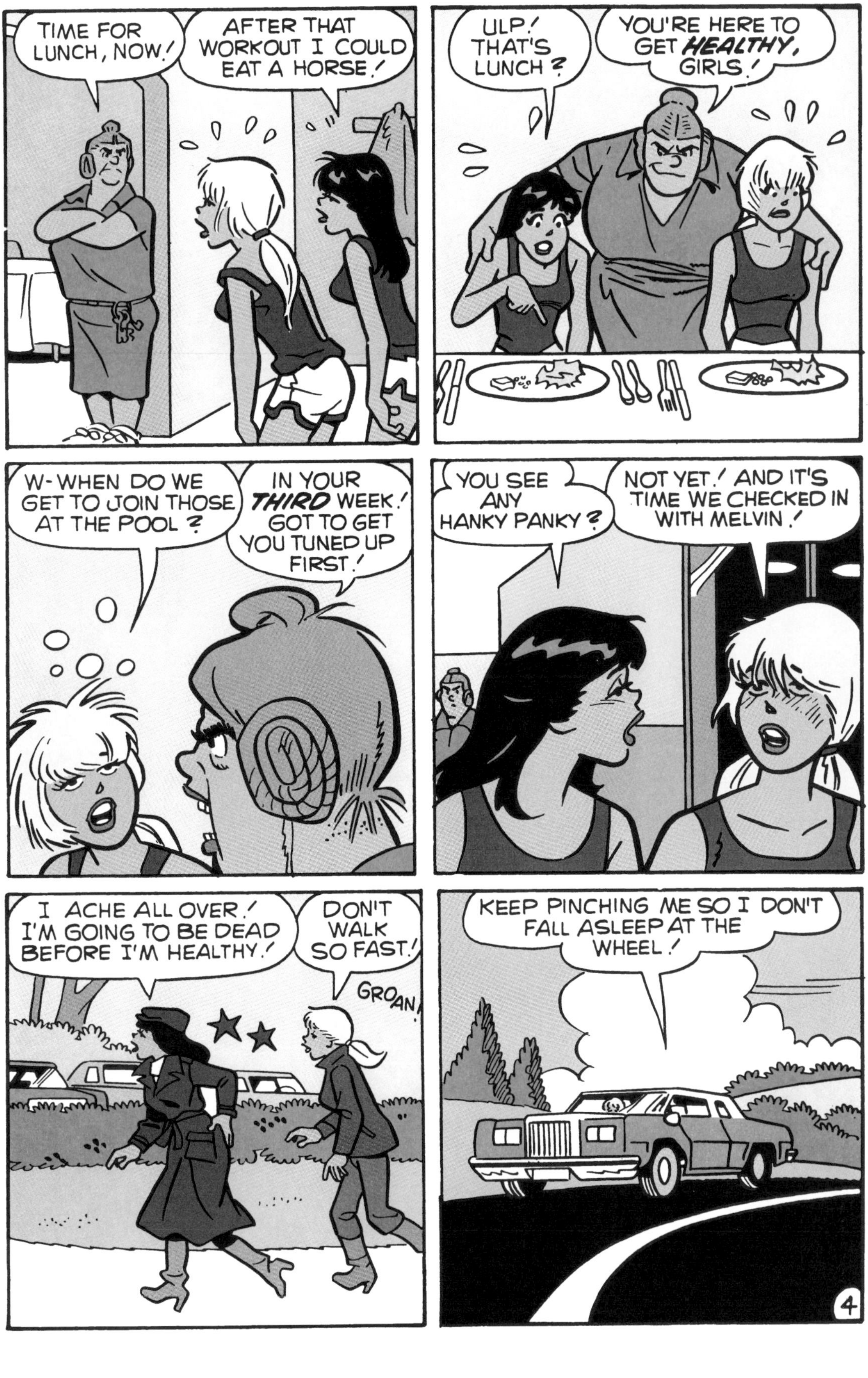
TIME FOR LUNCH, NOW!
AFTER THAT WORKOUT I COULD EAT A HORSE!
ULP! THAT'S LUNCH?
YOU'RE HERE TO GET HEALTHY, GIRLS!
W-WHEN DO WE GET TO JOIN THOSE AT THE POOL?
IN YOUR THIRD WEEK! GOT TO GET YOU TUNED UP FIRST!
YOU SEE ANY HANKY PANKY?
NOT YET! AND IT'S TIME WE CHECKED IN WITH MELVIN!
I ACHE ALL OVER! I'M GOING TO BE DEAD BEFORE I'M HEALTHY!
DON'T WALK SO FAST!
GROAN!
KEEP PINCHING ME SO I DON'T FALL ASLEEP AT THE WHEEL!
4

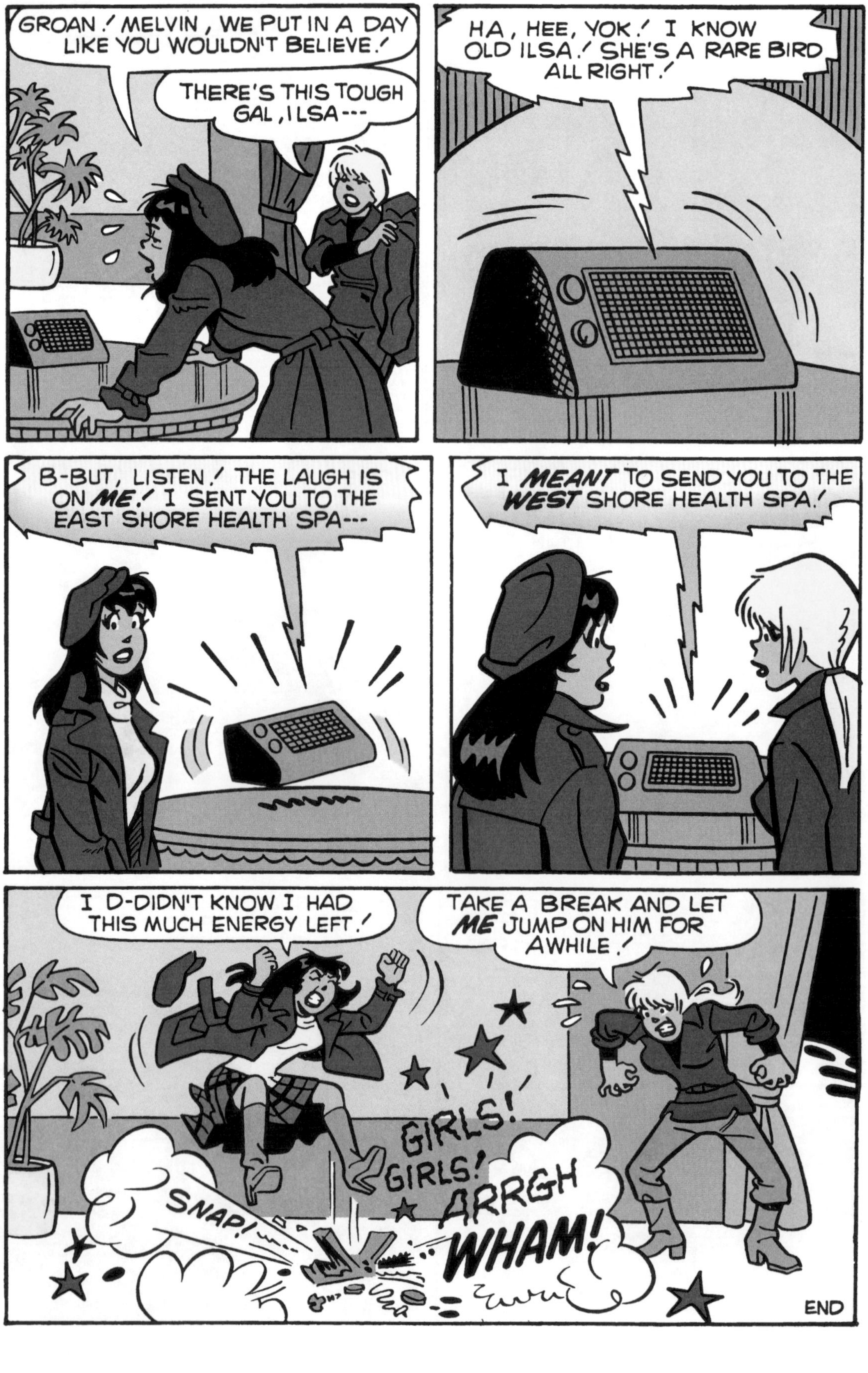
GROAN! MELVIN, WE PUT IN A DAY LIKE YOU WOULDN'T BELIEVE!
THERE'S THIS TOUGH GAL, ILSA---
HA, HEE, YOK! I KNOW OLD ILSA! SHE'S A RARE BIRD ALL RIGHT!
B-BUT, LISTEN! THE LAUGH IS ON ME! I SENT YOU TO THE EAST SHORE HEALTH SPA---
I MEANT TO SEND YOU TO THE WEST SHORE HEALTH SPA!
I D-DIDN'T KNOW I HAD THIS MUCH ENERGY LEFT!
TAKE A BREAK AND LET ME JUMP ON HIM FOR AWHILE!
GIRLS!
GIRLS!
ARRGH
SNAP!
WHAM!
END

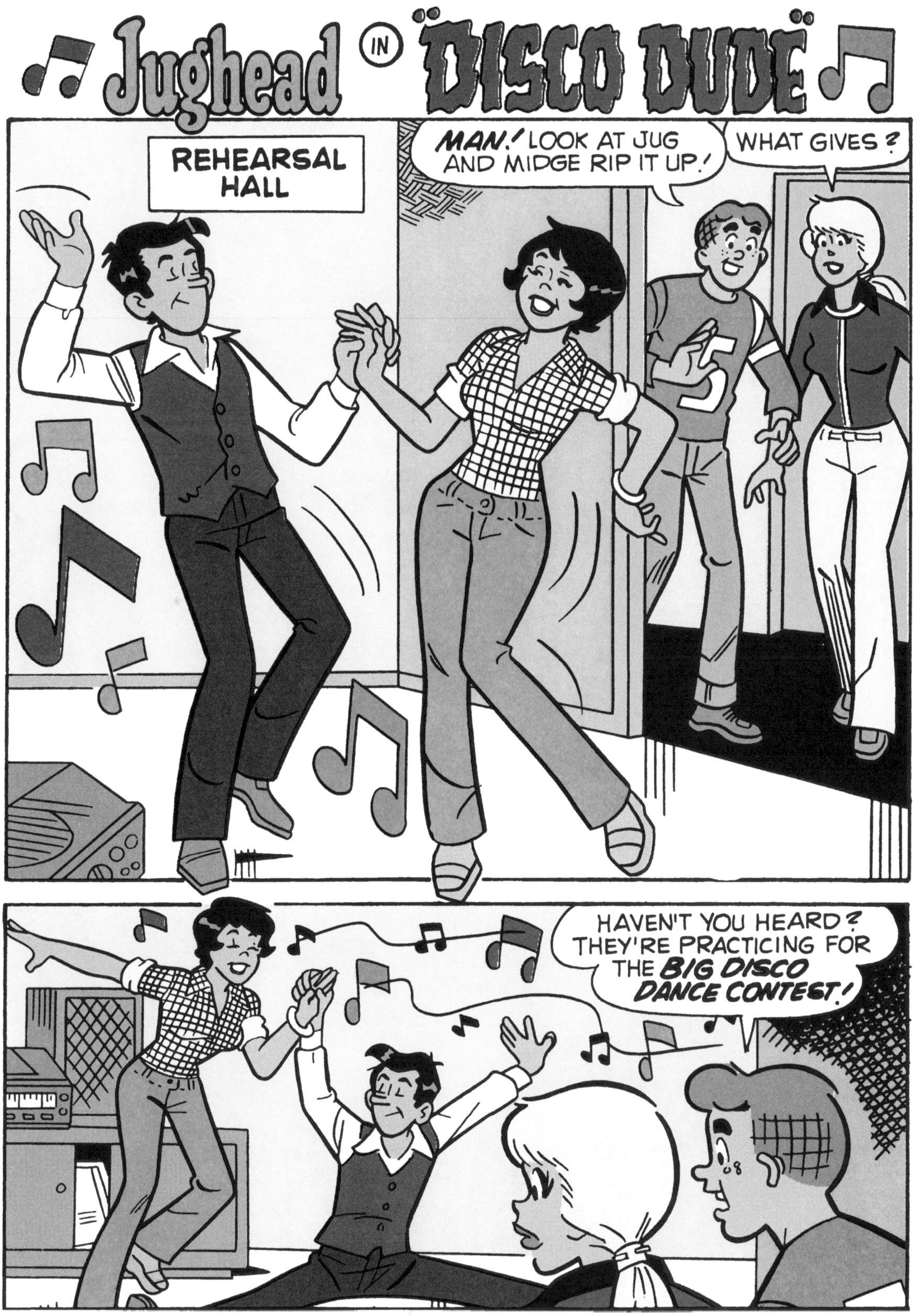
Jughead IN "DISCO DUDE"
REHEARSAL HALL
MAN! LOOK AT JUG AND MIDGE RIP IT UP!
WHAT GIVES?
HAVEN'T YOU HEARD? THEY'RE PRACTICING FOR THE BIG DISCO DANCE CONTEST!

Originally presented in LAUGH #343, October, 1979

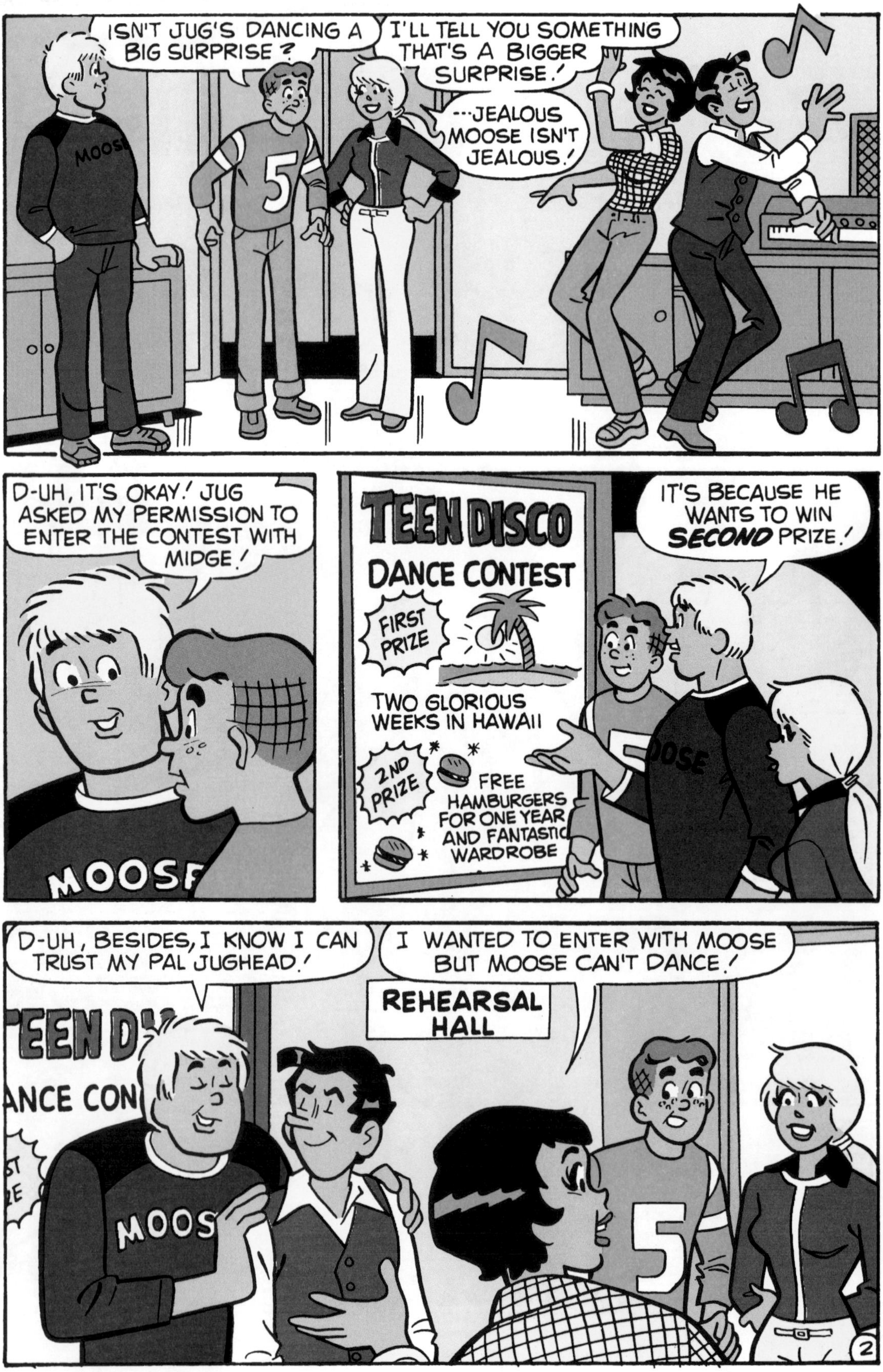
ISN'T JUG'S DANCING A BIG SURPRISE?
I'LL TELL YOU SOMETHING THAT'S A BIGGER SURPRISE!
...JEALOUS MOOSE ISN'T JEALOUS!
MOOSE
5
D-UH, IT'S OKAY! JUG ASKED MY PERMISSION TO ENTER THE CONTEST WITH MIDGE!
MOOSE
TEEN DISCO
DANCE CONTEST
FIRST PRIZE
TWO GLORIOUS WEEKS IN HAWAII
2ND PRIZE
FREE HAMBURGERS FOR ONE YEAR AND FANTASTIC WARDROBE
IT'S BECAUSE HE WANTS TO WIN SECOND PRIZE!
D-UH, BESIDES, I KNOW I CAN TRUST MY PAL JUGHEAD!
I WANTED TO ENTER WITH MOOSE BUT MOOSE CAN'T DANCE!
REHEARSAL HALL
MOOS
5
2

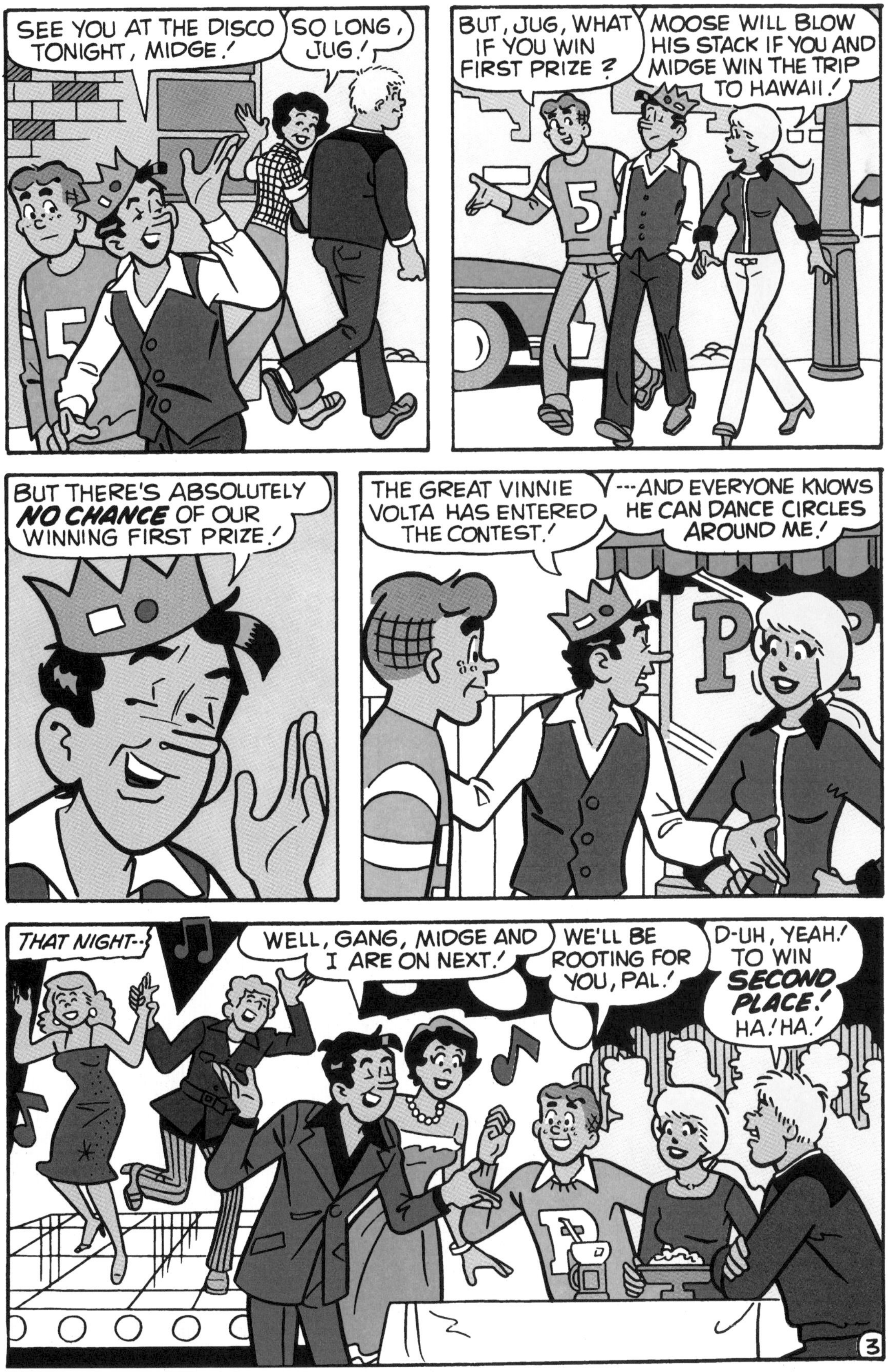
SEE YOU AT THE DISCO TONIGHT, MIDGE!
SO LONG, JUG!
BUT, JUG, WHAT IF YOU WIN FIRST PRIZE?
MOOSE WILL BLOW HIS STACK IF YOU AND MIDGE WIN THE TRIP TO HAWAII!
BUT THERE'S ABSOLUTELY **NO CHANCE** OF OUR WINNING FIRST PRIZE!
THE GREAT VINNIE VOLTA HAS ENTERED THE CONTEST!
---AND EVERYONE KNOWS HE CAN DANCE CIRCLES AROUND ME!
THAT NIGHT--
WELL, GANG, MIDGE AND I ARE ON NEXT!
WE'LL BE ROOTING FOR YOU, PAL!
D-UH, YEAH! TO WIN **SECOND PLACE!** HA! HA!
3

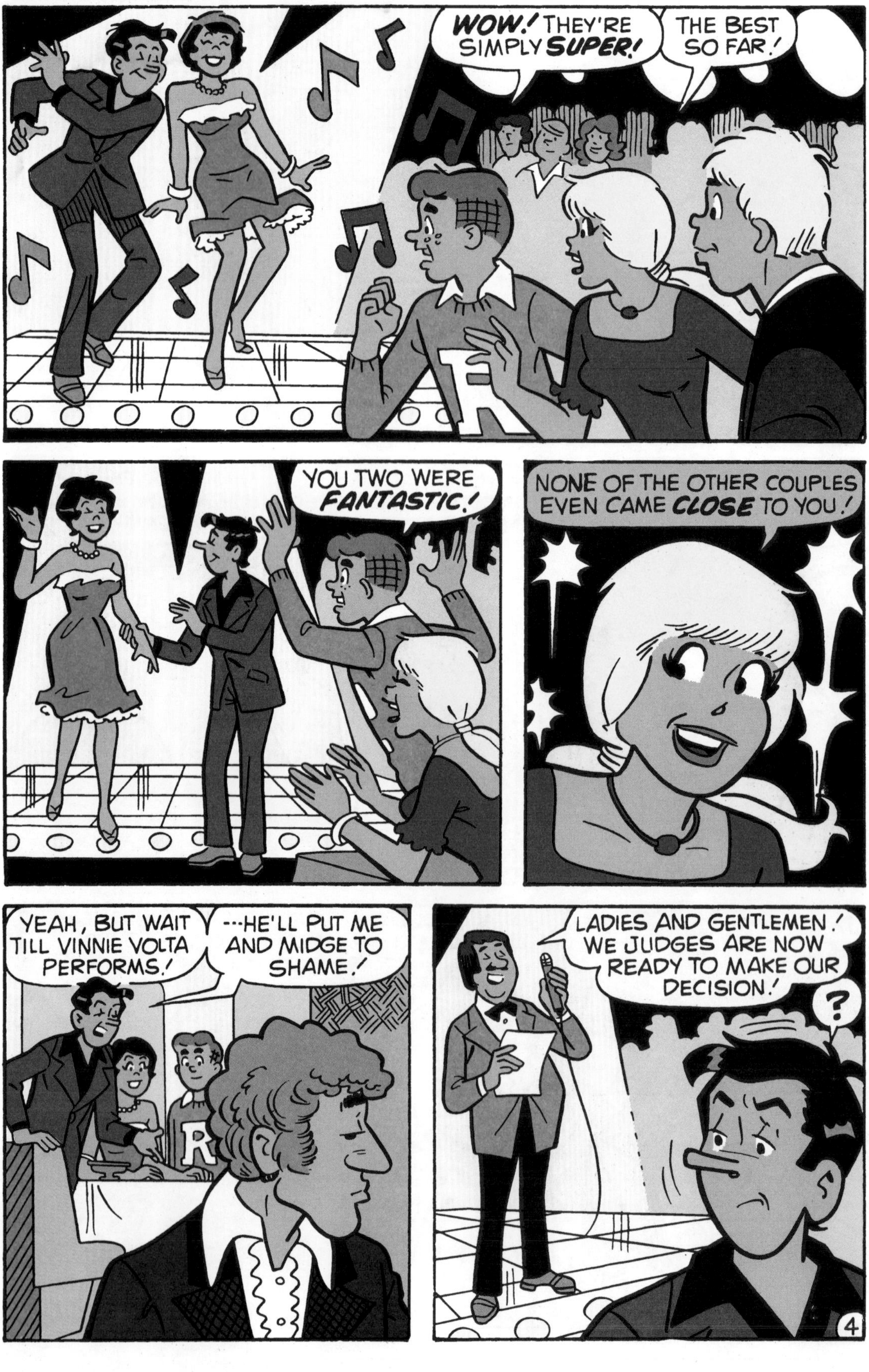
WOW! THEY'RE SIMPLY SUPER!
THE BEST SO FAR!
YOU TWO WERE FANTASTIC!
NONE OF THE OTHER COUPLES EVEN CAME CLOSE TO YOU!
YEAH, BUT WAIT TILL VINNIE VOLTA PERFORMS!
---HE'LL PUT ME AND MIDGE TO SHAME!
LADIES AND GENTLEMEN! WE JUDGES ARE NOW READY TO MAKE OUR DECISION!
?
4

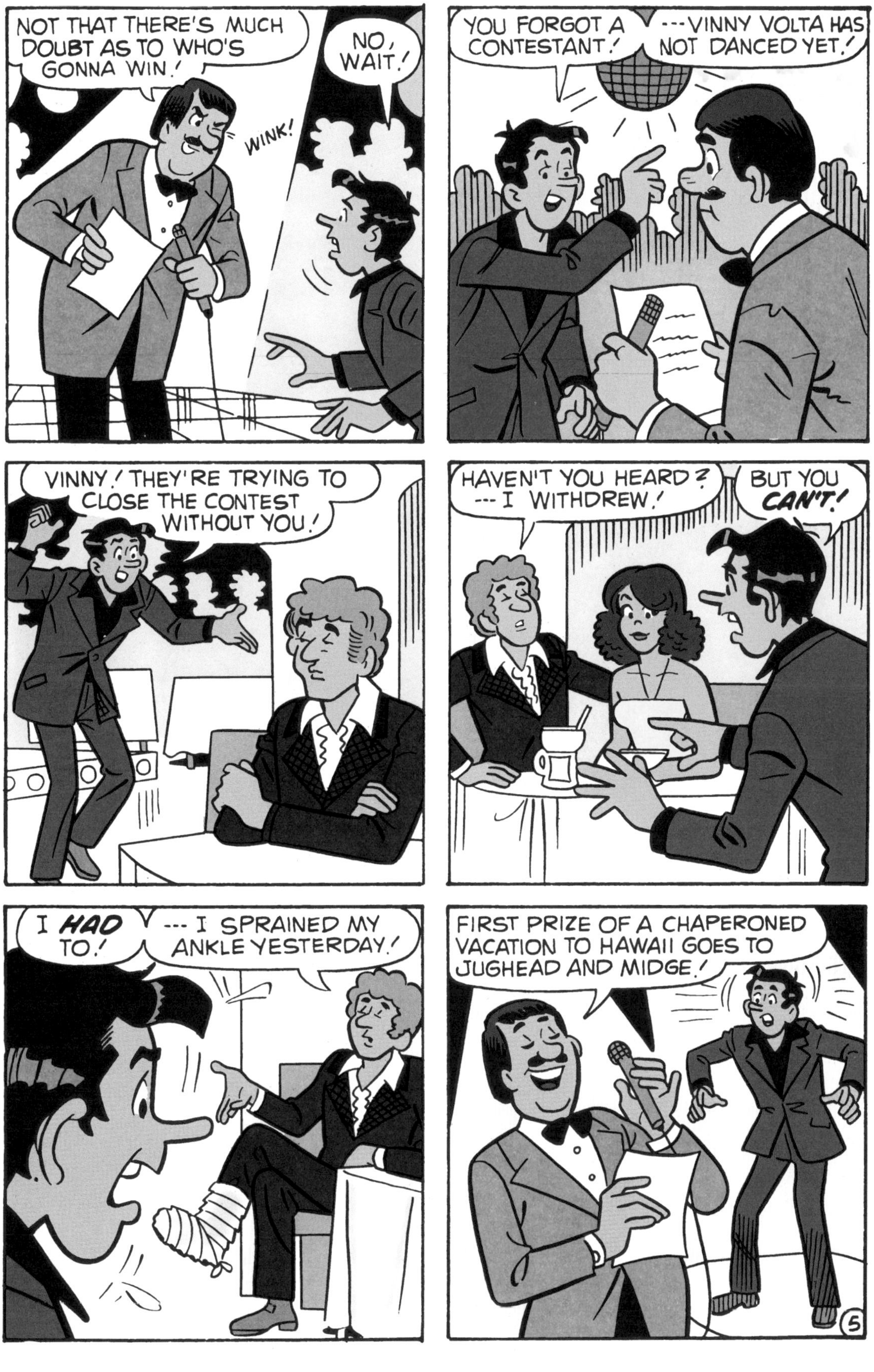
NOT THAT THERE'S MUCH DOUBT AS TO WHO'S GONNA WIN!
WINK!
NO, WAIT!
YOU FORGOT A CONTESTANT!
---VINNY VOLTA HAS NOT DANCED YET!
VINNY! THEY'RE TRYING TO CLOSE THE CONTEST WITHOUT YOU!
HAVEN'T YOU HEARD? --- I WITHDREW!
BUT YOU CAN'T!
I HAD TO!
--- I SPRAINED MY ANKLE YESTERDAY!
FIRST PRIZE OF A CHAPERONED VACATION TO HAWAII GOES TO JUGHEAD AND MIDGE!
5

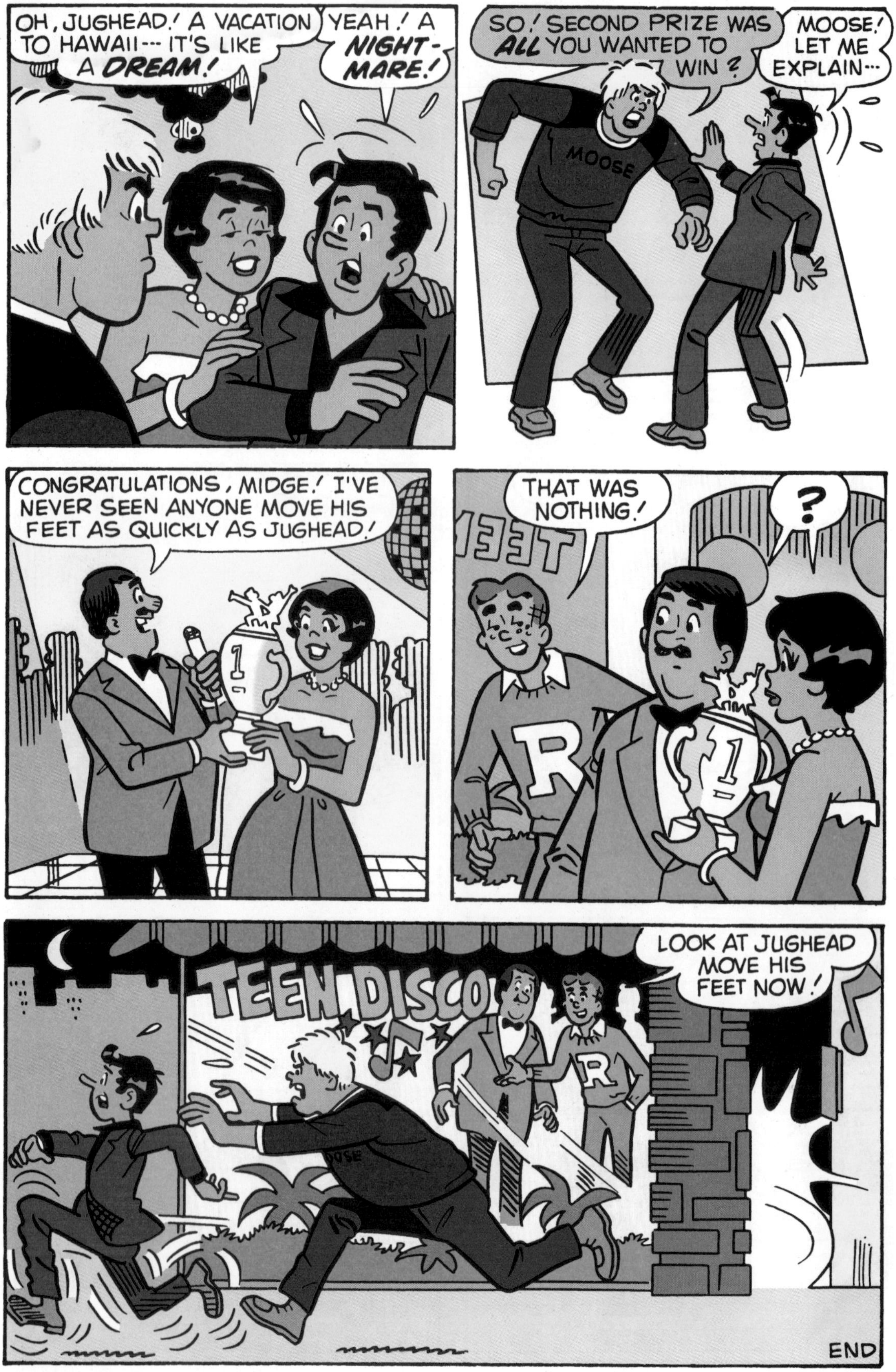
OH, JUGHEAD! A VACATION TO HAWAII--- IT'S LIKE A DREAM!
YEAH! A NIGHT-MARE!
SO! SECOND PRIZE WAS ALL YOU WANTED TO WIN ?
MOOSE! LET ME EXPLAIN---
MOOSE
CONGRATULATIONS, MIDGE! I'VE NEVER SEEN ANYONE MOVE HIS FEET AS QUICKLY AS JUGHEAD!
THAT WAS NOTHING!
?
TEEN DISCO
LOOK AT JUGHEAD MOVE HIS FEET NOW!
END